LILY DALE
CONNECTING

LILY DALE
CONNECTING

Wendy Corsi Staub

Walker & Company New York

First published in the United States of America in 2008 by
Walker Publishing Company, Inc.
Visit Walker & Company's Web site at www.walkeryoungreaders.com

For information about permission to reproduce selections from
this book, write to Permissions, Walker & Company,
175 Fifth Avenue, New York, New York 10010

Library of Congress Cataloging-in-Publication Data
Staub, Wendy Corsi.
Lily Dale: connecting / Wendy Corsi Staub.
p.   cm.
Summary: Now that Calla has finally accepted her ability to communicate
with the dead, ominous supernatural signs seem to imply that her mother's death
was not an accident, and Calla sets out to uncover the truth.
ISBN-13: 978-0-8027-9785-8 • ISBN-10: 0-8027-9785-7 (hardcover)
[1. Psychic ability—Fiction.   2. Psychics—Fiction.   3. Lily Dale (N.Y.)—
Fiction.   4. Mystery and detective stories.]   I. Title.   II. Title. Connecting.
PZ7.S804Lj 2008   [Fic]—dc22   2008019049

Typeset by Westchester Book Composition
Printed in the U.S.A. by Quebecor World Fairfield
2 4 6 8 10 9 7 5 3

All papers used by Walker & Company are natural, recyclable products
made from wood grown in well-managed forests. The manufacturing processes
conform to the environmental regulations of the country of origin.

*Dedicated in loving memory of my friend Stephanie Murphy
and to her husband, Tim, and their children, Ryan, Caitlyn,
and Maureen, in whom her joyful legacy will live on*

And to Brody, Morgan, and Mark

The author is grateful to agents Laura Blake Peterson and Holly Frederick, as well as to Tracy Marchini, all at Curtis Brown, Ltd.; to Nancy Berland, Elizabeth Middaugh, and staff at Nancy Berland Public Relations; to Peter Meuso and Ed Dintrone at Aquaint Interactive; to Morgan Doremus and Miss Media Productions; to Rick and Patty Donovan and Phil Pelleter at the Book Nook in Dunkirk, New York; to Emily Easton, Deb Shapiro, Beth Eller, Mary Kate Castellani, and everyone at Walker & Company; to Susan Glasier of the Lily Dale Assembly offices; to Dr. Lauren Thibodeau, PhD, author, and Registered Medium; to the Reverend Donna Riegel and members of her beginning mediumship class in Lily Dale; to Mark and Morgan Staub for their literary expertise and creative feedback; and most importantly, to Brody Staub, who came up with the title.

ONE

Lily Dale, New York
Wednesday, September 19
4:19 p.m.

"So, wait, let me get this straight—you've been dreaming about your mother, and now you're convinced she was murdered? Is this what you're trying to tell me?" On the other end of the phone line, Lisa Wilson's heavy southern accent is laced with disbelief.

"Not exactly." Calla Delaney paces across the creaky floorboards of her grandmother's northern living room, stepping around the sleeping pile of gray fur that is Gert, her new pet kitten. "I've been dreaming that I *am* my mother, and now I'm convinced she was murdered."

"Huh? You *are* her?"

Hearing a rumble of thunder in the distance, Calla notices

that the room has grown dim. Another autumn storm, rolling in from the west.

Fine with her. The gloomy weather suits her mood.

"I know it sounds crazy," she tells Lisa, "but in my dreams the past few nights, I've been reliving my mother's last moments—getting dressed for work, taking this manila envelope out from under the mattress, walking down the hall with it . . . then someone sneaks up and pushes me—her— down the—"

A hard lump of grief clogging her throat, Calla can't go on. She tries not to picture it all over again—from her mother's viewpoint in the dream, or from her own, in the real-life aftermath.

She, after all, was the one who found Stephanie Lauder Delaney on that nightmarish July afternoon, her broken corpse lying in a pool of blood at the bottom of the stairs.

There was no manila envelope near her body. Calla would have seen it.

"So, uh, what was in this envelope?"

"I have no idea," she says, well aware that Lisa's just trying to humor her, and wondering why she bothered to bring this up in the first place.

But when Lisa happened to call just now and asked how she's been, Calla found herself blurting it out.

"So the only place you ever saw this envelope was in your dream last night?" Lisa asks, and Calla hesitates.

Should she tell Lisa the rest of it—about the mysterious man who popped up on their Tampa doorstep back in March, carrying the envelope and asking for Mom? About how he was whistling the same unfamiliar tune Calla would later hear again here in Lily Dale—coming from Mom's girlhood music box, which, oh yeah, plays without being wound, has been known to open all by itself, and somehow contained Mom's emerald bracelet, which, the last time Calla saw it, was dropping off her own wrist and falling into Mom's grave?

No, she can't tell Lisa any of that. Not yet. And not over the phone. The whole thing is just too bizarre and complicated.

"The thing is, I know my mother had the envelope when she fell," she tells Lisa simply. "I saw it."

"In your dreams. And you saw someone push her down the stairs. Also in your dreams."

"I *felt* someone push her down the stairs."

"Because you were *her*."

"Right." Calla tries not to resent Lisa's skepticism. After all, if she were in her friend's shoes—which she *was* just a few months ago, before her own life back home in Florida was shattered—she'd probably react the same way.

But now, here in Lily Dale—a legendary open portal between the living and the dead—anything seems possible.

Lisa sighs. "I know the last few months have been really hard for you, and what happened to your mom was so totally unfair, no wonder you've been looking for some kind of—"

"No, Lisa—it's not that. I haven't been looking for anything. I wasn't even awake!" Agitated, she paces across the floor again, brushing against a towering stack of Odelia the packrat's books on the coffee table. "I mean . . . come on, haven't you ever dreamed that you were someone else?"

"Maybe Britney Spears back when I was, like, eight, and she was, like, famous for her singing instead of—"

"Come on, I'm serious."

"Sorry." Lisa sighs. "I mean . . . I don't know, Calla. It's not like I remember my dreams in all this major detail."

That, Calla figures, is because Lisa's dreams are only dreams.

Her own dreams—at least, the ones she's had since she arrived in Lily Dale—are actual visions.

She supposes she could try to explain to Lisa that when you're completely relaxed and asleep, you're much more open to spirit energy than during waking hours. So the dearly departed might take advantage of that state to pop in for a visit or send a message—like, you might witness something that happened in the past or will happen in the future.

When you think about it, it makes a lot of sense. To Calla, anyway.

It probably wouldn't to Lisa, a thousand miles away in Florida, where the veil to the Other Side is thicker than the southern sky before an afternoon thunderstorm.

"Lisa? You still there?"

"I'm here . . . just trying to figure out what else to say. I mean . . . oh my God, Calla. You're talking about *murder*."

"I know, but . . ." Calla trails off, her breath catching in her throat as she spots a flicker of movement in the next room and realizes she's not alone in the house. A shadowy figure is—

Oh! Thank goodness.

It's just Miriam, the nineteenth-century household ghost, drifting past the doorway. Miriam's husband built this house in 1883 and she spent the rest of her life here . . . and then some. She likes to keep an eye on things, though she's been known to tamper with lights and electrical appliances, apparently just as a gentle reminder that she hasn't moved out—or on.

Wait . . . did you just reassure yourself that it was just *the house-hold ghost?*

Okay, Lily Dale's definitely rubbing off on her. Next thing she knows, she'll be exchanging cake recipes with Marie Antoinette.

Around here, you really just never know.

It took her a while to figure out that she herself might be . . . gifted.

Might be? Um, hello, you definitely have a sixth sense and you really need to get used to it.

Yeah. Used to dreams that are more than just dreams. Used to knowing things she couldn't possibly know and seeing things no one else can see.

Like dead people.

Because lately, she's been . . . seeing things. People. Out of the corner of her eye, mostly. She'll think someone is there and turn her head just in time to catch a human figure before it disappears.

Occasionally, she can actually make out whether it's a man, a woman, a child. Most of the time, the figure is indistinct, although there have been a few who have come through so vividly that she thought at first they were alive.

Apparently, now that Calla's settled into Lily Dale, the ghosts who populate the earthly plane have decided to start showing themselves to her. Or maybe it's more that she's decided, subconsciously, to let herself see them. Either way, the situation is unnerving, compelling . . . and frustrating.

Take Miriam. She's often flitting around the house, but Calla has yet to get a good look at her. Odelia, Calla's eccentric grandmother, says she's shy. She also says that Calla will eventually fine tune her sixth sense and consistently be able to see Miriam—and the others—as clearly as if they were real live people.

At least Miriam sent Calla a message, through Odelia, on her first day here, reassuring Calla that she's harmless.

And I guess I bought it. After all, now she's just the household ghost.

But Lisa would never understand that . . . or anything else about Lily Dale.

"Listen, Calla . . . what you're seeing, with your mother . . . it's just regular dreams. Right? I mean, it's not like you're . . . one of them. Right?" Lisa sounds really, really hopeful.

One of them.

Them, as in Odelia and the rest of the spiritualists here in Lily Dale. When Lisa visited for Labor Day weekend, she wasn't exactly thrilled to find herself in a town filled with "kooky"—her word—mediums. Which is why Calla didn't dare mention that she herself had been seeing ghosts.

She definitely doesn't have to admit to that now, but she does need to tell someone she's been having these psychic visions about her mother's death all week. And Lisa is, after all, her best friend—a thousand miles away or not.

"It was a dream," she tells Lisa, "but it was real, too. It's kind of hard to exp—"

Startled by a noise behind her, Calla turns, wondering if Miriam is back.

But it's just Gert.

The kitten is up on all four legs, fixated on something just behind Calla. Her back is arched like that of a Halloween cutout cat, front paws poised as if ready to pounce.

No . . . you just never know.

Afraid to turn to see what, or who, might have come up behind her, Calla is certain that she and Gert are no longer alone in the room. The temperature seems to have dropped by about twenty degrees. Goose bumps ache on her arms beneath the thick sleeves of her hooded sweatshirt.

"Calla?" Lisa prods in her ear. "Are you there?"

"Uh-huh."

Gert's unblinking eyes remain focused on the spirit whose energy Calla fully senses now, directly behind her.

She swallows hard, takes a deep breath, and slowly spins around, hoping she's wrong and that the spot will be empty.

But it isn't.

T W O

The apparition has popped up a few times here in Lily Dale since Calla first spotted her at Mom's funeral in Tampa last summer.

As always, she's dressed in flowing white, with black hair pulled back from her exotic face and dark eyes that aren't unkind. Just . . . intense. Wafting in the air is the distinct floral scent that usually accompanies her—lilies of the valley.

Jacy Bly, who lives across Melrose Park from Odelia's house and knows all about these things, said she's probably Calla's spirit guide. He, like the locals, believes that everyone has guides, which as far as Calla can tell, are spiritualism's version of guardian angels.

"Calla?" Lisa is asking in her ear. "Hello-o?"

Aiyana.

The unfamiliar Native American word, which Jacy later told her means "forever flowering," popped into Calla's head out of nowhere one day. It's the spirit guide's name. Calla's not sure how she knows that; she just does. She's as positive about it as she is that Aiyana has been trying to tell her something.

Something about Mom's death.

That, Calla figured out—with Jacy's help—is why Aiyana's presence brings the scent of lilies of the valley, Stephanie's favorite flower.

If only she'd bring Mom with her.

A sorrowful tide of longing sweeps through Calla as she imagines what it would be like to come face-to-face with her mother again right here, right now . . .

Or anywhere, ever again.

She hears another distant boom of thunder and from the corner of her eye, sees a flicker of movement across the room.

Calla turns her head just in time to see a book fly off the stack on the coffee table and land on the floor, pages fluttering open as it lands.

Taken aback, she looks at Aiyana. "Did you do that?"

Aiyana just gazes at her, beginning to look a lot less solid than she did a few moments ago.

Calla read somewhere that it takes a lot of energy for a spirit to move an object around a room. Why would Aiyana even bother with a stupid parlor trick now?

Calla is long past needing proof of otherworldly powers. She gets it. Aiyana's from the Other Side. She doesn't need to throw books on the floor to prove herself.

"Wait . . . before you go . . . I just need to know what happened to her," she tells Aiyana fervently, realizing she's fading fast. "You have to help me. Please."

"Oh, Calla . . ." That's Lisa, on the other end of the phone line, suddenly sounding somber and emotional. "I will—I'll help you. Whatever you need. I'm here for you, I promise."

Calla wasn't talking to Lisa.

But all at once, Aiyana is gone, and Lisa is offering to help, and God knows she needs it.

"Remember how I told you I'd come to Florida to visit?"

"Yeah . . . please don't tell me your father changed his mind about letting you come." Calla's father, Jeff, is a physics professor on sabbatical at Shellborne College in California, and Lisa knows how overprotective he can be. Especially lately.

"No, it's just . . . if you really will help me do this . . . I need you."

"To do what?"

"When I get there, we can go over to my house and see if we can find any evidence that someone was out to get my mother."

"Evidence?" Lisa laughs nervously. "Who are we, CSI?"

"This isn't a joke, Lis'!"

"I know, I know, I'm sorry. I know it isn't. And I want you to come down so I can help you. Just . . . um, well, what about school?"

She's freaked out, Calla realizes. She doesn't want to get involved.

And I can't blame her, really.

"Listen," Calla says, "you don't have to do this with me. I know it's—"

"No, I want to help you," Lisa cuts in firmly. "Whatever you need. So, when are you coming?"

Calla smiles. Good old Lisa won't let her down. "I don't know . . . it'll have to be on a weekend. Maybe Friday?"

"This coming Friday? That would be—oh, wait, my parents said we might go up to Tallahassee to visit the campus again."

Florida State, Calla knows, is Lisa's self-proclaimed "safety" school—though her brother, Kevin, once privately told Calla that with Lisa's grades, even Florida State might be a "reach" school.

"But—ooh, I know! You can come with us and maybe we can both check out the sororities and—"

"No, I really just need to be in Tampa, to see what I can find out," Calla says impatiently. Lisa apparently doesn't grasp that this is a return to the scene of a crime and not a carefree vacation.

"What are you going to do there, exactly?"

"Well, my father said I can get my mother's laptop to use here, remember? I'm thinking there might be something in her files if I can get into them. She used her laptop for everything—work, paying bills, shopping, making travel arrangements. I feel like I might find out more about what was going on with her toward the end. My father told me she wasn't herself the last few months—she was really detached from him, but he wasn't sure why."

"Yeah, and the other thing is, once you have the laptop, we'll be able to stay in touch better, and you can get back onto MySpace," Lisa says excitedly, and Calla fights back a sigh.

Lisa truly doesn't realize that there's something far more significant at stake here than the Internet access that was so hard to live without when Calla first came to Lily Dale

More evidence that Calla really is part of a world far dif- .
ferent than Lisa's—and the one she herself left behind not so
very long ago. But it seems like a lifetime has passed since
Calla was living in the big, upscale Tampa home with both
her parents, going to private school, dating Kevin Wilson . . .

"Well, how about if you come down next weekend?" Lisa
suggests.

"Yeah, I guess I—" She breaks off, remembering.

"What?"

"That's the homecoming dance, and someone asked me to
go." Funny how something that seemed so important just days
ago now seems trivial.

Not to Lisa, though. She squeals in Calla's ear. "Who was
it? Blue or Jacy?"

Lisa, of course, knows all about the two local guys who
are, sort of, involved in Calla's love life at the moment. What
she doesn't know is that Calla still hasn't quite gotten over
Lisa's brother, Kevin, now a sophomore at Cornell. He dumped
her back in April, after he found a new girlfriend in college.
Last week, though, he popped up in Calla's e-mail, sounding
like he wants to be friends. Or maybe more.

"Blue asked me to homecoming," she tells Lisa, firmly
shoving Kevin from her thoughts.

"Blue—is he the hot one?"

"Actually, they both are." She smiles wistfully, thinking
about quiet, enigmatic Jacy, who almost kissed her once.

But Blue Slayton is the one who *did* kiss her, and who
asked her to the dance. And that's what counts, right?

Right. And it's really not that trivial. Calla has to have a
normal life, right? Despite living in this crazy town surrounded

by ghosts and people who can talk to them. Despite needing to know what really happened to Mom.

"So is Blue, like, the star quarterback on the football team for the homecoming game?" Lisa wants to know.

"I hate to burst your bubble, but no. He doesn't play football. He's one of the best players on the soccer team, though."

And Jacy runs cross-country.

She doesn't say that part out loud. They're not talking about Jacy; they're talking about Blue.

Funny, she's actually been considering going to one of Jacy's meets, but she hasn't had a chance—or, okay, much motivation—to get herself to one of Blue's soccer games.

They're playing away this weekend, but there's a home match the night before homecoming. She definitely needs to go.

Lisa asks a few more questions about Blue and the dance and what Calla's going to wear.

"Who knows? I'm clueless. It's not like I have a closet full of stuff to choose from, or a mall around the corner, or any cash if there were one."

"Well, maybe your grandmother will take you shopping for a dress. Just don't let her pick it out." Having visited Lily Dale, Lisa's met Odelia, with her red hair, cat's-eye glasses, and preference for loud, mismatched wardrobe colors.

"Ramona said she'd take me to the mall in Buffalo," Calla muses aloud, watching Gert curl up into a purring ball once again. The cat keeps one green eye open and focused on the spot where Aiyana appeared—and disappeared.

"Ramona?"

"Taggart. My next-door neighbor. My friend Evangeline's

aunt, who's raising her and her brother—I think I told you about them, right?"

"Mmm . . . maybe." Sounds like Lisa is losing interest. Or maybe she's jealous.

"Ramona's great, and she said she'd take me shopping, and she's going to treat me to a haircut, too. if I want. God knows I really need one." Calla shoves her thick, overgrown bangs back from her forehead and glances in the antique mirror above the chintz sofa.

Her long brown hair typically doesn't require much care, but she's definitely getting split ends from three months of neglect, and her streaks of gold highlights are fading fast here in generally overcast western New York State.

It's not just her hair that needs help after a month in Lily Dale. There are deep shadows beneath her wide-set hazel eyes, thanks to a string of restless nights. Her face is pale; the faint freckles that used to dust her nose are gone, thank goodness, but so is the healthy glow cast by the Florida sun.

If she's going to go to the homecoming dance with one of the most popular guys in the senior class, she'd better do something about the way she looks.

"So this woman you barely know is taking you shopping and for a haircut? That's really nice of her, especially now that you don't have . . ." Lisa trails off.

Your mom, she was going to say.

That hard lump is back in Calla's throat, aching so that she can't find the words to respond, even if just to tell Lisa that Ramona Taggart isn't someone she "barely knows."

For one thing, friendships form fast here in Lily Dale. For

another, Ramona knew Calla's mother well, having grown up right next door, just a few years younger than Stephanie. Calla has felt a connection to her from the moment they met—and to her orphaned niece, Evangeline.

Lisa changes the subject, sort of. "So, when can you come down here? Let's make a plan so I'll have something to look forward to."

Again, Calla bristles, wanting to tell Lisa that this is no vacation.

Instead, she says only, "I guess maybe I can come the weekend after homecoming, even though that seems way too far away. I'll check with my grandmother and my dad and let you know, okay?"

"Okay. But meanwhile, Calla . . . I feel like that place is really getting to you. Like you're dwelling on too much of this dark stuff all of a sudden. Maybe you should just, you know . . . leave."

Calla, who mere weeks ago wanted more than anything to get the heck out of Lily Dale, shoots back, "Leave? No way!"

Just the other night, she and her grandmother had that long conversation about why she needs to stay, and how Odelia is going to guide her, teach her how to handle this unwanted, obviously hereditary, so-called gift of hers.

She can't tell Lisa about the terrifying events that led up to the conversation, though. She and her grandmother agreed never to discuss with anyone what happened last Saturday night. Especially Dad, who would yank her out of Lily Dale immediately if he knew. The police promised to keep it out of the newspapers, for safety's sake.

So no one—other than Ramona, upon whose door Calla banged, hysterical, in the wee hours—had to know about the serial killer who decided to make Calla his next victim after she—with a little help from one of his victims on the Other Side—led the police to a teenage girl he'd left for dead.

Even now, over a week later, she shudders when she thinks about what could have happened to her at his hands.

But it didn't happen. I'm all right.

"I don't know how you can stand to live in a place like that," Lisa drawls on, "but if you're staying, I just hope you can manage to get past all this dark stuff."

"I will."

"Call me when you decide what day you're coming, okay?"

"Okay," Calla promises. "I'll see you."

"Yeah. And, hey, don't forget I love you."

"I love you, too," Calla returns, as always, before they hang up.

Hugging herself as if that can possibly banish the hollow feeling inside, she goes back over to the window.

The sky is blackening quickly beyond the leafy branches and gabled rooftops of Cottage Row. Calla turns her head, hoping to spot her grandmother attempting to beat the rain, hurrying home through Melrose Park from her afternoon mediums' league meeting.

No sign of Odelia, though; the street and park are deserted, as are quite a few of the shuttered, clearly abandoned pastel Victorian cottages across the green.

Just a few weeks ago, with the official summer season still under way, the town was teeming with activity.

Every July and August, people come from all over the world to visit the local mediums in search of their dearly departed or psychic counseling or spiritual healing. Then September rolls around, and not only does the steady stream of visitors cease—literally overnight—but a good many of the locals disappear as well.

Not Calla's grandmother. With maybe a hundred others, ODELIA LAUDER, REGISTERED MEDIUM—as the hand-painted shingle above her front porch refers to her—is a year-round resident of the gated little lakeside town whose claim to fame is being the birthplace of spiritualism and that remains almost entirely populated by psychic mediums.

Spotting movement across the green, Calla realizes it's not deserted after all.

A man has materialized, walking slowly along the street, leaning on a cane. For a few moments, Calla isn't sure whether he's alive or dead—his wind-whipped overcoat and brimmed hat could be from another era.

But having grown up in Florida, land of retirees, Calla realizes he might just like to dress in old-fashioned, formal clothes. A lot of elderly gents do.

She watches him stop at a house across the street, look at the sign that reads REV. DORIS HENDERSON, CLAIRVOYANT.

He hesitates only a moment before painstakingly making his way up the steps to the door.

Watching him, Calla doesn't have to be psychic to know Doris won't be home. She's at the mediums' league meeting with Odelia and just about everyone else in town.

Sure enough, after several knocks and a lengthy wait at

Doris's door, the man gingerly descends the stairs and shuffles on down the street.

He's looking for a reading, Calla realizes, as he stops at the next house that bears a shingle advertising a spiritualist in residence. No answer there, either.

Odelia's house is next on his path, and sure enough, he's heading deliberately—and with obvious effort—for her door, poor guy.

When Calla opens it, he's visibly relieved that the exertion wasn't in vain.

Tipping his hat to reveal a robust head of salt-and-pepper hair, he says, "Good afternoon, Ms. Lauder."

"Oh, I'm not her . . . I'm her granddaughter."

"Owen Henry." He extends a surprisingly firm handshake for such a feeble-looking guy. "Pleased to meet you."

"Calla," she supplies.

"Calla. Like the lily. And you're just as lovely."

Standing here in her jeans and hoodie, she doesn't feel as lovely as a lily, but he's a charming old guy and she can't help but smile and thank him.

"Is your grandmother home? I'm afraid I'm in need of her services to reach someone very dear to me."

Ordinarily—especially after what happened to her Saturday night—Calla wouldn't freely admit to being alone in the house, but this guy is obviously harmless. And in emotional pain, judging by the sad expression in his eyes.

"She's not here right now. Sorry. But if you want to leave me your phone number, I can have her get in touch with you and set up an appointment."

He brightens and offers a heartfelt, "Thank you. I'm desperate to get in touch with my wife, my sweet Betty."

As he says the name, a vision flashes into Calla's head. Just a quick glimpse of an elderly woman with a puff of white hair and gold-rimmed eyeglasses on a chain.

Betty?

She doesn't dare mention it. Not after what happened the last time she got involved with one of Odelia's clients, Elaine Riggs.

After taking down the man's name and phone number, she sends him on his way.

Then it's back to moping around until her grandmother comes home at last, about a half hour later. Thank goodness. It's hard to stay glum with Odelia around.

Today, she has on a bright pink-and-white polka-dotted raincoat that clashes with her dyed red hair and purple cat's-eye glasses, along with green rubber rain boots covered in yellow polka dots.

Calla, who was once mortified by her grandmother's wardrobe style, now knows exactly how Odelia's mind was working when she pulled together the outfit. The theme is polka dots—who cares about clashing colors? Not Odelia, who's also wearing red lipstick and toting a teal canvas bag. And—surprise, surprise—she's carrying on an animated conversation with . . . nobody.

At least, nobody Calla can see.

In any other town, the casual onlooker might decide her grandmother is in obvious need of a psychiatrist.

Here in Lily Dale, no one bats an eye at conversations with invisible partners.

Watching her grandmother throw back her head and laugh heartily at whatever it is the spirit is telling her, Calla can't help but grin.

Thank God for Odelia.

"Happy Monday," she calls cheerfully from the hall a minute later, shutting the door behind her. "I beat the rain, but just barely. What's new?"

"Someone came by for a reading. I told him you'd get back to him. He was a widower, and he's really desperate to reach his wife."

"Aren't they all," Odelia murmurs, shaking her head as she pockets Owen Henry's contact information. "How was school?"

"Fine," Calla says automatically.

Hmm, come to think of it, how was school?

Let's see, she got an A on her social studies test, an A– on her art project, and a D on her math quiz.

Okay . . . not so fine.

Odelia appears in the doorway. Her coat is gone, and Calla isn't surprised to see that she's wearing a navy-and-white polka-dotted blouse with her jeans, which are cuffed at the knees—the better to show off the rubber boots, naturally.

"I just saw Patsy Metcalf at the meeting," she tells Calla, "and she asked me if you'll be at her beginning mediumship class again tomorrow morning."

"What did you say?"

"What do you think? I said absolutely. I told her to enroll you for the rest of the course."

"Gammy, I don't know if I want—"

"Remember what we talked about the other night? I told

20

you I'm going to help you learn how to use your psychic abilities responsibly, and you're going to start with Patsy's class," Odelia says firmly, and steps around the book on the floor on her way to pet Gert.

Funny, Calla's mother would have stooped to pick it up. Most people would, actually.

Not Odelia. She's not the most meticulous housekeeper in the world, and her house is jam-packed with more stuff than any human being could ever use in one lifetime—not that Odelia believes in anyone having just one lifetime.

As her grandmother scoops the kitten into her arms, Calla leans over to pick up the book, then stops short.

It's one she checked out of the local library a few days ago, a thick, musty-smelling volume on the history of Lily Dale.

"What the heck is this doing down here?" she wonders aloud.

Odelia glances at it. "What is that?"

"My library book. I had it upstairs, on my bookshelf. Did you borrow it?"

"No."

"Then how did it get down here?"

"Miriam? Did you do that?" Odelia calls good-naturedly. No reply.

"What did she say?" Calla asks.

"She didn't say anything."

"Well, actually, she was just here a few minutes ago."

Odelia raises a dyed red eyebrow. "You saw her?"

"Sort of. I caught a glimpse of someone flitting by out of the corner of my eye, over there." She gestures at the doorway.

Odelia nods approvingly. "That's how it is, in the beginning. Sooner or later, you'll begin to see them more clearly."

Calla wants to remind her that she already *has* seen—and spoken to—apparitions.

But then she might be tempted to mention Aiyana, and she still isn't ready to share that with her grandmother. Not until she knows more about what might have happened to her mother.

Part of her reasoning is that Odelia, who has already warned her not to get involved in criminal cases, would be livid if she thought Calla was disobeying her orders, especially after what happened the other night.

The other thing is . . .

Well, Mom and Odelia didn't get along, and she isn't sure why. Out of a sense of loyalty to her mother, Calla needs to keep some things private for now.

"I'm going to go see if we have anything I can whip up for dinner," Odelia says, and heads for the kitchen with Gert in her arms.

As she picks up the book, Calla glances at the yellowed pages.

When it fell, it opened to a map of Lily Dale.

A mark jumps out at her—a circled X, made in old-fashioned sepia-toned ink.

She recognizes that it would be located in a wooded area near the pet cemetery and a woodland trail that leads through the Leolyn Woods to Inspiration Stump.

The first time Calla heard that an old tree stump, now encased in concrete, marks Lily Dale's most hallowed ground, she rolled her eyes. Leave it to the New Age freaks to pay homage to a nondescript hunk of cement.

Was that blatant disdain really only a few weeks ago?

Now she's been to the stump, buried deep in a grove of ancient trees, fronted by rows of benches as though it's a solitary performer on some eerie primordial stage. During the season, it's where the audience, hopeful of making contact with lost loved ones, gathers to be read by the mediums.

Maybe the constant collective wave of grief and longing contributes to the highly charged atmosphere there.

Or maybe it's something more mystical, more other-worldly than that.

"Do you want me to find that spot?" Calla whispers to Aiyana, wherever she is. "The place marked on the map? Is that why you dropped the book?"

The only answer is a flash of lightning, followed by a deafening boom of thunder and the rattle of rain on the roof as the storm moves in.

Leolyn Woods?

It'll have to wait.

THREE

Wednesday, September 19
6:52 p.m.

"Win some, you lose some . . . Guess I won't be making that again."

"Hmm?" Calla looks up to see her grandmother watching her pushing the remainder of her dinner around on her plate.

"Either you didn't like the pasta, or you aren't hungry."

It's a little of both, actually.

For a moment, the only sound is the steady dripping from the gutter outside. The storm took a while to pass.

Calla clears her throat, not wanting to hurt Odelia's feelings. "It's just . . . when you asked me if I thought snicker-noodles sounded good, I thought you meant cookies."

"No, those are snicker*doodles*," her grandmother says with

exaggerated patience, "and even I wouldn't feed you cookies for dinner."

No, but she *would* concoct a dish consisting of boiled spaghetti coated in some kind of peanut butter sauce and tossed with cut-up chunks of Snickers bars.

"Don't worry . . . I didn't like it either." Odelia stands and picks up her own plate, which even she didn't scrape clean for a change. "I was thinking it would taste kind of like those sesame noodles I had once at a Chinese restaurant."

"It might have—maybe without the candy bars."

"I know, but you seem so down today, I figured a little chocolate with your meal couldn't hurt."

Calla smiles faintly, carrying her own plate to the garbage can and dumping in the contents. "Usually I love your made-up recipes, Gammy."

"Well, every chef has an off night. Just like every psychic. And usually, I have a pretty good idea about these things, but tonight, I have no clue. . . . Are you sure you're okay?" Odelia asks again. She must have asked a dozen times as they ate—or pretended to eat, anyway.

"I'm fine," Calla answers again. "Just tired."

"I was hoping that was all it is. Like I said—off night. Psychicwise, and chefwise. I'm glad nothing's eating away at you."

"Nope." *Wow, Odelia really is having an off night, psychicwise.* "I've just been trying to figure out . . . the thing is, I really miss Lisa. I talked to her this afternoon. Do you think my dad will let me go visit her in a few weeks?"

"You have that airfare voucher Lisa gave you. I don't see why not."

"He's overprotective. That's why not."

"He is, but he let you come here, sight unseen, to live with me. Anyway, didn't he already say you could go visit Lisa?"

"Sort of. He said maybe."

Odelia shrugs, running water over the dishes in the sink. "When he calls tonight, ask him if you can book your flights."

"Can *you* ask him?"

"Nope. That's up to you."

"I'm afraid he'll say he changed his mind."

"He might. He might not. Why don't you call him right now and see?"

Calla looks at the stove clock, then remembers that it doesn't work. It broke years ago, and Odelia, who isn't big on keeping track of time anyway, didn't bother to fix it.

"It's probably about four o'clock, his time," she guesses. "I think he finishes teaching his last class of the day right around now."

Odelia hands her the phone. "Here, go ahead."

Calla dials the number as she walks with the phone into the next room, leaving Odelia washing the dishes and singing off-key.

In the living room, Gert comes to rub against her legs, purring. Calla balances the phone between her shoulder and ear and picks up the cat as the phone rings once, twice . . .

"Hello?"

"Dad? It's me!"

"Hey there! How's my girl?"

"Great!" She tries to sound as cheerful as he does, and wonders if he's faking it, too.

Hearing his voice makes her miss him. A lot.

She closes her eyes, picturing him wearing jeans and his ratty old Grateful Dead concert T-shirt Mom always hated.

In her mind's eye, he's standing in a small, unfamiliar kitchenette. Behind him, open shelving is lined with cups and plates in Mexican-style pottery, and a sunny window frames some kind of bright red blooming shrubbery. There's a fruit bowl on the counter, and as he holds the phone to his head with one hand, Dad is playing catch with a green apple in the other.

Listening to his familiar voice in her ear, it's so easy to picture him, she can almost believe she's right there with him. But when she opens her eyes, she's in Lily Dale, and Dad is a few thousand miles away, in a place she's never even seen.

"What's new?" he asks. "How was your weekend? How was school today?"

"Good. We had a senior assembly about college applications. I'm supposed to meet with my guidance counselor next week to talk about where I want to go."

"You and I are going to have to figure that out."

"I know."

Before Mom died, Calla had definite ideas about next year. Rather, her mother did. She was a strong believer in education, as, of course, is Dad. Mom, who had an Ivy League MBA, had high hopes for Calla, and they were going to visit college campuses over the summer.

Now it's time to start filling out applications, and she hasn't been anywhere or even given it much thought.

"I was thinking I'll come visit you the weekend after next, and we can talk about it."

"Oh . . . that's actually homecoming, Dad. I'm going to

be kind of tied up with that." She tells him about it, trying hard to sound carefree.

"I'm glad you're going," he says. "I'll just visit the following weekend, then."

"No, Dad—actually, I was planning to visit Lisa then, remember?"

"You were?"

Counting on his absentminded-professorness, she says, "You told me that I could."

"I don't like the idea of you flying around by yourself."

"I flew here by myself from Florida. I'll fly by myself when I come out and see you," she throws in for good measure, not that that's been discussed.

"I know . . ."

"Dad, I'm homesick. I miss my friends. Can't I please go to Tampa? It won't even cost me anything, and Lisa is really counting on me."

There's a long pause.

"All right. You can go."

Tears spring to her eyes.

Every time he feels her growing up a little more—up and away from him—he feels the ache of missing Mom even more.

She doesn't know how she knows that . . . she just does.

Same as with everything else.

"But Calla . . . if you're going to Florida because you're homesick . . . well, the thing is . . ."

"It's not home anymore. I know."

"It's not that I'm planning on selling the house anytime in

the immediate future, but I can't afford to hang on to it for-ever."

"I don't want you to. Whenever I think of it, I think of . . . what happened."

"I do, too. So I'll get us a new place. We can make a fresh start."

"In Tampa?"

"I don't know. Not out here, though . . . I'll tell you that much." He laughs. "I'm just not cut out for this California lifestyle."

"Give it a chance, Dad. I'm sure you'll be hanging ten on a surfboard and having your teeth whitened in no time."

He chuckles. "I doubt that. So listen, if you're tied up into October, I'll have to get there to visit you this weekend."

"But Dad, can you afford it?"

"Better than I can afford not to see my girl for almost a month."

"Really?"

"I miss you, Cal. I need to see you."

She swallows hard. "I miss you, too. That would be great, Dad."

"If you think Odelia's offer for me to stay there is still open, I'll save the money I spent last time on a hotel."

"Oh . . . I'm sure it's still open."

"You don't sound sure."

"No, I am. Gammy would love that."

The problem is, if Dad stays right here under Odelia's roof, he's more likely to pick up on the fact that it isn't your run-of-the-mill, nonhaunted household.

Maybe, Calla thinks hopefully, *he won't notice.*

He can be pretty forgetful.

And she'll definitely get her grandmother to take down the Odelia Lauder, Registered Medium shingle.

They talk for a few more minutes.

Then Calla says, "I'd better go start my homework."

"Good idea. Okay. I'll get online and buy myself a plane ticket to Buffalo for Friday." He bites noisily into something crunchy.

"Um, Dad? What are you eating?"

"An apple," he says. "I'm really getting into this California health-nut lifestyle."

Her heart skips a beat. "What kind of apple?"

"Granny Smith. Why?"

"No reason," she murmurs, well aware that Granny Smiths are bright green, just like the apple in her vision. "Hey . . . by any chance did you bring that old Grateful Dead T-shirt with you to California?"

He chuckles. "You bet. I'm wearing it right now."

She nods, pretty amazed with herself. No need to ask about the fruit bowl and the kitchen and the Mexican-style pottery and the blooming shrubbery.

Something tells her she's actually catching a glimpse of Dad on the opposite side of the country. Which is really more cool than scary, if you think about it.

"I love you, sweetheart. Be careful."

It's his standard sign-off, but tonight, the "be careful" resonates in her ears long after she hangs up and climbs into bed.

She just can't stop thinking about that manila envelope.

Whoever pushed Mom down the stairs stole it—Calla is positive about that.

A horrible accident.

That's what the police called it; that's what they had all believed: Calla, her father, her grandmother . . .

But I know the truth now.

Someone killed my mom. Someone was in our house with her and crept up behind her and gave her a hard shove. I felt those hands on my—on her—back. It was no accident. It was murder.

FOUR

Thursday, September 20
12:48 p.m.

Walking into the cafeteria, Calla looks around for Blue Slayton.

There he is, at his usual table, surrounded by his usual group of friends.

She hesitates before starting in his direction, first checking to see whether Jacy's here. Sometimes he skips lunch to go outside, which is against the rules—not that he seems to care. He told Calla he has a hard time getting through the entire day cooped up indoors.

"It's bad for the soul," was how he put it.

As luck would have it, he's here today, alone at a table with a sandwich and a book. Calla can't help but notice that he—unlike anyone else sitting solo in the cafeteria—looks perfectly content not to have company. In fact, he looks as though he actually prefers it that way.

She decides to go over to Blue first, figuring Jacy has yet to realize she's in the room—not that he'd do anything about it if he did.

"Hey, Calla," Blue says, in the process of devouring a double lunch. "What's up?"

As always, she's struck by his looks: gorgeous, wavy light-brown hair and piercing eyes that do justice to his name. It takes her a moment to remember what's up.

Oh, yeah.

Acutely aware that all his friends are listening in, she shifts her weight and says in a low voice, "You know how we're supposed to—"

"Wait, *what?*"

She clears her throat and begins again, louder. "You know how we're supposed to go out on Saturday night?"

"No," he says blankly, and for a moment, she thinks she's made an embarrassing mistake.

"I thought we were supposed to go to the movies Saturday . . ."

"Nope."

"Oh . . ." Not sure what to say, she wonders how she could have possibly screwed things up like this. Maybe it was just wishful thinking?

"Well, I guess I'll see you later," she says, and starts to walk away.

"Calla?"

She turns back. "Yeah?"

Blue breaks into a grin. "Gotcha."

"Oh." She chokes out a staccato laugh. "Yeah. You sure did. You got me."

And it's not really all that funny—to her, anyway. But Blue's friends are cracking up like they're watching some juvenile YouTube clip.

"So, what about Saturday night?" Blue asks, and at least he has the grace to pull his chair slightly away from the table. Not that his friends aren't continuing to listen in anyway.

"It turns out my dad's coming to visit this weekend."

"Again? Wasn't he just here?"

"Not 'just'—I mean, it's been a few weeks, and . . . he's coming tomorrow. So maybe we can go out a different night."

"You can't go out Saturday?"

"No, I just said, my dad's—"

"I know, but . . . I mean, you spend every second with him when he's in town?" Blue asks.

She wonders if the cocky attitude is for his friends' benefit or if he honestly doesn't get that she wants to be with her dad. It probably sounds immature to him, like she's some kind of daddy's girl.

"Forget it," she says, hating that she even cares what he thinks of her. "We don't need to go out a different night. That's fine."

"So, you can go Saturday?"

"No, I just told you I can't. I mean, forget it, forget it." She just isn't in the mood for this today.

Blue looks taken aback. "How's Sunday night? Is he gone then?"

"Yeah . . ."

"Then we'll go out Sunday. Okay?"

"Are you sure?"

"Not a problem." He flashes her his familiar, easy grin. She wonders if maybe she was too hard on him just now. He really is a good guy. He just likes to tease, and he doesn't understand what it's like when you never get to see your dad.

Then again . . .

Of course he knows what that's like.

His own father is always on the road.

All right, then maybe she struck a nerve with him.

Whatever.

"Sunday night's good," she tells him, and manages a smile.

"Great. I'll call you later, after soccer practice." With a wave, he goes back to his friends.

Relieved to have that over, Calla goes through the line to buy a salad, a yogurt, and a bottle of water, though she doesn't have much of an appetite now.

She's about to join her friends Willow and Sarita at their usual table when she remembers Jacy. Glancing in his direction, she catches him staring right at her over the top of his book.

Not wanting to drop her tray, she doesn't dare wave at him.

It doesn't matter; he's already focused on his book again. She decides to go over to say hello anyway. They haven't had much opportunity to talk in any of their classes lately, and she hasn't seen him outside of school.

"Hi, Jacy."

"Hey." He looks up only briefly.

"How've you been?"

"Pretty good." He turns a page in his book, obviously engrossed.

"That's good." She pauses. "Uh, what're you reading?"

He holds up the cover without comment.

She glances at the title. "*Into the Wild*. Wasn't that a movie a while back?"

He nods.

"I didn't see it. Or read the book. What's it about?"

"Wilderness survival."

"That sounds right up your alley—I mean, you're so into nature," she tells him lamely.

"Yeah," is all he says.

"Oh, well . . . I'll leave you alone then."

"See you."

"See you," she replies, hurt that he didn't try harder to make conversation, much less ask her to join him.

As she walks toward her friends, she reminds herself that Jacy is a loner. Everyone knows that. And when a person is reading a good book, he doesn't welcome interruptions.

Still.

"What's wrong?" Willow asks as Calla arrives at the table where she and Sarita are nibbling on their usual sparse lunches: apples and bottles of water.

"Do I look like something's wrong?"

"Yeah," Sarita says. "You do. What is it?"

"Nothing, it's just . . . I think Jacy just seriously dissed me."

"Jacy Bly?" Sarita shakes her chic short haircut and cuts off another chunk of apple, which she can't bite into because of her braces. "It wouldn't be the first time he's dissed someone. He's got a major attitude problem."

"Yeah, well, after what he's been through, he's allowed." Willow's wide-set brown eyes focus intently on Calla. "Are you and Jacy . . . ?"

"Friends. Yeah."

"Oh." Willow nods like she buys it—and really, it's the truth—but something tells Calla she suspects there might be more to it than that.

She's not going to elaborate, though. It's not that she doesn't trust Willow, who's become one of her closest friends at Lily Dale. Which is ironic, since Calla's first impression of her, unfairly based on her extraordinary beauty, was that she's standoffish.

She's not. She's just quiet.

Meaning Calla could probably confide her interest in Jacy and Willow would keep it to herself.

Maybe she will confide in Willow. Just not with Sarita here. She's more social, and if she mentions it, it'll get back to Evangeline, who has a not-so-secret crush on Jacy herself.

"Jacy really doesn't seem to be into making friends or getting involved in stuff here," Sarita points out. "I mean, he runs track, but that's pretty much it. And it's not exactly a big team sport, you know?"

Calla can't help but glance over at the table where Blue and his soccer buddies are laughing raucously. "Not everyone's into team sports."

"Right, and maybe Jacy's afraid to get too plugged in at this school," Willow says. "Maybe he's afraid he'll get yanked away from Peter and Walt and moved to a new foster home somewhere else or, God forbid, back to his parents."

"He probably is," Sarita agrees with a shrug, then resumes

their earlier conversation. "So, you're, like, positive you have to go to your dad's tonight?"

Calla looks up from her yogurt with interest. This is the first mention she's heard of Willow's father.

"I'm positive. I skipped last week because of the homecoming committee meeting."

"Did he even notice?" Sarita asks.

"Probably not." Willow tries to laugh it off, but Calla can see that Sarita's comment has struck a chord.

"Where does your dad live?" Calla asks.

"Dunkirk."

"With his new wife and her kids," Sarita puts in.

"Oh." Calla isn't sure what to say to that. "Well . . . that's good. Dunkirk's not so far away. Like, ten miles, right?"

"Less, but you'd think it was a hundred, the way her dad acts," Sarita says. "It's like he can't be bothered to come down to Lily Dale and pick her up. Half the time, he stands her up."

"Oh, Calla . . . I meant to ask you." Willow, obviously uncomfortable with the route the conversation has taken, blatantly changes the subject. "Are you ready for the math quiz this afternoon? Do you want me to go over a couple of problems with you, just in case?"

Mr. Bombeck has been on her case from day one, and quickly assigned Calla a study partner: Willow, who happens to be as brainy as she is beautiful.

At first, Calla was reluctant to work with her—after all, she's Blue Slayton's ex-girlfriend—but to her surprise, that didn't seem to matter much to Willow. Either she's long over him, or she's pretending to be, because she hasn't mentioned him, or the fact that he's dating Calla now. Willow must know about it, though. In a town the size of Lily Dale, everybody knows everything about everybody else.

"If you wouldn't mind going over some problems, that would be great," Calla tells Willow, sensing that she needs the distraction.

"Good. Let's do it."

As Calla reaches for her notebook, she glances over to see if Jacy's still over there, absorbed by his book.

He's there . . . but he's not absorbed by his book; he's looking right back at her.

When she catches him, though, he lowers his eyes again to the page.

Calla sighs inwardly.

After school, backpacks over their shoulders, hoods raised against the cold breeze, Calla and Evangeline trail a couple of other school kids along Dale Drive toward the entrance to Lily Dale.

At this time of year, nobody mans the gatehouse, with its sign that reads LILY DALE ASSEMBLY . . . WORLD'S LARGEST CENTER FOR THE RELIGION OF SPIRITUALISM.

Beyond, the winding lanes of the town are deserted against a cold gray backdrop. Clumps of late-summer flowers, blooming profusely in defiance of an almost perpetually sunless sky, bend and shift on fragile stems in a brisk wind off the choppy lake waters.

". . . so then I casually mentioned to him we might be out of town that weekend," Evangeline is saying, "just in case he was thinking of asking me. What do you think?"

"Hmm?" Distracted by a sense of uneasiness that's been nagging at her all day, Calla's barely been listening to Evangeline's long-winded account of what happened between her and Russell Lancione during study hall.

"Never mind. It doesn't really matter. It's not like I—hey, what are you looking at?" Evangeline follows Calla's gaze off to the right, in the opposite direction of Cottage Row and home.

Leolyn Woods is over there.

"Nothing, just . . . want to take the long way home today? I feel like getting some fresh air."

"Fresh air?" Evangeline asks dubiously, as a strong gust whips a clump of frizzy orange hair over her face. "You're joking, right? It's like a hurricane out here. Any more fresh air and we'll be dangling from a tree branch somewhere."

Her words are punctuated by the familiar, furious silvery clanging of metal wind chimes, as common above local doorsteps as medium shingles are.

And it isn't just wind chimes. Calla has no idea whether all Lily Dale residents are as big on indoor clutter as Odelia, Ramona, and a handful of others have proven to be, but they all seem to love outdoor clutter. Birdbaths, garden gnomes, fluttering American flags or smaller nylon ones imprinted with harvest pumpkins and autumn leaves. Now that election season is here, political signs have been popping up, too.

Calla hasn't been able to pinpoint any practical or spiritual reason for the jumble of exterior ornamentation. It simply appears to be, to the Lily Dale landscape, what neon-lit signs are to Las Vegas: part of the local tradition.

"The thing is," Calla tells Evangeline, with another glance

40

toward Leolyn Woods. "we always go the same way, every single day."

"Uh, maybe because that's where we live?" Evangeline frowns, shaking her head a little and longingly watching her brother, Mason, bear to the left up ahead, toward Cottage Row and home.

"I'm taking the long way today," Calla decides. "You don't have to go with me, though."

"But why do you—" Suddenly Evangeline's round face breaks into a grin. "Oh!"

"What?"

"I know why you want to go that way."

She does?

"You do?"

"Sure."

Then why is Evangeline smiling? There's nothing amusing about a ghost showing a person an old map marked with an X.

And anyway, how could she know?

How does anyone around here claim to know anything? Calla reminds herself.

Okay, Evangeline does claim to be a budding psychic medium, but as far as Calla can tell, she's got a long way to go. It's highly unlikely that she had a psychic vision of the book and the map.

Still, Calla decides to humor her. And in Lily Dale, you really just never can tell.

"All right," she says patiently. "Why do I want to go that way?"

"Blue."

"Blue? Blue what?"

"You mean Blue who. Blue Slayton. *Duh.* I bet he's hanging over at Jeremy's today, right? Jeremy lives there—on East Street." Evangeline gestures off in the distance, beyond the path toward the woods.

Actually, he isn't. He had soccer practice right after school. But Evangeline just gave her a good cover story, so . . .

"Oh . . . fine. You got me." Calla feigns a sheepish grin. "That's why I want to go that way. You coming?"

Evangeline hesitates.

Come on, Evangeline . . . come with me . . .

Calla really isn't anxious to go into the woods alone. She's been there before, and it's a creepy spot. The locals claim Inspiration Stump and its surroundings are a highly charged vortex of spiritual energy, and judging by her own reaction to the place, Calla suspects they're right.

"Why not." Evangeline shrugs and looks down at her chubby build, even more roly-poly than usual in her down jacket. "I could use some extra exercise. Let's go."

As they walk along, she resumes the saga of Russell Lancione and his unrequited crush on her, claiming not to care but spending an awful lot of time analyzing everything he's said and done.

Calla hates to cut her off, but they've reached the turn-off for Leolyn Wood, and as a conversational rule, Evangeline rarely pauses for air.

"Hey, let's walk through there!" Calla exclaims, as though she just thought of it.

Evangeline breaks off in the middle of a sentence. "What?"

"The woods. Let's go that way."

"That's a dead end. Why do you want to go in there?"

42

"It's just so . . . peaceful." Calla is getting sick of keeping up the act, but she still isn't ready to tell Evangeline the whole story. For all she knows, the map in the book, which is stashed in her backpack, is utterly meaningless.

But if not . . .

"We can't go in there right now," Evangeline says simply, shaking her head.

"It's okay, then, you go home, and I'll see you lat—"

"No." Evangeline grabs Calla's coat sleeve. "I mean, we *can't* go in there. Not that I don't want to. Not that I do, though."

"Why can't we?"

"Didn't you ever see the sign?"

"What sign?"

"Here . . . come on." Evangeline leads the way to the edge of the grove and points at, sure enough, a sign.

Do Not Enter Leolyn Woods in HIGH Winds

"What? That's crazy." Calla declares, even as she gazes overhead at the ominously swaying, creaking trees, their gnarled branches bony fingers grasping at the purple-gray heavens.

"Maybe, but it's just as crazy to ignore it, don't you think?"

"I don't know. I guess."

"Anyway"—Evangeline flashes her a smile—"I guarantee you Blue Slayton's not hanging in the woods on a day like today. In fact, I'm sure he knows you're about to walk past Jeremy's house, and I bet he comes outside looking for you."

"Why do you think that?"

"Because, duh. He's one of the most powerful psychics around here. Like his father."

Calla considers that. She hasn't exactly seen evidence of Blue's abilities since she's met him . . . but that doesn't mean Evangeline's claim isn't true.

"Come on, let's go." Evangeline hugs herself and stamps her feet a little. "I'm freezing."

Calla considers ignoring the warning sign and Evangeline, anxious to see what—if anything—lies in the spot marked by the map.

Then that nagging sense of uneasiness gets the better of her.

Another time.

Maybe she'll even get Jacy to go with her.

Though, now that she thinks about it, she's barely had a chance to talk to him lately. Today when she tried in the cafeteria, he seemed almost cold. But that was probably because he was reading, and she was interrupting.

Then again . . .

The more she thinks about it, the more obvious it seems that he's been avoiding her lately.

But why?

"Calla, you'll never believe this . . . guess what?" Evangeline breathlessly greets her on the telephone later.

In the midst of clearing the dinner dishes with her grandmother, Calla grins. Evangeline often begins her calls with that phrase, and her news is rarely anything anyone else would consider earth shattering.

"I can't even imagine," she tells Evangeline dryly, "so you'll have to tell me."

"My aunt is going to take us shopping at the mall tomorrow after school!"

"Really?" Calla perks up. "Wow, that would be—oh, wait. I can't. I forgot to tell you this afternoon . . . my dad's flying into Buffalo tomorrow to visit me for the weekend."

"That stinks. I mean, I know how much you miss him, but—hey, wait a minute. The mall is in Buffalo, too. What time is he coming in?"

"I think around eight." She looks around for the scrap of paper where she wrote down her father's flight information when he called earlier.

"We can all go to the mall, then pick up your dad at the airport! My aunt won't mind. Let me go ask her. *Aunt Ramona!*"

The phone drops with a clatter in Calla's ear before she has a chance to protest—not that she necessarily was going to.

After what she's been through lately, a trip to the mall would be a nice, welcome dose of *normal*.

She carries some dirty dishes over to the sink.

"What's going on?" Odelia asks, rinsing a sudsy glass.

"Evangeline said her aunt could take us shopping at the mall on Friday, then pick up Dad at the airport."

"That would be nice."

"I know. I just don't want Ramona to have to go out of her way."

"Oh, I don't think she'll mind," Odelia comments with a small, cryptic smile.

Seeing it, Calla remembers the strange sensation she had about Dad and Ramona when her father visited a few weeks ago and they met for the first time. The two of them couldn't be more different, but it was almost as if there was some kind of fleeting connection between them. At the time, Calla didn't know what to make of it, or even if it was just her imagination.

But now, looking at her grandmother, she gets the distinct impression that Odelia might somehow have the same crazy inkling.

Evangeline is back on the phone, sounding a little breathless. "Aunt Ramona said she'd *love* to pick up your dad at the airport Friday night!"

"She'd *love* it?" Calla echoes dubiously.

"That's what she said. Just get the flight information and tell him we'll be there! Aren't you psyched? I love how everything just falls into place, don't you?"

"Sure . . . I guess. Listen, I'll see you in the morning for school."

"See you then!"

Calla hangs up the phone to see that her grandmother is still watching her, looking as though she wants to say something. "What?"

Odelia shrugs. "Nothing, just . . . Ramona is a great person, don't you think?"

"Sure. I love her."

"Good."

"Good?" Calla echoes. "Why good?"

"No reason," Odelia replies as the doorbell rings. "That's Mr. Henry. Would you mind finishing the dishes for me?"

"Sure. You mean Mr. Henry from yesterday? The one who's trying to reach his dead wife?"

"That's the one." Odelia dries her hands and heads for the door.

A few moments later, she's escorting Owen Henry—

looking just as dapper as before, and just as feeble as he leans on his cane—through the kitchen on the way to the back room where she sees her clients.

"This is my granddaughter, Calla."

He smiles and pauses to lean on the cane with his left hand while tipping his hat with his right. "Lovely as the lily. We met."

"Good luck," she says, and goes back to the dishes as he and Odelia disappear into the back room.

She's upstairs doing her homework when they emerge an hour later. After hearing her grandmother show him out the front door, she goes to the top of the stairs.

"Did you get through to Betty, Gammy?" she calls down.

"Nope."

Surprised by her grandmother's flat response, she descends the stairs halfway to find Odelia frowning.

"What's wrong?"

"I wasn't getting anything at all from him. It happens sometimes."

"Was he disappointed?"

"Yup. He kept insisting that I try harder to reach her. I explained that it doesn't work that way—that it's not like a telephone where you just dial up the spirit of your choice."

She's said that countless times to Calla. It doesn't help to ease the frustration.

I know how you feel, Owen Henry, Calla thinks as she climbs slowly back up the stairs. *I've lost someone I love, too. And I'd do anything to connect with her again.*

In the shadowy second-floor hall, she rounds the corner—and cries out when she comes face-to-face with a stranger.

Oh, okay . . . she's not real. At least, she's not alive—or of this century, or even the last. She's wearing a long dress with a snug bodice and high collar, and her hair is pinned back severely, Victorian-style.

"Miriam?" Calla asks instinctively, and the woman smiles delightedly before drifting through the wall—in the very spot where there was once a doorway to an upstairs sitting room, Odelia told her.

"What happened?" Odelia calls, hurrying up the stairs. "Are you okay?"

"I'm fine, Gammy. Actually, I think I just met Miriam."

"You mean you *saw* her?"

"Yup." And her heart is still pounding from the scare.

"That means your psychic awareness really is growing stronger every day," her grandmother informs her.

Maybe so.

And maybe she's getting closer to being able to glimpse the one person she longs to see again.

Because what good is it for her to be able to see dead people if the one person she's lost and needs most of all isn't among them?

One of the Lily Dale mediums—Althea York, Willow's mother—did actually see Mom standing beside Calla. It should have been comforting, and it was, in a way, but it was also incredibly frustrating to know Mom was right there and yet not be able to make the connection on her own.

She tried to convince herself that it was enough just to know her mother's still with her.

But it isn't.

She longs to see her, the way she's seen other spirits, like the woman, Miriam, in the hall just now. She longs to speak to her mother.

"Your pain is so overwhelming . . . it may be acting as a barrier," Althea told her. She went on to explain that in time, when Calla learns to accept her loss—and to become more expert at opening herself to spirit energy—her mother might be able to come through to her.

Not exactly promising.

Calla can't imagine ever accepting that her mother's been ripped from her life so unfairly—and deliberately.

In Mom's girlhood bedroom, she closes the door behind her and kicks off her shoes.

It's taken a while, but Calla finally feels at home in this room, with its vintage furniture, whitewashed beadboard, wallpaper, and carpet in soft shades of sage and rose.

The bureau and shelves are filled with Mom's books, framed photos, and other mementos of the girl she once was. On the bed is a quilt Odelia made of fabric squares from Mom's old clothing. Whenever Calla climbs into bed and wraps herself in it, she likes to imagine being wrapped in her mom's arms again.

When her homework is done, Calla changes into pajamas and does just that, hoping she'll get through a night without nightmares for a change. The one about Mom being pushed down the stairs, or the other one . . .

The one that keeps popping up to remind Calla that something tore Odelia and Mom apart for good, years ago. She's been hearing snatches of their terrible argument in her dreams since she got to Lily Dale.

At first, before she knew about her "gift," she assumed she must have witnessed it, as a toddler.

But now she wonders if she was really there at all. Maybe she's been channeling the emotion-charged past.

". . . because I promised I'd never tell . . . ," Mom sobbed.

". . . for your own good . . . ," Odelia said, and then, ". . . how you can live with yourself . . ."

Then one of them, Calla isn't sure which, declared, with chilling certainty, *The only way we'll learn the truth is to dredge the lake."*

Calla has grown pretty sure they must have been talking about Cassadaga Lake, just yards from Odelia's doorstep. Her grandmother inexplicably forbade her to set foot in its waters when she first got to Lily Dale in August.

Calla can't help but wonder if whatever secrets might lie in its black depths could possibly have something to do with her mother's death.

With her murder.

When at last she falls asleep tonight, she does dream, but not about Mom and Odelia.

She dreams about a gothic-looking house perched high on a cliff, with an octagonal stained-glass window in its square center turret and a widow's walk above.

And she dreams about a woman with a puff of white hair and gold-rimmed glasses on a chain.

Odelia may not have been able to get through to Owen Henry's lost love . . . but somehow, Calla has.

There was no specific message, though. Just the house and Betty.

With the school day ahead and her father on the way,

there's nothing to do but file it away with all the other spirits she's met in passing.

For now, Owen Henry will have to keep on longing, keep on waiting, keep on hoping for a connection.

Just like me.

FIVE

Buffalo, New York
Friday, September 21
4:33 p.m.

For the first time since she left Florida back in August, Calla finds herself in utterly familiar surroundings.

Okay, so she's never actually set foot inside Buffalo's Walden Galleria before today.

But the sprawling suburban shopping mall could be back in Tampa, with its chain stores and food court restaurants, echoing high-ceilinged corridors teeming with trendy teenagers, stroller-pushing moms, slow-moving senior citizens.

Looking around, Calla can't help but feel relieved to be back among the living . . . so to speak.

It's not that she doesn't appreciate the ambiance in quaint, rural Lily Dale, with its ramshackle gingerbread cottages and picturesque lakeside location. But strange things happen to her there.

After another restless night, she was planning to tell Jacy about the map and ask him to go to the woods with her. She hasn't been able to bring herself to go alone.

She also wanted to know more about those visions of his.

But Jacy wasn't in school today.

Probably just as well.

Maybe she doesn't need to know any of the gory details—hopefully, a figurative expression.

Anyway, they wouldn't have had much chance to talk about it during classes, and Ramona was parked out front at dismissal to drive Calla and Evangeline straight to the mall.

Best to put it all behind her, at least for now.

Not until this minute did Calla realize just how homesick she's been for the real world, all the modern conveniences she used to take for granted—not just a computer and the Internet, but cell phone service, TiVo, takeout delivery, swimming pools, a car at her disposal . . .

And gorgeous shopping malls filled with clothes.

This was the first year she didn't get to go back-to-school shopping with Mom and her Platinum American Express card.

But you don't want to get all upset thinking about that now, do you?

You just want to have fun for a change, right?

Definitely. Today, if she can help it, she's not going to dwell on Mom's death, or Jacy's troubling warning, or anything to do with Lily Dale. She's going to shop, and then she's going to get to see her dad.

"Okay, where do you two want to start?" Ramona asks as they pause beside the directory map.

"How about if you decide where to go first, Calla," Evangeline suggests, adding a little wistfully, "You're the one who needs to get a dress for homecoming."

Evangeline was hoping someone would ask her to the dance, too. Well, someone other than Russell Lancione, her one prospect, whom she plans to say no to if he does ask.

It's not just because Russell is "blah," as Evangeline claims. No, Calla suspects she's been holding out, hoping the elusive Jacy Bly will suddenly decide to sweep her off her feet.

Yeah . . . aren't we all.

Of course, Evangeline has no idea that Calla's also got a secret crush on *her* secret crush—much less that Jacy and Calla have . . .

Well, really, nothing has actually *happened*. It's not like Jacy's kissed her, or asked her out. And it's not like he ever will, now.

Calla feels her face grow hot just thinking about her misunderstanding yesterday afternoon—and what she inadvertently admitted to him.

Fishing in her oversized fringed suede purse, Ramona announces, "I have a coupon for twenty percent off something at Lord and Taylor. And I bet they have some great dressy dresses if you want to go look, Calla."

"Oh, that's okay . . . I don't think I'm going to get something to wear to the dance today," Calla replies, with a guilt-ridden glance at Evangeline.

"Why not? I'm sure you could find something that would look gorgeous on you." The well-padded Evangeline, still wistful, shakes her head at Calla's slender build.

"I doubt I'll be able to afford much of anything. Anyway, you should use your coupon for yourself, Ramona."

"Do I *look* like I shop at Lord and Taylor?" Ramona wrinkles her nose, and Calla can't help but laugh.

In her ragged-bottomed jeans, dangly earrings, and a brown suede jacket, Ramona looks, as always, like a throwback to the flower-child era. A strikingly pretty throwback, at that. She's even wearing makeup tonight.

Calla wonders if that has anything to do with the fact that Ramona's going to be seeing Dad tonight. Somehow, she doubts it.

A cute older guy in a business suit checks her out as he passes, but she seems oblivious. Probably just as well. Ramona's not shy about discussing her disastrous love life, and Calla knows all about her talent for falling for the wrong kind of guy.

Meaning, any guy who doesn't embrace her habit of communicating with the dead.

"Once they figure out what I do for a living, they head for the hills," Ramona likes to say, and she doesn't seem to be exaggerating much. A couple of romantic prospects have already come and gone since Calla arrived.

Dad has no idea she's a medium—yet.

But once he finds out, any spark of attraction between the two of them—if there even is such a possibility—is sure to fizzle.

"Let's go take a look at Lord and Taylor. I'm sure there will be lots of stuff on sale," Ramona tells Calla. "Plus, I'm paying for your haircut next week, remember? And you said you've saved up some babysitting money, right?"

"Right."

It was Ramona who hooked Calla up with a regular after-school babysitting job for Dylan and Ethan, her friend Paula's two sons.

She does have almost a hundred dollars in her wallet. But that'll go fast when she picks up the essentials, namely, more long-sleeved shirts and sweaters and another pair of jeans.

Her Florida wardrobe of shorts, flip-flops, and sleeveless T-shirts barely saw her through the remainder of a chilly northeastern August. When Dad visited a few weeks ago, he did take her shopping at T.J. Maxx in nearby Dunkirk. By that time, though, Calla had figured out that Dad was broke without Mom's banking salary, so she picked out only a down jacket and a sweater.

Meanwhile, she's been shivering her way through the increasingly chilly days. If she's going to stay in Lily Dale, she needs a wardrobe of warmer clothes, and she can't ask Dad to buy it for her. He's spending enough money flying here for the weekend.

"I just need a lot of everyday stuff," Calla says as the three of them start walking through the mall. "A dress is kind of last on my list right now."

"But you need that, too," Evangeline tells her. "I mean, you can't go to homecoming with Blue Slayton dressed in jeans and sneakers, right?"

"No, but . . . how dressy is homecoming, anyway?" Calla asks. "Are we talking *gown* dressy? Like a prom?"

"It used to be like that," Ramona says, "when your mother and I went to school there. But now I think it's just semiformal."

"It is," Evangeline confirms. "Not that I know from experience."

"Calla, how about if we schedule your haircut for the day of homecoming? Instead of just getting it cut, you can have it styled, too, for the dance. And you can have your makeup done, too."

"Oh . . . you don't have to do all that."

"Let me. I want to. Your mom would want me to," Ramona adds with a sad smile.

"Do it, Calla," Evangeline says. "Come on. How fun will it be to get a fancy hairdo and makeup for the dance?"

"I don't know . . . maybe." She can't help but be a little overwhelmed by Ramona's kindness. It's like she's trying to help make up for Mom's not being here to do mother-daughter things with Calla.

Last spring before the junior prom, Mom treated Calla to a manicure, pedicure, facial, and fancy hairstyle. Too bad Calla was too miserable to enjoy the pampering—or the prom, for that matter. Her date—platonic, of course—was nice, smart, height-challenged Paul Horton, whom all the kids called Paul Shorton.

When she thinks back to how many tears she shed over the breakup with Kevin, as though it were the worst thing that could happen to her—not realizing the real nightmare was still ahead . . .

"You know," Ramona cuts into her thoughts. "I just thought of something, Calla. Maybe you could . . ."

Ramona stops walking, tilts her head and frowns.

"Maybe she could what?" Evangeline prompts.

Apparently lost in thought, Ramona doesn't reply.

Calla and Evangeline exchange a glance and a shrug.

"Never mind," Ramona says abruptly, and starts walking again. "Hey, look—the Gap is having a sale."

"The Gap is *always* having a sale," Evangeline replies, but she asks Calla, "Want to check it out?"

"Definitely."

"You two go, and meet me at the food court in a half hour," Ramona tells them. "I need to pick up some books in Barnes and Noble for that Crystal Healing seminar I'm teaching next week."

Twenty minutes and sixty-seven dollars later, Calla has a new pair of jeans, two long-sleeved tops, and a soft pumpkin-colored yarn sweater that has a small rip in the neckline. Ramona said Odelia will be able to sew it for her, no problem.

Evangeline got a sweater, too—same exact style, but no rip and in a different color, saying the pumpkin was too close to the shade of her hair and freckles.

"You know what? We should wear them to school on the same day, like twins!" she tells Calla as they settle at a table with an Orange Julius, two straws. "Hey, let's buy some other matching stuff!"

Calla raises an eyebrow and fumbles for something polite to say.

Evangeline bursts out laughing. "I'm just kidding! You didn't think I was serious, did you?"

Relieved, Calla grins. "Only for a second."

"Come on. I might be a loser, but I'm not *that* much of a loser."

"You're not a loser at all."

"Sure I am," Evangeline says cheerfully, then takes a sip from her straw before adding, "Good thing I have one cool friend."

"Who?"

"Duh. You!"

"Me! *I'm* cool?"

"Yeah, and the cool thing is"—Evangeline grins broadly—"you don't even know it."

"No way. I am so not cool."

"Think about it Calla. You're gorgeous, too—come on, don't shake your head like that, you know you are—and you waltz into Lily Dale out of nowhere and fit right in, and now you're going to homecoming with this hot guy every girl in school wants to go out with, and you're having lunch with Willow York and Sarita Abernathie every day."

"So?"

"So, they're gorgeous." True. Willow, with her porcelain skin and delicate features, and Sarita, with her dark skin and exotic beauty, are two of the prettiest girls in school.

"Plus, they're cool," Evangeline adds.

"So that . . . what? Makes me cool by association?"

"Ha. If it worked that way, I'd be cool by association with you," Evangeline points out wryly. "Listen, all I mean is, people like you, and they admire you. Things are going great for you here. You should enjoy it."

While it lasts.

She doesn't say that last part, but Calla hears it in her own head, accompanied by an inexplicable twinge of foreboding.

"Dad, you remember my friends Evangeline and Ramona." Calla leads him over to where they're standing at the top of the airport escalator

They held back when she spotted her father coming through the gate just now, obviously wanting to give her time for a private reunion.

"I remember. Nice to see you again." Dad shakes their hands.

Calla can't be certain, but his eyes might linger a little longer on Ramona than is absolutely necessary . . . and vice versa.

The airport is jammed with people on this Friday night.

Calla realizes, as they head for the escalator, that not all of them are alive.

It's just a flash, but she just had a pretty clear vision of a young boy, maybe ten or eleven, wearing Depression-era knee breeches, argyle socks, a vest, and a flat newsboy-type cap.

He's there, and then he's gone, haunting her without so much as a "*Boo*."

"Your dad is hot!" Evangeline whispers to her as the four of them take the escalator down to the short-term parking lot. "How come I didn't notice that before?"

"Um . . . because he wasn't?"

Calla herself is caught off-guard by the change in her father's appearance. His hair is longer than usual, shaggy, as if it needs to be cut, but it actually looks better like that. He looks younger. He's shaved off his beard, which had a lot of gray in it. And he's not wearing his glasses, but he is wearing a casual short-sleeved cotton button-up shirt and loafers—no socks—with his jeans.

Wait till Mom sees him, Calla finds herself thinking, before she remembers, with a sharp pang of grief, that her mother is gone.

Will this ever stop happening to her?

"I was just telling Jeff we haven't eaten yet, and he hasn't either," Ramona tells Calla and Evangeline as the four of them step off the escalator and head toward the car. "So we're all going to go get some wings, if you two aren't too tired."

"Too tired? Are you kidding?" Evangeline grins. "That sounds great! You haven't had real wings yet, have you, Mr. Delaney?"

"No, only the synthetic ones."

Calla is used to her father's dry sense of humor, but it takes Evangeline and her aunt a while to figure out that he's joking. When they do, they laugh. Hard. Especially Ramona.

"You can sit in the front with me, Jeff," she says when they reach her car.

Evangeline nudges Calla. "Are you thinking what I'm thinking?" she whispers as her aunt and Calla's father climb into the front seat together.

"That depends . . . are you thinking you're starved and you have to pee?"

"Calla!" Evangeline swats her arm.

"What? That's what I'm thinking."

Evangeline rolls her eyes and gets into the backseat.

Okay, it isn't what Calla was thinking.

But she doesn't want to let on to Evangeline that she, too, has noticed some kind of connection between her father and Ramona.

Oddly, it isn't that Calla feels as though he's betraying her mother in any way . . . though maybe she should.

No, the thing is . . .

They're wrong for each other.

Dad is a level-headed professor who on his last visit referred to a couple of Lily Dale mediums as "New Age freaks."

No way would he ever in a million years be interested in Ramona.

Then again . . .

Just months ago, Calla couldn't have imagined him clean-shaven and wearing loafers without socks, either.

Still . . .

People change their looks far more easily than they change their minds.

No way, Calla thinks stubbornly, settling into the backseat as her father and Ramona laugh together about something. *Absolutely no way.*

SIX

Saturday, September 22
10:25 a.m.

"Calla Delaney! You've decided to join us again, I see. Welcome." Petite, middle-aged Patsy Metcalf—who, in her trim jeans and beige turtleneck looks more like a suburban mom than a medium and metaphysics class instructor—takes her place among the circle of chairs in the octagonal mediums' league building.

Calla returns the pleasant smile and wishes she could edge her chair closer to Evangeline, sitting beside her, and ask if people are allowed to leave halfway through the class if they aren't entirely comfortable.

She tried to get out of it this morning, with her grandmother.

"I wasn't going to go, with Dad here," Calla protested in a whisper as they got breakfast ready.

"I think you should. Don't worry about Jeff. I'll keep him occupied while you're gone. I could use a man to do a few things around the house for me."

"Dad isn't exactly handy," Calla pointed out. "And anyway, where are we going to tell him I went?"

"To a study group. That's what it is," Odelia said innocently. "Right?"

So that was the story they gave Dad, over Odelia's rich creme brulee French toast. Calla wasn't in the mood for it, having had a late, heavy dinner of chicken wings, followed by a gooey dessert, but she ate it anyway.

She definitely wasn't in the mood to come to class, either, but here she is.

"You liked it last week," Evangeline pointed out to Calla as they walked over. "And anyway, you need help figuring out how to deal with your gift."

No denying that, considering how many stray spirits have been popping up around her lately.

Though Calla wishes Evangeline, and everyone else around here, would stop calling it a gift. Mostly, it feels like a curse.

Brooding, she stares at the flickering candle in the middle of the circle, unable to glean much from the class discussion about billet reading. She does learn, though, that it's a century-old exercise once used by mediums to hone their skills and refute skeptics.

She also catches glimpses of people in the room who aren't really here, and wonders if she's the only one who sees them: the matronly woman in a hoop skirt, the gorgeous

Hispanic-looking man in the seersucker suit and straw hat, even a ghost dog scampering about beneath the chairs.

No one else comments.

It's just me, Calla realizes uneasily.

When Patsy announces that it's time for the class to give billets a try, Calla shifts her weight on the folding chair and raises her hand halfway.

Patsy, busy gathering paper and pencils, doesn't notice.

"What's wrong?" Evangeline whispers.

"I need to get going."

"Home? Why?"

Calla shrugs. "I just have to go."

"You can't. We're in the middle of class."

"I know, but . . . I don't know how to do this."

"What? Billets? It's really cool. You need to try it."

The woman on Calla's other side nudges her. She's middle-aged, with a pale, drawn face and telltale scarf tied over her head. Cancer, chemo. You see a lot of that around Lily Dale, the desperately ill in search of healing.

She holds out a handful of pencils and smiles. "Hi. I'm Anne. Take one, pass the rest on."

Calla hesitates.

She's here. She might as well stay, ghostly visitors and all, rather than disrupt the class by walking out in the middle.

"All right, does everyone have a pencil and a slip of paper?" Patsy asks a few seconds later. "Notice that the papers are all exactly the same size. And we're going to fold them exactly the same way—in half, and then in half again. Everyone needs to write a question on the paper, then fold it and put it into the basket when I pass it to you. Got it?"

Almost everyone nods.

"What kind of question?" asks Lena, a girl who's a year behind Calla at Lily Dale High.

Sitting cluelessly with her pencil poised on the paper, Calla was wondering the same thing and is glad she didn't have to be the one to ask.

"Anything at all," Patsy tells them. "Something you've been wondering about, or wrestling with. Something you'd like Spirit to provide the answer to."

Whoa. Now she gets it. She knows exactly what question she wants answered.

Where can I find Darrin Yates?

Then, thinking better of writing his name, which will probably be familiar to these locals, she erases it. She could just write his initials, but someone might still figure it out.

Instead, she replaces the name with *the man who calls himself "Tom"?*

That, after all, is the fake name he gave Calla when he came to see Mom back in March. Spirit will probably know that. Spirit knows everything, right?

Wondering if she really believes that, Calla folds her paper as instructed and puts it into the basket Patsy passes around the circle.

Then she turns off the lights and, in the flickering candle-light, passes the basket around the circle again.

"Everyone take a slip of paper. Don't unfold it. Just hold it in your hands."

When everyone has a folded billet, she leads the class through a series of relaxation exercises, telling them to open their minds to Spirit and ask Spirit to give them the answer to the handwritten question they haven't even read.

With her eyes closed, Calla does her best to focus on the paper in her hand.

In her mind's eye, she sees a train speeding toward a mountain tunnel. She can hear the whistle blaring, then it becomes muffled as the train is swallowed into the darkness, until all is silent.

What does it mean?

Calla has no idea. Maybe the person who wrote the question asked whether there's a railroad journey in the future. If so, it looks like the answer is yes.

If not, I'm clueless.

She wonders—not for the first time this morning—why she's here.

They begin.

An elderly woman with puffy dyed black hair begins. "Spirit is showing me a springtime meadow," she says, eyes closed in concentration. "I know it's springtime because I see tulips and daffodils growing. I see a woman's left hand, wearing a gold wedding band and feeding some long grass to a young colt." She opens her eyes. "That's all."

"All right, open the paper and tell us what it says," Patsy commands.

"It says, 'Will I carry this baby to term?' "

A choking sound, almost a sob, escapes a young woman on the opposite side of the circle. Her hand, wearing a gold wedding band, Calla notices, flutters to her mouth.

"That's mine," she manages to say, her voice choked with

emotion. "I've lost two pregnancies now, and . . . I'm due in April."

Patsy smiles. "I think you just got good news, Emily."

Everyone claps.

Calla joins in, but she's not so sure they should be celebrating just yet. It's not as if the old woman saw Emily cradling a newborn.

Then again, Patsy has mentioned a few times that often the spirits will deliver a sort of symbolic message, conveyed in what some locals like to call psychic shorthand. Patsy said every medium has her own shorthand symbols.

Calla's received plenty of messages from Spirit since she got to Lily Dale, but she's never tried to give an actual reading. She has no idea whether she has shorthand symbols in her repertoire. Maybe she does. Maybe for her, trains stand for something else. Something that doesn't involve travel. Who knows?

Patsy decides that whoever has just been read will do the next reading.

Emily says that she saw a boat on a choppy sea, taking on water.

Calla listens for the response with interest, wondering if Emily's boat—and her train—symbolize something else.

The question:

Would it be a mistake to give my brother
a loan?

"That's mine," says a middle-aged man with a red beard and a blue flannel shirt stretched tightly across a pot belly. "Wow, that's good. Freddie—he lives in Rhode Island—he's a fisherman. His trawler was damaged in a Nor'easter a while back. He wanted to borrow some money for repairs—you know, get back on his feet. He's never been good with money, and me . . . well, I've never had much. I'd have to cash in some stuff to get it for him. I guess it's a bad idea?"

"That depends on your interpretation of what Emily saw. What do you think, Emily?"

"I think it means he's not supposed to lend the money," she tells Red Beard. "The boat was sinking."

"Was my brother on it? Because maybe it means I'm supposed to rescue him with the money."

"I don't know I didn't see him."

Either way, Calla realizes, it's pretty clear that a boat is just a boat. At least this time.

And now it's Red Beard's turn.

"I don't know why," he says, "but I keep seeing a statue of a bear in a fountain. I mean, not *a* statue, *the* statue. There's only one that I've ever seen. It's up in Geneseo—my cousin's daughter went to college there, and I saw it when we went to her graduation."

He pauses, rubbing his beard, eyes squeezed shut.

"I'm seeing a house, too—it's Victorian, you know . . . with a mansard roof and gingerbread porch and shutters and all that. It looks like something you'd see here in the Dale, but . . . it's not familiar to me. Maybe it's up there in Geneseo, I don't know. The thing about it is, it's painted purple. Not, you know, lavender. Bright purple. Neon." He laughs and opens his eyes. "Never saw anything like it."

Patsy smiles. "Don't think I have, either. Read the question, Bob."

Red Beard—Bob, apparently—unfolds the paper and reads, "Where can I find the man who calls himself 'Tom'?"

Calla's eyes widen.

"Whose was it?" Patsy looks around the room.

"Uh . . . it was mine," Calla manages to say.

Evangeline kicks her gently and whispers, "Who's Tom?"

Calla ignores her, thoughts reeling.

"Sounds like Geneseo might be a good place to start looking for this guy," Red Beard tells her. "That, or start looking for purple houses."

"Maybe so," Patsy agrees, "or maybe not. Remember, we aren't always meant to interpret messages so literally. The color purple, the bear, even just a fountain—those could be symbols for something else. Calla, do they mean anything to you?"

She shakes her head. "Where's Geneseo? I've never heard of it."

"It's a college town, about an hour and a half, two hours away from here."

Calla isn't sure how she's going to get there, or when. It seems impossible, considering that she's flat broke and without a car.

But if there's the slightest possibility Darrin Yates is there, then that's where she's going to go. She'll just have to find a way.

"Odelia, that dinner was great." Dad pushes back his chair and pats his stomach. "Normally I don't like cereal on my chicken, but it was absolutely delicious."

"It's an old family recipe. You just dunk it in egg and roll it in crushed cornflakes, then fry it."

"Really? Steph never made chicken this way."

"Calla tells me she was something of a health nut. Right, Calla?"

"Mmm-hmm" She pokes her fork halfheartedly at the barely touched chicken on her plate.

All she can think about is what happened in her class this morning.

Not just all those spirits she saw hanging around, or Red Beard's clue about Darrin Yates—although that's been the main reason for her preoccupation.

But she's still feeling just as unsettled about what happened next, when it was her turn to read.

She described her vision of the train speeding into the dark tunnel and confessed that she had no idea how to interpret it.

Patsy assured her that was okay.

Calla was momentarily stumped when she read the question written on the paper in her hand: *Am I going to make it?*

"Whose is it?" Patsy asked, and Anne, sitting right next to Calla—the obvious chemo patient—raised her hand. It was trembling.

Calla's heart sank.

This time, Patsy assured them all that the vision might not be symbolic at all—that it quite possibly was meant to be interpreted literally: Anne might be going on a train journey sometime in the near future.

"I've always wanted to take the Orient Express," she replied, but her laugh was hollow.

She knew, and Calla instinctively knew, that the answer to her question was no. She wasn't going to make it.

"Calla," her father says now, "are you okay?"

She looks up to find both him and Odelia watching her.

"Sure . . . I'm fine."

"You don't look fine," her father decides. "What's up?"

"I'm just . . . you know, worried about school." That's always a good catchall source of angst.

"What *about* school?"

"You two sit, I'll clear," Odelia murmurs, and stands to begin taking plates away from the table.

"You know, college," Calla improvises. "I have no idea where I want to go, and the guidance counselor said we should be in the final stages of narrowing things down."

Mrs. Erskine, her guidance counselor, really did tell her to put together a list of schools to discuss with her father this weekend—reach schools, target schools, and safety schools, about ten in all.

Calla can't think of even one . . . other than Cornell.

"I thought you were thinking Cornell." Apparently, her father is a mind reader.

"I was, but . . ." But that was mostly because of Kevin. "I doubt I can get in there."

"It can be one of your reach schools. You never know."

Great. So, one down, nine more to go. And if by some miracle she does manage to get into Cornell, she can see Kevin and Annie every day. Yippee.

"There must be some other schools you're interested in."
Calla shrugs.

"Why don't I fly back here in a few weeks, and we can go look at some campuses?"

"Around here?"

"Here, in New England . . . that's what your mother was planning to do with you. I'm just sorry we're getting such a late start."

"Won't it be too late, though, in a few weeks? I thought I had to have my applications in then."

Her father puts a reassuring hand on her arm. "It'll work out. Figure out where you want to go, and get started on the applications, and we'll narrow it down when we see the campuses."

"What if I want to go to . . . I don't know, the Midwest? Or California?"

"Do you?"

No. She doesn't. And she doesn't know why she's making this so difficult. She just can't seem to help herself.

"I told you—I don't know what I want, Dad!"

She sees her father and Odelia exchange a glance.

Then Odelia says, "You know what? I made a devil's food cake for dessert, and I think it would be really nice if we invited Evangeline over to have some with us. Maybe we can all play cards or something."

"That's a great idea!" Dad exclaims. "And we can invite Ramona, too . . . if she's around."

"I'm sure she's around." Odelia looks pleased. "What do you think, Calla?"

"Sure, why not."

Later, sitting around the table playing Ten Penny with the Taggarts, including Mason, and her father and grandmother, Calla finds it impossible to stay bummed out about anything. It's almost like a party. And Dad still has yet to catch on that her grandmother and Ramona are both mediums.

At one point, Calla sees Miriam drift amiably into the room as if to investigate the source of the rowdy laughter. Clearly, both her grandmother and Ramona have spotted her as well. Calla sees their raised eyebrows and can almost hear the unspoken conversation between them.

Odelia is telling Ramona not to acknowledge anything in front of Dad, and Ramona is assuring her that of course she won't.

"I don't know when I've laughed so much," Ramona declares at the end of the night when they're saying their good-byes. "Jeff, it really is too bad you live so far away. We could all do this more often."

"That would be great," Dad says, so fervently that Calla looks at him in surprise.

Remembering that he told her he was having a hard time adjusting to life on the West Coast, she finds herself wondering if he's even planning to stick it out.

When the Taggarts are gone and Odelia has disappeared upstairs, she finds herself alone with her father in front of the television.

"Nothing on but the news," Dad says, channel surfing. "And there's never anything good about that. I suppose we could just turn in, but I'm still on LA time."

"I'm not that tired yet, either." Calla hesitates, then asks, "Dad, is there any chance you're not going to stay in California for the rest of the school year?"

Of course I'm going to stay there.

That's what he's supposed to say, anyway.

But what he really says is, "I'm lost there, Calla."

"You mean, you're lonely?"

He nods. "It's just not what it was supposed to be. I keep wondering what I'm doing there—probably the same way you feel here."

"That's how I used to feel, but not anymore. Now I like it. It feels like home, almost."

"Yeah . . . I can see that. I wonder if it would feel like that for me, too."

"You mean . . . are you thinking of coming *here*?"

"I don't know what I'm thinking. It's just . . . there's more for me here than there is in California . . . or in Florida, for that matter."

She's silent, digesting that.

Maybe he's right.

And maybe part of the reason is that he's interested in Ramona.

She didn't miss the little glances and smiles the two of them exchanged all night. There's no question that there's some kind of connection between them.

"What do you think I should do?" her father asks.

"Me?" She's definitely not used to him asking her advice. He's the parent. Shouldn't he know what to do? "I . . . I'm not sure, Dad."

She doesn't even know what she should do.

For a moment, she considers spilling the whole story to him—about the dream, and Darrin, and everything else connected to Mom's death.

But that would mean admitting too much.

And it's not like her father's going to give her the green light to go off and investigate on her own.

More likely, he'll tell her to start packing her bags.

It always comes down to that.

You're completely on your own, Calla tells herself grimly. *It's up to you to either find out what happened or put it to rest and move on.*

You just have to decide which it's going to be.

SEVEN

Monday, September 24
3:09 p.m.

"Jacy!" Dumping her math notebook into her backpack, Calla hurries to catch up with him as he strides out of the classroom after the last bell. "Wait up!"

Jacy doesn't stop walking, and he doesn't look back, but he does slow down enough to let her fall into step beside him.

"What's up?" he asks tersely.

Maybe this wasn't such a great idea after all, she concludes, fumbling with the zipper on her backpack, then slinging it over one shoulder.

Bold confrontation's never been her style.

But then, it's not like she and Jacy aren't friends, right? If nothing else.

And friends talk to each other.

Which Jacy hasn't done at all today. Or last week, either, for that matter.

She's been trying to convince herself that it might be her imagination that he's been standoffish. But the other day, he was less than friendly in the cafeteria, and today, when she was really paying close attention, she couldn't help but notice that he didn't talk to her or sit near her or even glance in her direction.

Which is odd, considering where they left off that night on Odelia's front porch, when Calla was 99.9 percent sure Jacy would have kissed her good night if Evangeline's brother, Mason, hadn't ruined the moment.

A few nights later, Jacy jogged by Odelia's house as she was waiting for Blue Slayton to pick her up for a date. Of course, he didn't know that was where she was going . . .

Or did he?

Jacy, like everyone else around here, is a gifted psychic.

Anyway, Lily Dale isn't just a small town filled with psychics; it's a small town, period. Word gets around.

So Jacy probably knows all about her and Blue—maybe he saw her talking to him in the cafeteria yesterday, even—and now he's giving her the cold shoulder, because . . .

Well, because he's jealous, which seems out of character. What else can it be, though?

Anyway, if he's such a gifted psychic, shouldn't he realize that Calla isn't only interested in Blue Slayton? Doesn't Jacy realize that she likes him just as much? Or maybe even more?

There's something about lanky, soft-spoken Jacy—with his sensitive mouth and exotic dark hair, eyes, and complexion—that has physically appealed to her from the first time they connected, back in August.

Yes, and even then, as they shook hands, Calla was literally jolted by . . . something. Some kind of static electricity, sizzling up her arm.

Early on, Jacy—bronzed and usually barefoot—had a way of popping up when she least expected it, kind of like the many spirits who tend to hang around Lily Dale. And, like the spirits, his presence tends to rattle Calla—tie her tongue in knots and make her heart beat faster, though not for the same reasons.

The foster son of a pair of local male mediums, Jacy's a relative newcomer to the Dale himself. But Calla never would have guessed that, considering his insight into how things work around here—and on the Other Side.

Until she spilled her suspicions to Lisa the other day, Jacy was the only one who knew about Calla's theory that her mother's death was no accident. He's the one who helped her decipher the spirit messages that led to that conclusion, and he's been helping her try to track down the long-missing Darrin Yates, her mother's long-ago boyfriend.

Maybe he's just being a good friend and nothing more.

He did hold her hand as they walked home together after that troubling confrontation with Darrin's parents . . .

But that was probably because he felt sorry for her, after the way the Yateses treated her—as if her mother possibly had something to do with Darrin's disappearance years ago.

Anyway, Blue's the one who's been asking her out, not Jacy. It was Blue who kissed her good night, and Blue who invited her to homecoming, and if she had any common sense, she'd get over Jacy right now.

Uh-huh. Good luck with that.

"What's up with you lately?" she asks him over the chaotic chatter that echoes through the crowded corridor.

"The same. Homework. Running."

Running. He's on the cross-country team.

"Is it my imagination, or have you been avoiding me lately?" She waits for him to deny it, but he does the opposite.

"No," he replies evenly, "it's not your imagination."

Caught off guard, she wonders what she's supposed to say to that.

"Did I . . . um, do something to make you mad?"

"*Mad?* No."

Jealous, then?

She doesn't dare ask that.

She has a moment to think of something else to say as they take opposite routes past a handful of girls gathered around someone's cell phone in the hallway, laughing about a text message one of them is typing in.

"Hi, Calla," a voice calls from the group as she passes.

It's Pam Moraco, a petite, sharp-featured blonde who might be more attractive if her smile ever reached her close-set eyes.

"Hey, Pam," Calla says briefly, and is glad, and not at all surprised, to see that Pam and her friends are much more interested in the cell phone than in her.

She moves past them and meets up with Jacy again on the other side, still wondering what she's going to say to him. But before she has a chance to come up with something, he stops walking and turns to her.

"What?" she asks, taken aback by the accusation in his narrowed black eyes.

"I know what happened last Saturday night."

"Last Saturday night, I was at home playing cards with my dad and my grandmother and the Taggarts," she tells him, confused. "Is that a problem?"

"No . . . *last* Saturday night. Not this past one."

Last Saturday: her date with Blue, and Blue asking her to homecoming . . .

So she was right. He's jealous.

"Well, it's not like you didn't have the opportunity to do it yourself," she shoots back, not sure whether to be irritated or flattered by his blunt honesty.

Something flickers in his expression, but he says nothing.

"I was actually kind of hoping you would," she goes on, "but he beat you to it."

There. Total honesty in exchange for his. It's only fair.

Now what?

Now, most likely, Jacy will tell her how much he regrets missing his chance, and that he hopes to make up for it.

If he asks her out now, she'll definitely say yes, Blue or no Blue. They might have a homecoming dance date, but it's not like she can't go out with anyone else in the meantime.

She glances back at Pam and her gossipy friends, to see if any of them are paying attention to her and Jacy.

It doesn't seem like it, but you never know.

Calla might be free to talk to other guys, or even date them, but she really doesn't need anyone running back to Blue and starting trouble.

"Come on," she tells Jacy. "Let's go."

Jacy obliges, but he's wearing a confused expression. "What do you mean, 'he beat you to it'?"

"I mean, he asked first. What was I supposed to do, say no because I'd rather go with you?"

"Go where?"

Suddenly uneasy, Calla asks slowly, "What do you mean, 'go where'?"

There's a long pause.

"I, uh, don't think we're talking about the same thing."

"You said . . . last Saturday night."

"Right. I was up late that night, and I saw the cops over at your place, and—"

She gasps, pressing her hands to her flaming cheeks. "*That* was what you meant?"

"Some lunatic breaking into Odelia's house and attacking you. Yeah. After I warned you to be careful."

Totally mortified, Calla shakes her head, barely hearing his words.

So he wasn't talking about Blue, and her love life, and his wishing he had asked her out.

No, he was talking about that lunatic killer coming after her.

Meanwhile, I just basically told him that not only do I have a thing for him, but that I'd much rather go to the dance with him than Blue.

It's a wonder he's even still here talking to her, but he is, not that she can really even grasp what he's saying.

"I told you I thought there was something . . . I just had a bad feeling. I knew you were in trouble. You should have been more careful. If you had just—"

"I, uh, I'm really sorry," she cuts in, glad her locker is just around the corner. She needs to get there, fast.

"You're sorry for what?"

"For everything." *Mostly, being a total loser and opening my big fat mouth and sticking my big old foot in it.*

Quickening her pace, as if she'll somehow be able to just lose him, she makes the turn around the corner—and slams right into someone, who immediately drops what he's carrying with a deafening slam and clatter.

Donald Reamer. And the world's biggest, loudest wooden chessboard, along with an entire collection of pieces.

"Oh . . . I'm so sorry!" she tells Donald, a hugely obese kid whose looks aren't helped by thick glasses and a line of dark fuzz on his upper lip, which is quavering as he looks down at his chess set.

Oh, no. No, Donald, please don't cry.

Of all the people she could crash into, it had to be poor Donald, the resident scapegoat?

He's always tripping, bumping into furniture, dropping things . . . probably because he's so nervous about the kids who constantly make fun of him. Of course, the clumsiness only fuels the teasing—a vicious, cruel circle.

Sickened by the snickers around them as Donald grunts and struggles to bend his hefty body, Calla tells him, "No, it's okay, I'll get your stuff."

But Jacy's beat her to it, already on his knees, handing the board to Donald and reaching to retrieve the scattered pieces.

Calla drops beside him and crawls around grabbing what she can, aware that a bunch of kids have stopped to watch and, of course, make some mean-spirited comments about Donald.

She sees Donald bend to pick up a black pawn in time for a clean white Nike to kick it out of his reach.

Furious, she looks up to see a wiry, smirking freshman attached to the sneaker.

"Oops, sorry," he tells Donald.

Laughing with his idiot friends, he's poised to kick a white rook when an arm snakes around his ankle and gives a sharp tug.

The kid goes down hard, sprawled face-first on the floor.

"Oops, sorry," Jacy says, then calmly and swiftly retrieves the white rook, the black pawn, and the few remaining pieces.

He stands and hands them to Donald with a casual, "Here you go," as the freshman would-be bully slinks away with his henchmen and Calla gets back on her feet and dusts herself off.

"Thanks." Donald is focused on the pieces, taking inventory.

Calla notices an older man, then, heavyset and bearing quite a strong resemblance to Donald. He's standing just behind him, leaning over Donald's shoulder and looking silently into the box.

He must be a teacher. Calla wonders why he didn't say anything to the kids who were taunting Donald. She's noticed that faculty members, aware of what goes on with him, usually step in to stop the bullying if they're around.

"Got everything?" Jacy asks, and Donald nods. "Good. Chess club meeting today, huh?"

"Yes." Donald nods, then offers awkwardly, "One Christmas, my dad made me this board and carved all the pieces. It took him months to do it. He's the one who taught me how to play, when I was little."

"Seriously?" Jacy leans in to get a better look. "That's really a great set."

"Do you play chess?"

"A little."

"Really? You should come to chess club."

"I don't like clubs," Jacy tells him with a shrug. "But I'll play you sometime, if you want."

"Okay." Donald's obvious disappointment isn't lost on Jacy.

"Tomorrow," Jacy tells him. "At lunch. We'll play. Okay?"

"I don't go to lunch on Tuesdays. I have French Horn then."

"Then Wednesday. You bring the set."

Donald brightens immediately. "Sure."

"Good. See you then."

Donald lumbers away with the oversized male teacher protectively trailing along behind him, clearly intending to see him safely to chess club.

Calla, still momentarily distracted from her own problems, stands with Jacy, watching them go.

"I wonder why he didn't give that kid detention," she murmurs.

"Who?"

"The teacher."

"What teacher?"

She points, then realizes that the man walking with Donald is no teacher. There's something about the way he drifts along, almost weightless despite his obese build . . .

"You don't see him, do you." It's not a question, and as Jacy shakes his head, she acknowledges the truth.

The man is yet another spirit.

"I'm never going to get used to this," she mutters with a sigh.

"What does he look like?" Jacy asks, and she briefly describes him. "That's Donald's father, I bet. I heard he died a few years ago. Heart attack, I think."

Calla's heart sinks.

So Donald is part of the sad little club, too; he knows what it's like to suddenly lose a parent.

She swallows hard, picturing Donald's father lovingly carving a chess set for his son, and knowing Donald lost one of the few people in this world who had been kind to him.

She's been here long enough to know that the Reamers don't live in the Dale but somewhere on the rural outskirts. It doesn't necessarily mean Donald isn't psychically aware, but she figures the odds are against it.

He probably doesn't realize his father watches over him from the Other Side. He's not aware that his father sees how the other kids torture his son, how he tries to protect him. All he knows is that he's been robbed of the parent who loved him.

She realizes she's about to cry.

It's just too much. She can't handle this. Any of it.

"I've got to go," she tells Jacy abruptly. "I'm babysitting for Paula Drumm's kids today, and I can't be late."

Jacy says nothing, just keeps up with her as she resumes her sprint down the hall.

Arriving at her locker, she reaches for the combination lock, but Jacy puts his hand on her arm. "Wait. There's something I need to tell you."

"What?" Something tells her it's not going to be a heartfelt declaration of true love.

"It's been bugging me all week, ever since I found out about that guy attacking you."

"Wait . . . how *did* you find out about that?"

"I asked one of the cops."

"But they said they weren't going to let it get out!"

"Not to the public. But I know this guy, Figeroa, he's sort of a friend of mine."

"You have a friend on the police force?" she asks dubiously, then sees his expression and remembers that he's been through a lot more than most people his age.

"Figeroa knows I'm not going to say anything to anyone, and he knew I was worried, so . . ." He shrugs.

He was worried about me.

But that doesn't mean he has feelings for me.

"Whatever, Jacy." She pulls her arm from his grasp, then forces herself to look at her watch, as though he's keeping her from an engagement far more pressing than babysitting.

Yeah, like hurling herself off the nearest tall building—not that there are any for miles around.

Looks like you'll just have to carry on indefinitely in sheer humiliation. Nice going.

Jacy touches her arm again, more gently this time. "Calla . . . I'm sorry I haven't talked to you all week. Bad way to handle things—maybe I suck at communication. What can I say? But I'm trying to talk to you now."

Okay, that's encouraging . . . not that it takes away a shred of her embarrassment.

"Can you please just . . . what is it you need to tell me? Because I really have to get to Paula's."

He clears his throat. "Last week I told you I was worried about you because I'd had a vision of you in some kind of trouble."

"No, you didn't."

"Yeah, I did. I told you that night after we went to see the Yateses, remember?"

Remember? It was when he was holding her hand, right after he almost kissed her . . . how could she forget?

Except he didn't say anything about a vision.

"You just said you were worried," she reminds him, "and that I should be careful."

"Oh. I guess I didn't mention the vision. I didn't want to scare you with the specifics."

"So you saw a man coming after me?"

"I saw . . . listen, the details aren't important. When I heard what happened to you Saturday night, I figured that must have been what I was seeing. But . . . it wasn't."

A chill slips down her spine. "What do you mean?"

"I mean, I still have this feeling that you're in some kind of trouble, or . . . more like danger. And it's been getting stronger every day. Every time I see you."

"You've been having more visions about me?"

"Yeah."

"What are they?"

He sidesteps that again. "I've been trying to figure out what it all means, whether what I'm seeing is supposed to be interpreted literally, or if it's some kind of psychic shorthand."

"What do you think?"

"I honestly don't know."

"Why didn't you say anything to me before now?"

Another shrug. "You didn't listen to me last time."

Exasperated, she says, "But I didn't—"

"Wait, just listen. I told you to be careful. You weren't. You walked into the house alone that night, with that guy waiting there, and you almost got yourself killed."

"That's not *my* fault. It's not like I knew someone was there."

Or did she?

She remembers the overwhelming feeling of foreboding as she crossed the threshold that night. It grew stronger by the second. If she had listened to her instincts, she might have walked right back out again.

But she didn't.

She pushes her self-doubt aside, though, needing to settle this with Jacy, who's acting as though she personally offended him. Which is ridiculous.

"So that's why you haven't been talking to me? Because you think I should have heeded your big, dramatic, ominous warning?"

She's being sarcastic; she can't help it. She just feels like she's in way over her head with him and there's no getting back on solid footing. Not anytime soon, anyway.

"I said it's not all your fault," he reminds her. "It's mine, too. It's—look, I don't like feeling like this, okay? I'm not good at it."

"Feeling like what?"

He looks away, obviously uncomfortable.

Whoa.

Jacy, who's managed to maintain a level of emotional detachment since they met, is no longer entirely in control.

Looking at him, she glimpses for the first time the wounded child whose alcoholic, troubled parents lashed out at each other and at him one too many times. The authorities intervened, took him from his home, and placed him in the system.

Peter and Walt are good to him; according to Evangeline, they want to formally adopt him, and his parents are prepared to sign away their rights.

How does that feel? For your own parents to hurt you, badly, and then be willing to cut all ties?

No wonder Jacy spends so much time alone—running, fishing, hiking in the woods.

He's got a lot to think about. So much pain to absorb, a tremendous amount of healing to do . . .

He probably doesn't want to be too close to anyone after what he's been through. He probably needs to keep the world at arm's length.

Gazing at Jacy, aching for him, Calla wills him to turn his head and look at her again.

He does, and she clearly sees the vulnerability in his eyes.

That lasts all of a few seconds before some defense mechanism kicks in and they flash with anger.

"Hey, it's not like I *want* to worry about you," he snaps at her.

"So don't." She shrugs, clenching the straps of her backpack with both hands so he won't see them shaking.

"Doesn't work that way, in case you hadn't noticed."

They stare at each other in silence.

Locker doors slam all around them. People are laughing, talking, oblivious.

Then Jacy says, "You've got this thing hanging over you. I see it whenever I look at you."

"What thing?"

"I'm not sure. I just feel like someone's going to try to hurt you."

"Again?" she asks, heart pounding in dread.

He nods. "It has nothing to do with the other night. This is someone else. A stranger, I think. And I feel like it has something to do with your mother."

EIGHT

Tuesday, September 25
3:31 p.m.

Walking into an empty house after school, Calla finds a note on the kitchen table.

At the vet with Gert. Back by Six.
Love, Gammy

Calla goes straight to the adjacent sunroom, where Odelia does her readings.

Rare afternoon sunlight streams into the bright room with windows on three walls, unadorned by curtains or shades. The color scheme here, unlike the rest of the house, is a soothing beige. And unlike the rest of the house, the room is relatively free of clutter. The only furniture is a trio of wingback chairs, all facing each other in the center of the room, and one table that holds a box of tissues, a couple of candles, a tape recorder, and her grandmother's appointment book.

Calla opens it, hoping that Odelia is more organized in her professional life than she is in her private one.

Surprisingly, she is.

On last Thursday's date, beneath Owen Henry's name in the 6:30 p.m. slot, is a phone number.

Calla goes to the kitchen, picks up the phone, and dials the number before she can chicken out.

Yes, she knows her grandmother warned her not to meddle with her clients.

Yes, she knows that the results were almost disastrous when she disobeyed that warning.

But the poor, grieving man deserves to know that someone has at least glimpsed his wife on the Other Side. That Betty hasn't just disappeared into some black void. Maybe it'll bring him comfort to know that she's there, and that she showed Calla a house—presumably, the earthly home she and sweet, feeble Owen shared in their twilight years.

When a male voice answers the phone with an almost curt-sounding "Hello?" Calla assumes she's reached the wrong number. Figures Odelia wouldn't be as organized as it seemed there for a minute.

"I'm sorry," Calla says, "I was trying to reach Mr. Henry . . . ?"

"This is he."

It is?

He sounds more brusque over the phone than feeble and sweet, as he was in person. "Who's calling, please?"

"This is Calla Delaney." *Lovely as the lily,* she wants to add. *Remember?*

Apparently he doesn't, until she prompts, "Odelia Lauder's granddaughter? From Lily Dale?"

"Oh! Calla. Right. What can I do for you?"

Might as well not mince words. "I'm a psychic, Mr. Henry, like my grandmother. And I know she couldn't put you in touch with your wife, Betty, but I think I . . . um . . . saw her. Did she have white hair and gold glasses on a chain?"

There's an audible gasp on the other end of the phone. "That's her. What did she say?"

"She didn't actually *say* anything," Calla admits uncomfortably.

"What did she do?"

"She didn't, uh, *do* anything, either."

Maybe she shouldn't have called. After all, she doesn't really have anything specific to share, other than having seen Betty and the house.

But maybe that will be enough. Mr. Henry is in the same boat she is. It might bring him comfort.

"I thought you'd just want to know that she's alive and well . . . I mean, on the Other Side. And she's still with you."

There's a pause.

Mr. Henry clears his throat. "Calla, my dear, you've made this old man very happy. I'd like to know more about my dear Betty. Let's set up an appointment."

"Oh, I don't do readings," she says hastily.

"I thought you said you were a psychic."

"I am . . . I mean, I see things, but I don't . . . you know . . . work. As a medium. I'm just . . ."

94

Just what? A kid? Confused? Sticking my nose where it doesn't belong?

No, she definitely shouldn't have called. Didn't she learn her lesson the hard way with Elaine Riggs?

"It would mean the world to me if you would just sit down with me for a short time and put me in touch with Betty," Owen Henry says fervently. "Please. I have a few questions for her. Questions only she can answer."

"But . . ."

"I'll give you one thousand dollars if you'll do this."

Calla's voice lodges in her throat.

One thousand dollars?

"I'm sorry. I can't," she manages to croak.

Really, she can't. It wouldn't be right.

"Please. I'm begging you."

One thousand dollars.

With that kind of money, she could definitely figure out a way to get herself to Geneseo and back. There must be a bus or something.

"Calla, you're the only one who can help me," Mr. Henry is saying, his voice sounding as if it's going to give way to tears.

"All right."

She has to help him.

But not for money.

"I'll see what I can do," she says. "But you can't pay me."

"I insist."

"I, um, insist that you don't."

Tempting as it is, that would be wrong.

"I just want to help you," she tells him, "because I know what it's like to lose someone."

"All right, then. I'll come right over," he says eagerly.

"No!" she all but screams into the phone.

"No?"

"Not here. And not, um, today. I'm tied up."

"Tomorrow?"

"Tied up again." She really is, with babysitting and working with Willow on her math.

"Thursday," he says firmly. "Where shall we meet?"

She hesitates, then tells him she'll meet him at the diner over in Cassadaga, about a mile down the road from the Dale. She can walk there after school. There's always a chance that someone from the Dale might walk into the diner, but at that time of day, it's pretty unlikely.

"You're a lifesaver, Calla," Owen Henry says warmly before hanging up, and she decides she might have done the right thing after all.

NINE

Wednesday, September 26
7:56 p.m.

"Okay, that was pretty good." Willow leans back in her chair and stretches. "Want to take a break before we do the extra-credit stuff?"

"Definitely." Calla slaps her math textbook closed and tosses her pencil aside. "Thanks for showing me how to solve that last problem to the second derivative. I don't know if I'm ever going to get the hang of calculus."

"You will. You said math was one of your best subjects back in Florida."

"Yeah, but not here. It's like I'm starting from scratch. And Bombeck is so tough, it doesn't help."

"Maybe it does," Willow contradicts. "He's tough, but he's good. He's not going to let you slide through, you know?"

"Definitely not."

"Want another bottle of water?"

"Sure."

"Come on into the kitchen. I could use something to eat—how about you?"

"My grandmother made the world's hugest meal tonight," she tells Willow as she follows her through the small, cluttered house. "Lasagna, meatloaf, mashed potatoes . . . I'm still stuffed."

"Meatloaf *and* lasagna?"

"Yeah, she said she bought too much ground beef, so she made the extra into a meatloaf. I'm surprised she didn't make hamburgers to go with it. She likes to eat. And she's a great cook, even if some of her concoctions are a little . . . out there," she adds, remembering the snickernoodles.

"Like my mom. She used to be a great cook, too, before . . ."

She got sick.

But she doesn't say it, and Calla wonders why Willow never mentions her mother's obvious illness. The perpetual lineup of orange plastic prescription bottles on the counter betray Althea York's daily battle with whatever it is that's shortening her breath and confining her to her bed during most of Calla's visits.

Tonight, though, she's surprised to find Althea in the kitchen, pouring hot water over a tea bag. Her enormous body is swathed in a light blue terry-cloth robe, and her short gray hair is standing on end.

"Calla, how are you?"

"Fine, thanks . . . how are you?"

"Just fine." Althea nods decisively, double chins wobbling.

And really, she doesn't appear to be at death's door.

Still, every time Calla sees her, she senses illness radiating from Althea, along with the sorrowful knowledge that her days are numbered.

She's never mentioned it to Willow, though. She just feels a silent kinship with this beautiful girl who may or may not realize that she and Calla will someday have far more in common than schoolwork.

It's like Willow's going to be joining their sad club, Calla thinks—not for the first time. A club that includes Evangeline Taggart, Blue Slayton, Jacy Bly, even Donald . . . almost all the kids she's met here in Lily Dale are bereaved one way or another, just as Calla is.

Quite a few of her friends back home have divorced parents, but there's nothing like this.

Is it mere coincidence that Lily Dale seems to draw far more than its share of those who have lost their closest loved ones?

The longer she's been here, the more certain Calla has become that there are no coincidences.

"Would you like some tea, girls?" Althea asks, still holding the steaming pot. "It's jasmine."

"I will, thanks, Mrs. York. It smells good."

"I'll get it. Mom, you go back and lie down." Willow takes the teapot from her mother's hands and takes two more cups from the cupboard.

"I'll lie down in a minute. For now I'll just sit and visit with Calla." Althea sinks into a chair at the kitchen table as though she doesn't have the strength to make her way out of the room just yet. "How's the math homework going tonight?"

"It's . . . going," Calla tells her. "I don't know what I'd do without Willow."

Hands clasped around the hot mug, Althea inhales the fragrant steam and nods. "She's a good girl. I don't know what I'd do without her, either."

Willow smiles faintly and plants a kiss on her mother's head, then sets a cup of tea in front of Calla and sits down with her own.

They talk about tea and homework and the weather, and Calla can see that Althea is getting wearier by the second, though she tries to keep up a good front.

"Come on, Mom." Willow pushes back her own chair. "You should go rest. Let's go. Calla, I'll be right back."

"It was so nice seeing you, Calla," Althea says. "Come again soon."

"Oh, I will, unfortunately." She forces a laugh. "You're going to be pretty sick of me by the time the semester is over, if I don't get the hang of this calculus stuff."

She tries not to notice how heavily Althea leans on her daughter as Willow walks with her toward the doorway.

With tears in her eyes, Calla thinks of her own mother. What she wouldn't give for the chance to walk beside her again, even knowing—as Willow must—that their days together were numbered.

Back at home, Calla is completely absorbed in the math homework she and Willow couldn't finish, when Odelia knocks on her bedroom door.

"Calla? Can I talk to you for a minute?"

Uh-oh.

Did she find out, somehow, about Calla's plan to meet Owen Henry tomorrow?

"Sure," Calla says with a gulp. "Come in."

"I hate to interrupt you when you're doing your homework . . ." The door opens with a loud creak and Odelia sticks her brassy red head into the room.

She doesn't look irked. That's a good sign.

"I brought you a snack," Odelia says amiably, and it's all Calla can do not to heave a huge sigh of relief.

"Thanks."

"Ants on a log. Your mother always loved it."

"Ants . . . ?"

Odelia sets a paper plate on the desk, and Calla is relieved to see that it contains celery sticks filled with peanut butter and dotted with raisins.

With her grandmother, you just never know.

She's still not hungry after that huge supper, but it was so sweet of Odelia to bring her a snack that she probably should at least attempt to eat it.

"I just got off the phone with Ramona," Odelia says as Calla crunches into a piece of celery, "and I need to talk to you about something."

"Ramona?" Calla stops crunching. "What happened?"

"No, nothing *happened*. Why?"

She breathes a silent sigh of relief. "Just the way you said it, I thought . . ."

"Honey, you've got to stop this."

"Stop what?"

"Worrying."

Calla opens her mouth to protest, but her grandmother cuts her off with a wagging index finger, sporting an iridescent purple manicure. "I know you worry all the time."

"No, I don't," Calla mutters halfheartedly, and her grandmother shakes her head, bending over to squeeze Calla's shoulders.

"The way you jump every time the phone rings, like you're expecting it to be bad news . . . after everything you've been through, I understand why. But it's not good for you."

Calla stares at her calculus problem, wishing Odelia would go away.

Or maybe that she could find the words to agree with her grandmother's assessment of her mental state, and tell her about the various warnings she's received lately. She could even ask Odelia for help.

Help? Like what, a shrink?

She doesn't need a shrink to figure out that her anxiety stems from the trauma of losing her mother so suddenly and violently, or from people warning her that she herself might be in danger now. Maybe she was never exactly happy-go-lucky in the old days, but she sure didn't worry about disaster striking on a daily basis.

"I promised both of us that I'd take good care of you if you stayed here," Odelia says. "And I wasn't just talking about getting you into Patsy's class. I'm here for you, whatever you need. You know that, right?"

Calla nods, pretending to be looking over her calculus problems.

Odelia reaches down, cups Calla's chin, and turns her head so that she can't help but meet her grandmother's gaze.

"What?" Calla asks.

"Just making sure you're listening."

"I am."

"Good. So here's the other thing. When I talked to Ramona, she said she's taking you to get your hair and makeup done on Saturday before the dance."

"I know she said she wants to do that, but really, all I need is to get a haircut. I've needed it for a few weeks now." She shoves her overgrown bangs off her forehead.

"You should have told me. I don't notice that sort of thing—on my own head or anyone else's. It drove your mother crazy when she was your age. Sometimes I don't think she wanted to be seen with me in public."

Calla can't help but grin at the thought of Mom, always so meticulously put together, next to Odelia, with her wacky wardrobe and wild red hair, which usually does need some attention—from a hairstylist or even just a brush.

The smile fades when she realizes that she never did get to see the two of them together—not that she really remembers, anyway. She was too young the last time Odelia visited them in Florida to recall much of anything.

For all she knows, Mom and Gammy's falling out started over something really minor—like Gammy dropping and not rinsing red gobs of Close-up from the bathroom sink after brushing her teeth, which would have driven Mom crazy and drives Calla crazy now.

Yeah, and maybe they never screamed at each other about a secret Mom promised someone never to tell, and dredging the lake to find out the truth about . . . something.

Calla's not even sure anymore if she actually overheard the

argument—the one that keeps coming back to her in her dreams.

Maybe she was just channeling something that happened in the past, something she didn't witness. Mediums do that all the time.

But you're not a medium, she reminds herself.

Or is she?

What would she call herself, if not that?

A psychic? That's what she told Owen Henry. It seemed less . . . threatening.

Medium is just such a strong label. Even here in Lily Dale, where everyone and their brother is one.

Calla isn't registered with the Assembly, and she doesn't have a shingle or a business card, but . . .

But you do what mediums do.

Deal with it.

Deal with the fact that your "normal" life ended the day Mom died.

"Anyway," Odelia goes on, "it's very sweet of Ramona to want to take you to the salon on Saturday. I'd take you myself, except I've got a Thought Exchange meeting that afternoon."

"It's okay, Gammy." Calla wonders if that's why she's here, to apologize for not doing girly things with her.

"Ramona also mentioned that you got a few things at the Gap when she took you to the mall on Friday, and that you tried on some dresses at Lord and Taylor, but you didn't buy one."

"No. I didn't really find anything I loved." Which is a lie, and one Calla repeated to Ramona and Evangeline at the mall, too.

In reality, there were a couple of dresses she loved, and they did look good on her. But she simply didn't have enough money, even with Ramona's coupon, so she returned them to the rack.

Ramona kept asking if it was because of the money, and she wanted to lend some to Calla for a dress, but Calla wasn't comfortable doing that on top of the haircut. It's not like Ramona's rolling in cash, with two kids to support and an old house to maintain, all on a Lily Dale medium's modest earnings.

There was no way she was going to ask her father for the money, either. He probably spent his last dime just getting here for the weekend and treating Ramona and Evangeline to dinner Friday night.

Poor Dad.

Poor me.

Maybe she should have told Owen Henry she'd take his thousand dollars after all.

Odelia's gaze is sharp behind her purple cat's-eye glasses. "I know you need something to wear to the homecoming dance, Calla. And I'll be happy to buy you—"

"No, Gammy," the recently reclaimed childhood nickname spills so easily from her lips, "you don't have to do that."

"I want to. You need a dress. And I know you need other things, too. Like warm clothes—winter's coming."

"I'm fine."

"You can't parade around here in flip-flops and T-shirts. The snow will be up to your waist before the year is out. Trust me."

Calla laughs. "I'll get boots and gloves and stuff. I promise."

"I don't know why I didn't notice any of this before now.

It's not like I've never had a teenage girl in the house." Her smile is bittersweet. "I guess I've been wrapped up in other things, as usual."

Other things . . . meaning the Other Side. Even off season, Odelia is one of the most sought-after mediums in the Dale, constantly busy with readings for regular clients, conducting home message circles, participating in healing services, going to various meetings . . .

Even so, it's not as though she's much better off, financially, than Ramona.

In fact, only one local medium seems to be raking in a hefty income: David Slayton, Blue's father.

"The homecoming dance is a pretty big deal, Calla . . . and I know you really like Blue, don't you?"

"Um, sure." But it's suddenly Kevin's face that's flitting through her mind.

"You don't sound convinced."

"Gammy! Of course I like him. I'm going to the dance with him, aren't I?"

The way her grandmother is peering at her through those glasses, Calla could swear she's trying to read her thoughts.

Can she tell Calla is thinking about her lost love?

She hurriedly tries to push Kevin from her mind and winds up picturing Jacy instead.

He hasn't necessarily been avoiding her at school, but he's definitely kept a polite distance. There were a few times when she thought she could feel him watching her. But whenever she turned her head, he quickly looked away.

Whatever.

No—not whatever! You need him.

She really wanted to tell Jacy about the map indicating that spot in Leolyn Woods. So far, she's been too busy—and all right, too chicken—to check it out.

Jacy's the only one who could possibly understand and maybe have some insight. Calla was planning to corner him in the cafeteria at lunch, but he spent the whole time playing chess with Donald Reamer—whose father, Calla had noticed, was looking on, pleased.

"Listen, Calla, about the dance . . ."

She looks at her grandmother. "What about it?"

"Ramona had a suggestion. And it's a good one. If you'll go for it."

"What is it?"

"It's . . ." Odelia hesitates. "Come on. I'll just show you."

Curious, Calla follows her across the small second-floor hallway to her own room, which, like the rest of the house, is cluttered with belongings. Odelia's packrat habits probably didn't thrill Mom, either.

Watching Odelia open her closet door—and immediately duck as something topples off a shelf—Calla suppresses a smile and wishes, not for the first time, that she'd had the chance to discuss her grandmother with her mother. But Mom didn't like to talk about Odelia, and she certainly never mentioned that she was a medium, much less that her hometown was filled with them.

Odelia's closet is, not surprisingly, crammed from floor to ceiling. She's wedged herself halfway inside and appears to be hunting for something.

"Here they are!" a muffled voice announces, and a moment later, she emerges with several plastic-shrouded hangers.

Calla eyes them dubiously. "What are they?"

"Your mother's fancy dresses. Ramona told me all that vintage stuff is popular again, and she thought you might be interested."

"In wearing one of Mom's . . . ?" The room swims beyond Calla's tears and her throat is once again clogged by that hard, painful lump that makes it almost impossible to push the words out. "I . . . I don't know."

"Oh, honey." Odelia hugs her, hard. "I'm so sorry. I didn't mean to—"

"No, it's not—I mean, I'm just . . . I miss her."

"I know. Let it out."

She sobs on her grandmother's shoulder, and Odelia strokes her hair and murmurs all the comforting things Mom used to say to her: *It'll be all right, go ahead and cry,* and, most importantly, *I love you.*

Finally spent, she blows her nose, mops her eyes, and sighs. "I didn't mean to fall apart."

"Everyone needs a good cry now and then." Odelia picks up the hangers and carries them back toward the closet.

"Wait—what are you doing?"

"Putting them away. I'm sorry I—"

"No, wait, Gammy. Let me see them."

"Are you sure?"

Calla nods. The dresses are another little piece of her mother. She'll take what she can get.

Together, they lay the dresses out on the bed and look them over: a sleeveless ice-blue gown, a black velvet sheath, and a copper-colored iridescent taffeta dress with a full skirt that would be perfect, Calla realizes, for a fall dance.

"This one." She holds it up. "Can I try it on?"

Odelia nods, clearly moved—and caught up in a memory.

Calla carries it across the hall to her bedroom, passing Miriam in the hallway. This time, she isn't even all that startled to see her.

In her room, she strips off her jeans and T-shirt and pulls the dress over her head. It smells a little musty but not bad.

She checks the mirror and isn't surprised to find that it fits perfectly. Mom was a size 6, just as she is, and they have the same slim, long-waisted, long-legged build.

"You look gorgeous. Just like her. She wore that to a dance when she was about your age. Or maybe it was a prom, now that I think about it."

Calla turns to see Odelia standing in the doorway, looking misty.

"I think there's a picture of her in it around here some-where," she goes on, gazing around the room.

There is.

Calla knows it well: it's the framed photograph of Mom—all dressed up, with big eighties hair—and her boyfriend, Darrin Yates.

She goes over to the dresser, picks up the frame, and hands it to Odelia.

"Oh, yes." She studies it for a minute, then hands it back wordlessly.

"Was he her boyfriend?" Calla asks, as if she didn't know.

"Yup. Darrin Yates."

"Didn't you like him?"

"Why do you ask?"

Calla shrugs. "It doesn't sound like it. The way you said his name."

"You're right." Odelia shrugs, as if it's no big deal. But it is. Calla can tell. "I didn't like him. He was trouble from day one."

"Why? What did he do?" Drugs, Calla knows, were a part of it. Ramona told her about that.

Odelia looks at her for a long moment, then shakes her head. "Some people just have negative energy. He was one of them."

"But why? What did he do that was so bad?"

"He did some things I didn't like."

"Drugs?"

"Some things are better left in the past, Calla."

"Where is he now?"

"I have no idea, and I don't care."

Frustrated by her unwillingness to talk about him, Calla blurts, "Well, I think he was at Mom's funeral."

Odelia's red eyebrows disappear beneath her hairline. "He *what?*"

She shouldn't have said anything. She never intended to get into this with her grandmother.

Well, it's too late now. You put it out there. You can't take it back.

"He was at Mom's funeral," she admits reluctantly. "You must not have seen him. Or maybe you did, and you forgot. You were really upset."

"We all were. But believe you me, I wouldn't have forgotten running into Darrin Yates again after all these years." Odelia shakes her head darkly. "I guess I just didn't see him. I cried so much that day I couldn't see my own hand in front of my face, and anyway . . . I didn't know any of the people who were there, so I wasn't really looking. People who were in Stephanie's life now . . . they were all strangers. I wasn't a part of it."

Her grandmother looks, and sounds, like she's going to cry.

"But she always loved you, Gammy. No matter what happened between you."

"I know. And I always loved her, no matter what she had done. I never meant to—" She breaks off, looking as though she just realized she's said too much.

No matter what she had done.

"Did Mom do something you didn't like, too? Is that why you two didn't get along?"

"She did a lot of things I didn't like, and vice versa, I'm sure. Mothers and daughters . . . you know how it is."

But it's more than that. The way Odelia said it—*no matter what she had done*—obviously, Mom did something specific that drove her and Odelia apart.

"Are you sure Darrin Yates was there? At the funeral?" Odelia asks again, almost sharply.

"Pretty sure." Realizing there's only one way she's going to draw more information out of her grandmother, Calla admits reluctantly, "He was at our house, too, a few months before Mom died. On Saint Patrick's Day."

"What?!"

"Only, he told me his name was Tom. But this is him. I'm positive." She waves the framed snapshot at Odelia. "And he was whistling a song . . . the same song that plays on that music box." She points to the carved wooden jewelry box on Mom's dresser. "Maybe he gave it to her. Did he?"

"I don't remember where she got it. You say he was at

your house in Florida?" Odelia is obviously not thrilled to hear it. "Was it just a friendly visit? Did he just pop in out of the blue? What did he want?"

"I don't know. Mom didn't seem all that surprised to see him there—I mean, it wasn't like she opened the door and there he was, after twenty years or whatever."

"So you don't think that was the first time your mother had seen him lately?"

"I don't think so." Although it's troubling to think of her mom being in contact with another man when she was so busy with her job that she barely had time for Dad and Calla. "Oh, and he gave her an envelope, I think."

"An envelope! What was in it?"

"I don't know. She didn't tell me. I didn't think anything of it—I figured he was just someone from work. But Mom was pretty upset that day when he came over. She burned the soda bread, and you know my mom—she never burned anything."

Her grandmother seems to be digesting this news.

"Was your father there?"

"When Darrin came over? No." Calla carefully sets the picture back in its spot on the dresser. "Why?"

"I wondered if Stephanie told Jeff about him. That's all."

"You mean that he was her boyfriend when she was growing up? I don't think so, Gammy. She never talked about the past."

"Maybe she did with your father."

"Nope. He used to tease her about that. He said she must want to pretend her life started the day she met him."

"So you're saying your father didn't know Darrin existed? And I guess that means he doesn't know he was at the funeral? And at your house before that?"

"No. Do you think . . . should I tell him?"

Odelia pauses. "There's nothing to tell, really. Is there?"

"No," Calla murmurs, staring at her mother in the picture, and then at herself in the mirror, wearing the same dress. "There's nothing to tell."

TEN

Cassadaga, New York
Thursday, September 27
3:28 p.m.

Sitting at a booth in the window of the diner, Calla sips a watery fountain soda through a straw and keeps an eye on the rain-soaked parking lot for Owen Henry.

He's due any second now, and she hopes he won't be late. She told her grandmother she had to stay after school for extra help in math, which would get her home shortly after four at the latest.

She felt bad lying to Odelia, but there was no way around it. Her grandmother wouldn't understand that Calla *needs* to do this for Mr. Henry. That maybe, in a way, it's part of her own healing process to maybe help someone else pierce the smothering black veil of unbearable grief.

And anyway, what good is being able to do what she can do if she doesn't use the gift to help people? Isn't that what Lily Dale's philosophy is all about, in the first place?

Oh, good. A battered, oversized black sedan is splashing into the lone parking spot reserved for disabled customers, a telltale blue handicapped parking sign dangling from the rearview mirror. That has to be Owen Henry.

Instead, an elderly woman emerges from the driver's seat and helps an even more elderly lookalike out of the passenger's seat with a walker. As they make their way to the diner, step by fragile step, huddled beneath a big black umbrella, Calla sees that they're being followed by a filmy-looking woman with a Prohibition-era pin-curled bob and long-waisted dress.

Watching the scene, Calla decides the women are sisters. And that's their mother, watching over them from the Other Side. And there's a kind of faint aura of light around the older sister, the one with the walker, and something about the way the mother is hovering close to her . . .

It means it won't be long before the older sister passes on, Calla realizes without understanding quite how she knows any of this but absolutely certain it's the truth. The older sister is close to crossing over to the Other Side, and that's what the light means, and her mother is waiting for her.

She plucks a paper napkin from the holder on the table and hastily wipes tears from her eyes as the sisters settle themselves into the next booth. They order hot tea and whole-wheat toast from the waitress, who calls them Dora and Edna and asks what they're doing out on a day like this.

"Oh, a little rain never hurt anyone," says Dora, the older of the two.

"And you know how my sister looks forward to her tea and toast after bingo every week," Edna declares with an affectionate smile.

So Calla was right. At least about them being sisters.

She turns her head slightly and sees that their mother is still there, still watching, still waiting.

"Calla?"

Startled, she looks up to see Owen Henry at her table. He's wearing his usual hat, along with a rain-spattered trenchcoat, and leaning on his cane.

Glancing toward the window, she sees that the newest addition to the parking lot is a large, relatively new SUV. Not what she'd expect him to be driving. Funny how sometimes her instincts are dead-on, like with the sisters, and other times, she's dead wrong.

"Let's get down to business, shall we?" Owen asks, draping his coat on the hook above the booth and sitting across from her. He's wearing a suit with a bow tie.

"Okay," Calla agrees, not sure how to even begin. She doesn't see Betty hanging around him today.

"Hello there. What can I do you for?" the waitress, a plump, friendly woman with blond hair and black roots, pops up to ask Owen.

"Just a cup of black coffee."

"How about some pie to go with that?"

"No, thanks."

"Or a cinnamon roll?"

He shakes his head.

"Are you sure? They're delicious. I've had two of them myself today," she adds with a conspiratorial wink.

Calla wishes Owen Henry would at least crack a smile, but he's obviously impatient for the waitress to leave them alone. She guesses she can't blame him. He's focused on Betty, and he wants to get on with it.

"I have a few questions for Betty, if you don't mind," he says as soon as the waitress has taken the hint and silently deposited his coffee on the table in front of him.

"I don't mind, but . . . I mean, I don't see her spirit here, so I'm not sure I can reach her."

"You can try, though . . . can't you?" he asks, and there's such an air of tense desperation around him that she realizes she's going to feel terrible if she can't come up with something.

"Of course I can try."

"Okay. First, tell her I love her."

Calla smiles and nods. Then she closes her eyes and tries to meditate, the way Patsy taught them in class. She does see Betty's face in her mind's eye, but she can't tell if it's just the memory of seeing her the other day.

Whatever. *Owen loves you,* she silently tells the mental image of Betty, feeling a bit silly.

Opening her eyes, she expects Owen to ask if she got a response.

"I have a question," he says instead. "Can you see if you can answer it—if not through Betty, then with your psychic abilities?"

She nods. "What is it?"

"I inherited some stock certificates a few years ago from my cousin Elmer, and it turned out they were a lot more valuable than I ever imagined. Betty always kept them under the mattress in the guest bedroom, but after she died, I looked for them, and they weren't there."

Okay, this isn't at all what Calla was expecting. "So you want me to ask her where they are?" she asks slowly.

"Can you? Poor thing was suffering from dementia in her last days and got so paranoid, she thought people were trying to steal things from her."

Calla nods, remembering. That's exactly what it was like with her grandfather Poppy Ted, who had Alzheimer's disease before he died. He was convinced that the nurses were stealing his hospital bed out from under him, piece by piece. Toward the end, when he didn't recognize his own sons—Dad and Uncle Scott—he even accused them of robbing him. It was horrible.

"I'll see if I can find out where the stock certificates are," Calla tells Owen sympathetically, having some idea of what he must have been through with Betty.

"Thank you." He leans forward in anticipation, his coffee still untouched.

Calla glances around the diner. The two elderly sisters are sipping tea in the next booth, their mother sitting silently beside Dora, who's still glowing faintly. The waitress is wiping down the counter, oblivious to a pair of truckers who sit eating eggs . . . because they aren't really there, Calla realizes, noticing that they're getting a bit transparent before they vanish altogether.

Ghosts.

They're everywhere.

With a sigh, she closes her eyes.

Just focus on the spirit you need.

Breathe in . . . breathe out . . .

Come on, Betty. Show me where the stock certificates are.

That same house pops into her head. The gothic one on the cliff, overlooking the water.

Okay, maybe she's getting somewhere.

Is the stock hidden in the house? she asks Spirit.

Nothing new.

Just the image of the house again, stubbornly filling her head. She senses a pointedness to the vision, though.

"It's in the house somewhere," she tells Owen, opening her eyes to find him waiting anxiously.

"Which house?"

"Um . . . your house, I'm assuming. Yours and Betty's?"

He nods. "It's a brick cape. So the stock is there after all?"

"Brick cape?"

"That's the house. Brick. Cape Cod–style."

She shakes her head. "No. The house I'm seeing is more like a mansion. Really old-fashioned. On a cliff above the water."

He frowns. "Which water?"

"I don't know . . . I thought it must be the sea, because there's a widow's walk."

"No. Betty's house—mine and Betty's house—is on a cul-de-sac, right down the highway in Fredonia. No widow's walk. Tell me more about the house you're seeing."

She describes it in as much detail as she can. When she mentions the big square turret and octagonal stained-glass window, it's as if a lightbulb has suddenly gone on in Owen Henry's brain.

"Well, how do you like that," he says, and reaches into the pocket of his suit.

He pulls out a ten-dollar bill and hurriedly tosses it on the table in front of Calla. "There . . . that's for my coffee, the rest is for you. Thanks. You really helped me."

"But . . . I mean, is that all?" she asks, watching him shove his arms into the sleeves of his damp overcoat and plunk his hat back on his head. "You don't want to ask Betty anything else? Tell her anything else?"

Maybe, one more time, that you love her?

"No, that's it. Thanks again," he says, and is gone.

Watching him scurry out into the rain, Calla has a sinking feeling.

She should have listened to Odelia.

Getting involved with this man wasn't the right thing to do. Not at all.

Out the window, Owen Henry jumps into the shiny SUV and starts the engine with a roar. The tires screech a little as he pulls out onto the highway, heading north, toward Fredonia.

It isn't until Calla stands up that her gaze falls on Owen's cane, propped where he left it against the side of the booth.

Her heart seems to stop short in her chest as she remembers how he left the diner just now.

He was striding, without the slightest sign of a limp.

Dear God, Calla. What did you just do?

"You're just in time!" Odelia calls from the living room when Calla arrives home.

"For what?" Calla hangs her backpack on the newel post and pokes her head in to see her grandmother sitting in her favorite chair, knitting in front of the television, with Gert at her feet.

"There's a great movie starting on Lifetime. Want to watch? Loni Anderson is in it."

"Who?"

Odelia sighs. "Sometimes, my dear, I forget just how young you are. Sit down and watch anyway. I could use some company."

Right now, she just isn't in the mood to be around anyone, not even Gammy.

"I have a ton of homework. Sorry."

"A girl's gotta do what a girl's gotta do," Odelia says as Calla bends to give her a peck on the cheek.

She's halfway up the stairs when her grandmother calls after her, "Oh, Calla? I forgot! You have mail!"

"I do? Where?"

"Somewhere. Maybe in the kitchen. Check the counter," Odelia advises with typical scatterbrained vagueness.

With a silent sigh, Calla heads to the kitchen. The counters and table seem to hold everything *but* the mail.

"I can't find it, Gammy," she calls.

"Did you look in the fridge?"

"The fridge?"

"I brought it in when I was putting away the milk and eggs. It might be in there."

"Of course it might," Calla mutters, shaking her head.

And of course it is, a card-sized envelope, addressed to her, lying on the shelf next to the Tupperware filled with leftover snickernoodles no one is ever going to eat.

Recognizing the handwriting, Calla gasps.

Kevin.

Why is he sending her mail?

"Did you find it?" her grandmother calls.

"Mmm-hmm." She's already tearing into the envelope and pulling out a card.

On the front is a photo of a herd of sheep. One is wearing a clownish red bow tie, and the caption reads, *"Adding to my misery, no one here thinks I'm funny."*

Smiling to herself, Calla opens the card and reads Kevin's handwritten note:

Hey, Calla—Saw this and thought of you. I really miss your laugh. And a lot of other things. I e-mailed you a while back to tell you I've got the car here in Ithaca now and maybe I'll take a ride to Lily Dale to visit you some weekend. I never heard back from you. My sister said you can't check your e-mail very often from there so I figured you probably didn't get it. Bet you didn't know I knew how to use the regular mail. Gasp! I even had a stamp. Call my cell (same number) if you want me to come see you or if you need anything.

xoxo, Kevin

She did get that e-mail he sent—and chose not to reply after Lisa told her that Kevin is thinking of bringing his new girlfriend, Annie, home to Tampa for Thanksgiving.

If he's so crazy about her, why does he keep writing and wanting to visit me?

In all fairness, she supposes Kevin might just want to stay in touch for old times' sake . . . as friends. After all, they've known each other most of their lives. She was Lisa's best friend before she was Kevin's girlfriend and spent almost as much time in the Wilsons' house as she did in her own.

That's why it was so strange, after the breakup, to have him more or less erased from her life. She didn't just miss him as a boyfriend. She missed him as her closest confidante.

Calla glares at the sheep in the red bow tie.

So where were you when I needed you most?

Yes, he was at her mother's funeral, and he even tried to talk to her afterward.

But he didn't tell her he still loved her, and he didn't ask her to be his girlfriend again. Most likely, he just felt sorry for her.

He probably still does.

I don't need that. I don't need him.

She tucks the card into her backpack and wearily climbs the stairs to start her homework.

ELEVEN

Friday, September 28
7:17 p.m.

For the second time today, Calla walks along Dale Drive toward Lily Dale High . . . only this time, it's dark, and she's alone.

Evangeline was planning on coming with her to Blue's soccer match tonight, but instead, she's out dress shopping with her aunt.

Russell Lancione finally worked up his nerve to ask her to the homecoming dance, and Evangeline decided to go with him.

"A last-minute date with someone you only like as a friend is better than no date at all, right?" she asked Calla on the way home from school.

"Sure," she said, remembering her junior prom and Paul "Shorton" Horton.

"You don't sound very convincing."

"You'll have a great time." Who knows? Maybe she will.

"Not as great a time as you. Everyone's in love with Blue, and you get to go with him. You're so lucky."

Maybe . . . but she's definitely not in love with him.

She's barely even seen Blue the last few days. He's been busy with soccer, and she's been busy with schoolwork and babysitting and seeing ghosts around every corner and . . .

Owen Henry.

She feels sick every time she thinks of what happened yesterday.

She keeps trying to convince herself that he really was a sweet, frail old widower, but . . .

Aren't sweet, frail old widowers more interested in telling their late wives how much they miss them than in missing stock certificates?

And how do you explain his magically being able to toss the cane aside and pretty much run out the door?

Magical Lily Dale healing?

Ha.

There's nothing Calla can do about it now, other than put it behind her.

Tonight, she's vowed that all she's going to allow herself to think about is Blue, and soccer, and staying warm.

It's so cold out that she can see her breath, and the wind is gusting off the lake, as usual. She's shivering even in three layers and a fleece jacket.

A fat harvest moon hangs in the sky, and in the distance, the lights from the athletic field cast a welcoming yellow haze. But it's dark and lonely here on the deserted country lakeside road.

Lonely . . . but she isn't alone.

Hearing giggling along the side of the road, she spots two spirit children running along, pushing a wooden hoop with a stick.

They're harmless . . . still, she's spooked.

And spooked again when she hears a faint jingling of silvery bells and turns her head just in time to see an old-fashioned sleigh glide past in a swirl of phantom snow, filled with laughing young people in Victorian bonnets and caps.

Okay, it's cold . . . but not that cold.

A little farther down the road, a man in some sort of military uniform gallops past on horseback.

Either the ghosts are out in full force tonight . . . or her powers of perception are growing stronger, like Odelia said.

Is this how it's always going to be? Spirits constantly around her, coming and going and hanging around?

She's read enough to know that it probably is . . . and that she has to learn how to tune them out, or they're going to drive her crazy.

Not that she would ever get involved with drugs or alcohol, but . . .

Ramona told her that some people here—especially teenagers—aren't comfortable with their sensitivity.

"It can be a frightening, isolating feeling to discover that you have an awareness of spirit energy," Ramona said. She told Calla that some people—like Darrin, when he was younger—self-medicate to escape what they can't accept or control.

I didn't get it then, but I do now, Calla thinks uneasily, eyeing a little girl in a frilly turn-of-the-century dress and a big, floppy hair bow.

She finds herself picking up her pace, almost as if she can outrun them. All of them.

But she can't.

They're everywhere. A couple of teenage boys chugging past in a 1930s car with an *ah-ooga* horn, a fifties housewife pushing a baby carriage, a fleet-footed Native American brave hunting game with a bow and arrow.

She probably shouldn't be out tonight. She should be home, in bed, trying to fall asleep so that she can escape the three-ring spirit circus for a little while.

But she told Blue she'd be there, and anyway, she's found that it's easier when people are around or she's busy. She doesn't notice the ghosts so much when she's distracted by conversation or schoolwork.

Out here alone at night on the country road, though, there are no distractions.

Too bad her grandmother wasn't around to give her a ride to the school—or home, at least. But Odelia is conducting a workshop up in Buffalo tonight, on vibrational healing. She won't be back before midnight.

"Be careful walking over," was the last thing she said to Calla before heading out the door earlier. "It's dark, and cars fly through there at night."

"I'll be careful," Calla promised wearily.

Be careful. Be careful.

That's all anyone ever says to her anymore.

She's *always* been careful.

But that doesn't mean you're safe.

Even as the thought enters her head, she hears footsteps shuffling in the dry leaves behind her.

Running footsteps.

Bearing down on her.

Another ghost?

No.

"Jacy!" Talk about a welcome sight.

"Calla!"

He stops running, asks breathlessly, "What are you doing out here?"

"Going over to the school."

She doesn't bother to ask him what he's doing; it's obvious from his shorts, running shoes, sweat band, and Lily Dale Track T-shirt.

"You must be freezing," she says, and realizes he's wiping sweat from his face. Duh. He's working out. Of course he's not freezing.

"No, but you look like you are."

The wind kicks up, and she shivers—not so much from the cold, though.

It's more . . .

Well, out here alone in the dark with him—it's not like it should be the least bit romantic under the circumstances, and she's sure it isn't, for him, but . . .

Stop that. You've got to get over him. He's obviously not interested. He barely even speaks to you.

"So what's going on at school tonight?"

"Soccer match."

He nods. "Going to see Blue play?"

"Yeah." She wants to ask him when his next track meet is and tell him she'll be there, too, but that seems more than a little ridiculous. Better to keep her mouth shut as much as possible, especially after the way she stuck her foot in it last week.

But the awkward silence that falls between them is almost worse.

She has to say something. Anything.

"Hey, you haven't had any more dreams about me, have you?"

Anything but *that*.

"I mean . . . not *those* kinds of dreams," she blurts, which definitely sounds even worse.

"I mean . . . you know . . . visions," she amends, and is glad it's so dark. She has no desire to see the look on Jacy's face, and it's a good thing he can't see hers, because her cheeks are flaming hot.

Why does she always say the wrong thing around Jacy?

Come on. You know why.

It's because she's so physically aware of him—especially now, alone together in the dark, all that lean muscle and masculine sweat—that she can't even think straight.

At last, Jacy speaks. "I've had a few."

A few . . . a few . . . a few . . .

What is he talking about?

"A few . . . ?"

"Visions. About you."

"Oh!" *You idiot. You just asked him about that.* "Well, can you tell me what they—?"

She breaks off with a startled cry and clutches Jacy's arm as a rush of noise and flashing light swoops toward them out of nowhere.

"It's okay, it's just an ambulance." He pulls her closer to him, away from the edge of the road as the rescue vehicle, sirens screaming, barrels past and disappears around the bend.

"Was it real?" she asks.

"Real? What do you mean?"

"Nothing, I thought . . ." Calla forces a nervous laugh. "I don't know what I thought. Sorry. I've been pretty much a nervous wreck lately."

She starts to let go of his arm, but his other hand comes down on top of hers. "Hey . . . are you all right?"

"Not really."

"What's wrong?" he asks softly.

"What isn't?" Her heart is pounding . . . but no longer in fear.

Something's happening between them. Something that started with the electrical current the moment they met; something that just moments ago seemed impossible, but now feels . . . inevitable.

"I'll help you," he tells her. "I know you feel alone . . . but you're not."

The breeze stirs and her bangs fall across her eyes. Before she can brush them away, he reaches out and gently pushes the strands back. His fingers are warm against her forehead, and they linger, so that he's cupping her face, almost as though . . .

He's going to kiss me.

There's no time for her to grasp the idea; no time to stop it from happening.

Jacy leans in and their lips meet, and the autumn chill gives way to the Fourth of July with an explosive shower of sparks.

"That was a long time coming," he says when he pulls away from her.

"It was?" she can't help asking, shocked to discover that he felt that way, too—and glad he made no apology, though that, she suspects, wouldn't be his style.

"You don't think so?"

"You know what I think." She offers him a taut smile. "I bared my soul to you the other day, remember?"

"I remember."

"You don't know how much I wished I hadn't said anything."

"You don't know how glad I am that you did." At last, he removes his hand from her face. She's disappointed, until she feels him grasping for her hand.

"But . . . you've barely talked to me since," she points out, lacing her fingers with his, scarcely able to believe this is really happening. Did Lacy Bly really just kiss her? Are they really holding hands in the moonlight?

"I told you . . . it's complicated."

"Because of what you've seen. Because you think I'm in danger."

"That . . . and everything else."

"You mean, you don't want to get involved with me."

"I don't want to get involved with anyone," he says bluntly.

She doesn't blame him, after all he's been through, but it's not easy to hear.

"So what now?" she asks him.

He shrugs. 'How about if you just tell me what's been going on?"

"You mean, with Blue?"

Long pause.

Uh-oh. Oops.

"I meant, with everything else," Jacy says gently. "You said you weren't okay . . . I didn't think that had anything to do with Blue."

No, it had a lot to do with you.

Sighing inwardly—will she ever get it right with him?—she fills him in on all that's happened since they last spoke: the ghosts, the billets, the bear fountain and Darrin Yates, the book and Leolyn Woods, Aiyana.

Jacy is quiet for a long time, thinking it over. Then he asks, "You said the fountain is in Geneseo?"

"I think so. Have you ever been there?"

"No, but I know where it is. We should go check it out."

Her heart skips a beat. "You'd go with me?"

"You can't go alone."

No, she can't. For starters, she has no way of getting there.

"Do you have a car?" she asks. "Because I don't want to tell my grandmother about it and ask to borrow hers. There's no way she'd let me go."

"Walt and Peter lend me their car on weekends sometimes. I'll ask them."

"You can't tell them where we're going, though. They're friends with my grandmother. It'll get back to her."

"I won't tell them. We'll make something up. Want to go tomorrow?"

"Yes!" she exclaims, then, "No. I can't. It's homecoming."

"Oh. Right."

"Sunday for sure, though. Okay?"

"Can't. Track meet."

"Oh. They won't let you borrow the car during the week?"

He shakes his head. "That's one of their rules. They don't have many, but . . . I guess it'll have to wait until next weekend."

"I'm going away," she tells him. "To Florida. I already have my plane ticket."

Hearing another siren in the distance, they look at each other, then toward the school. "Something must have happened there," Calla says anxiously.

"Sounds that way."

"I hate sirens. They remind me of . . ." She closes her eyes, trying to shut out the horror of that awful day. But the memories come anyway: walking into the house to find Mom's body, running screaming into the street, one of the elderly neighbors dialing 911, the sirens.

"I know. I don't like them either." Jacy squeezes her hand, and she remembers that he's had his own share of sorrow.

"So . . . I guess Geneseo will have to wait," she says reluctantly.

"Yeah. But for now, I think I should tell you . . ." He hesitates.

"What?"

"About what I've been seeing. With you. You know . . ."

"The visions?"

"Yeah. Just so you know, because you're going to Florida, and . . . well, it's about water."

Her heart stops. "Water?"

"Don't go in the water in Florida, Calla. Promise me."

133

Dread creeps over her as she remembers Odelia's cryptic warnings about not going into the lake here. "Why not?"

"When I see you . . . you're in the water. Struggling."

"You mean . . . drowning?"

"I'm not sure. But I don't feel like it's an accident."

TWELVE

Saturday, September 29
9:32 a.m.

"Calla, you'll never believe this . . . Did you hear what happened last night?" Evangeline asks breathlessly in her ear.

"Yeah. I heard." Calla sinks onto the couch, clutching the phone, her hand trembling.

"I can't believe it. You must be so upset!"

"Yeah. Poor Blue." Renewed guilt threads its way into her brain as she thinks of him, laid up at Brooks Memorial Hospital down in Dunkirk, his left foot fractured.

The ambulance that had raced past Jacy and her was real, all right. And it was going to rescue Blue. He'd collided with a beefy player from the opposing team on the wet soccer field, and had gone down hard with the other guy on top of him. It was a freak accident, according to everyone who witnessed it.

Such a freak accident that if Calla didn't know better, she might think she had somehow willed it.

Or maybe she doesn't know better. What if she—or Jacy—did have something to do with it?

No. Blue had already been injured before they even discussed going to Geneseo. It was a freak accident, and nothing more.

Not like Mom's death.

"Poor Blue," Evangeline is echoing, "and poor you. It's so unfair that this had to happen now, before the dance. I can't believe you don't get to go."

You have to tell her.

"Evangeline . . ."

"Ramona and I were really looking forward to the three of us going to the salon today. I mean, you should still come. I know it won't be the same, but—"

"Evangeline, I'm going."

"To the salon? Great! At least you can still get your hair cut, and—"

"No, not the salon . . . to the dance."

"Really? You're going alone?"

"No." Guilt, guilt, guilt. So many reasons to feel guilty right now, mostly for the web of lies she's about to spin, not just to Evangeline, but to her grandmother, and Ramona . . .

But you have no choice. It's the only way.

She takes a deep breath. "Jacy Bly is taking me. Just as friends," she feels compelled to add, hoping that makes it easier, not just on Evangeline, but on her.

Silence.

"Evangeline?"

"That's . . . I, um . . . I think that's nice. Of him. And, uh, for you."

"We're friends, Evangeline. He felt bad when we heard what happened to Blue last night, so he . . . you know . . ."

"Yeah. He's a good guy. You'll have fun with him."

"It's not like that. We're not . . . you know."

"Yeah. You said. Just friends." Evangeline's voice is tight. "Well, I'm glad you get to go. I guess I'll see you when we go to the Hair Wharf. I think the appointment is for two."

"What about class?"

"Class?"

"Patsy's class. You're going this morning, right?"

"Oh . . . I am, but I'm going to be a little late. Go on over without me, and I'll see you there, okay?"

"Okay. Sure."

She doesn't want to walk over with me, Calla thinks, hanging up the phone.

Does she really blame Evangeline for being upset?

She has a date for the dance—supposedly, anyway—with the guy her friend likes.

Okay, so it isn't really a date.

But what's gone on between her and Jacy isn't platonic.

He kissed her last night.

Not just that first time, but later, too. Even after they had walked over to the school just in time to see Blue Slayton being loaded into the ambulance.

He didn't see Calla. He was obviously in too much pain to notice much of anything.

But he did call her, late, from the hospital.

"I know," she said, when he told her what had happened. "I was there. I saw you. Are you going to be okay?"

"Eventually." He sounded groggy from the medication. "But I won't be doing any dancing tomorrow. They're not even letting me out of here until at least Sunday."

She told him how sorry she was, and told him to get some rest.

"Yeah, I will. It was such a freak thing, you know? That guy came at me out of nowhere. I can't believe this happened to me. All I've been thinking about lately is that you and I were going to have a great time at the dance, and now look."

She couldn't help but remember what Evangeline said about Blue being a powerful psychic, like his father. Shouldn't he have had an inkling that something was going to happen to him on the soccer field that night?

Maybe not. It's not a precise science, by any means.

She hung up with Blue and turned to Jacy, who had walked her home and come inside.

"He can't go," she told him.

"Then let's do it."

They had already hatched a tentative plan at that point.

Now it's in full swing.

There's no going back.

"Good morning!"

Calla turns to see her grandmother in the hallway, at the foot of the stairs. She's wearing the orange satin kimono she uses as a bathrobe, and yawning.

"Hi, Gammy."

"Today's the big day." Odelia pads into the room in her purple terry-cloth scuffies. "How do you feel?"

Might as well get it over with.

"Um . . . the thing is, Blue got hurt last night on the soccer field, so I'm not going with him. Jacy Bly is taking me instead."

Odelia levels a long gaze at her.

She knows I'm lying.

Calla feels sick inside.

Then her grandmother breaks into a smile. "It's not that I wish anything bad for Blue," she says, "but this is how it was supposed to turn out."

"What do you mean?"

"You and Jacy. I knew it. I've felt it all along. I knew you two were going to connect, even before I ever introduced him to you."

No way.

"Gammy we're just going as friends," she says, thinking of Evangeline.

Odelia waves that notion away with her hot-pink-polished fingers. "Don't give me that. I know there's more to it."

"Really . . . there isn't. And please don't say anything to Ramona, or . . . Evangeline."

"She likes him. I know."

Calla nods glumly.

"She'll get over him. There's someone else for her out there."

"Russell Lancione?" Calla asks, brightening. "Do you have some kind of premonition about the two of them, or something?"

That would be great, and it would let her off the hook with Jacy.

"No premonitions. There's just someone for everyone. Including Evangeline. And Jacy Bly isn't her someone."

Is he really mine? Calla wants to ask but doesn't dare.

"The thing about Jacy," Odelia says, "is that he's been through hell and back. His parents—they really hurt him. He built up a lot of walls because of that. Likes to shut people out. Is afraid of losing even more than he already has."

It's just like Calla thought. He doesn't want to let her in, doesn't want to care about her—or anyone.

"Walt and Peter have made a lot of progress with him, but . . . some kinds of hurt take a long, long time to heal. And some don't ever heal," Odelia adds sadly, shaking her head and thinking, Calla suspects, not just of Jacy.

"You go easy on him, and you'll see. He'll come around."

"Gammy . . . it's just a dance."

No. It's not even that.

"I'm so happy for you, Calla. What I wouldn't give to be your age again, going to a dance with a boy I'm crazy about."

Great. Calla can only hope her grandmother never finds out she and Jacy never made it to the dance.

Evangeline will notice, that's for sure.

I'll have to figure out something to tell her, Calla promises herself.

For now, she can't think past tonight, and getting to Geneseo with Jacy.

"Well? What do you think?"

Calla looks up from the gossipy pages of the *Us* magazine

she's been trying, with little success, to read for the last forty-five minutes. Mostly, she's just been staring out the plate-glass window of the Hair Wharf salon at the dark gray waters of Lake Erie off the Dunkirk Pier.

Standing in the doorway of the salon waiting room, Evangeline does a mock-modeling spin, turning this way and that to show off a face full of makeup and her new hairdo, an elaborate mass of curls falling from a black satin headband.

"Wow . . . you look gorgeous!" Calla exclaims sincerely.

"Thanks. What do you think, Aunt Ramona?"

"Oh, honey . . ." Sitting beside Calla, Ramona is obviously emotional. "I think you're growing up. And you're beautiful."

"That's what I told her." Leslie, the pretty, dark-haired young stylist, looks on proudly, a can of hairspray still in hand.

"You don't think I look like a Disney princess?" Evangeline wrinkles her nose—the freckles oddly buffed away by a thick layer of foundation.

"Not in a bad way," Calla assures her.

"Wait till that kid sees you. He isn't going to know what hit him," Ramona declares.

"Who? Russell?" Evangeline's nose wrinkles even more. "I don't want him to like me that way."

"I hate to break it to you, but I don't think you have a choice. He already does."

Evangeline flashes a smile at Calla's comment, though Calla can't help but notice it isn't quite as warm as in the past.

She hasn't exactly been cold-shouldered by her friend today, but it's been clear that Evangeline isn't thrilled she's going to the dance with Jacy.

She made no effort to mask her jealousy during their

awkward walk home from Patsy's class, and she asked a million questions, most of which Calla couldn't—or wouldn't—answer.

Evangeline wanted to know exactly how their date had come about. In detail. She wasn't entirely satisfied with Calla's explanation: that she had run into him at the soccer field, and after they both witnessed Blue's accident, Jacy just naturally asked her if he could take her in Blue's place.

"Jacy never goes to anything but track meets," Evangeline pointed out. "I never see him at dances, or football games, or soccer. And believe me—I look for him. Everywhere. I guess I'm just surprised that he was around last night, and that he wants to go to homecoming tonight."

Calla almost told her then that it wasn't really going to happen, that they aren't really going to the dance, but in the end, what difference would that make?

She's still going to be with Jacy later, and it might be even worse if Evangeline realizes that something more compelling than a date for the dance is drawing the two of them together. Not even just the physical attraction, which Calla doesn't dare acknowledge to her, but the mystery surrounding Darrin Yates.

She doesn't want to tell Evangeline about that, either.

Better to just leave things the way they are, for now.

And later, after she doesn't show up at the dance with Jacy . . .

I'll just make up something else. Another lie.

"All right . . . it's your turn." Leslie gestures at Calla. "Ready?"

"Sure." Trying to muster casual enthusiasm, she puts the magazine aside and follows Leslie to the next room.

There, Calla spots a filmy pair of women whose hair is set on big fat rollers, with a few loose tufts taped to their cheeks. They're both wearing baby doll negligees and false eyelashes. On the far side of the room, a buff and fabulous—and nearly transparent—young male stylist snips an invisible patron's hair.

Oblivious to the spirits, Leslie keeps up cheerful small talk as she washes and trims Calla's hair. The weather, food, Hollywood gossip.

Calla tries to relax and get into it, but she can't. She's too distracted by the ghosts and worried about tonight.

"You're so tense," Leslie comments. "You must be thinking about the dance. I hear you have a hot date."

"Where'd you hear that?" Calla asks, knowing full well.

"Evangeline told me. Sounds like she wants to switch dates with you."

Calla tries to laugh, but it comes out sounding kind of strangled.

"Okay, it's time to make you fancy. Hair, makeup . . . the works. What kind of dress are you wearing?"

"It's . . . vintage."

"Vintage—like Victorian? Or more like the seventies? Not that I was around then," she adds slyly.

No, but the two women in the fat rollers and false eyelashes probably were, Calla thinks, glancing again in their direction.

"Um, more like the eighties," she tells Leslie.

"Ooh, I love the eighties!" declares Leslie, who couldn't have been alive for much of that decade either. "What color is it?"

"Kind of a reddish brown."

"That'll be gorgeous with your coloring. Do you know what kind of style you want?"

"I'm not sure. I guess you can just surprise me."

"Are you kidding? Really?"

"Go for it."

"Okay. I live for customers saying that . . . not that anyone ever does."

Calla shrugs. Her heart isn't in this, and she just can't pretend.

"I'm spinning you this way, okay?" Leslie twirls the chair so that Calla's back is to the mirror. "If you're going to give me free license with this gorgeous face and head of hair, I don't want you to change your mind halfway through. You can see it when we're done, and believe me, you'll love yourself."

Leslie intently paints her face while holding a makeup kit like it's a painter's palette, dabbing on a little of this, a little of that.

"You totally look like a supermodel," she tells Calla, who cringes a little inside. Maybe it wasn't such a great idea to let Leslie do whatever she wants. Calla usually goes for a natural look.

Oh, well. Too late now. As Leslie combs and curls and teases and gels and sprays her way around Calla's head, Calla goes over, and over, what's going to happen later.

Jacy is planning to pick her up at Odelia's and go along with the homecoming dance charade. Odelia said something this morning about checking to see if she has batteries in her camera so she can take pictures of the occasion, which made Calla feel even more nauseous than she has been.

But she has to do this—has to lie—for her mother's sake. Maybe this hunt for Darrin Yates in Geneseo will wind up to be a wild-goose chase, but on the off-chance that it isn't . . .

"Okay. You're done." Leslie spins the chair back toward the mirror with a ceremonious, "Ta da!"

Calla catches a glimpse of her reflection and sees her jaw drop in the mirror.

"Don't you love how retro you are? I thought your look should go with the vintage dress. What do you think?" Standing over her, Leslie proudly surveys her handiwork.

Staring into her own eyes, rimmed by a thick layer of shadow, liner, and mascara, and gazing at the carefully upswept pile of hair riding high over her forehead, Calla struggles to find the right words. Or any words.

"I think . . . I think . . ."

"I know!" Leslie gloats. "Quite a transformation. It's like looking at a stranger, isn't it?"

No. It isn't like that at all.

For Calla, it's eerily like looking at her own mother, the night she wore the copper-colored dress and went to the dance with Darrin Yates.

THIRTEEN

Saturday, September 29
7:10 p.m.

"He's here!" Odelia calls up the stairs to Calla.

That's funny. She didn't hear the doorbell ring. Dressed and ready, she's been listening for it, but—

Oh.

There's the doorbell now.

Calla wonders whether Odelia glimpsed Jacy coming up the porch steps or simply "felt" him approaching.

Does it really matter? That sort of thing happens all the time around here.

Yes. Tonight, it matters.

It would be nice to think that Odelia's having an off night, as far as her psychic abilities and premonitions go.

That way, Calla wouldn't be wondering if there's any significance behind her grandmother's earlier warning to be extra-careful tonight.

"Just make sure you keep your wits about you," Odelia said as Calla nibbled on the sandwich her grandmother insisted on making her.

"Not that I don't always do that anyway . . . but why?" Calla asked.

"Because you're going out alone at night in a car with a boy, even though the dance is almost just around the corner."

Calla pushed aside a familiar nagging guilt, along with the fear that her grandmother's warning might stem from something more ominous than pure maternal concern.

Now, that it's time to go, her misgivings are back full force.

What if something terrible happens to her tonight?

What if she backs out of the whole thing because she's scared?

What if she never finds out what really happened to Mom?

I have to do this. It's that simple.

She slips the framed photo of her mother and Darrin into the beaded evening bag Odelia unearthed from the bottom of a cedar chest. It was the same bag, she told Calla, that Mom carried when she wore this dress to her high school prom. On Calla's wrist is a familiar emerald bracelet. It doesn't match the dress, but who cares? It was Mom's . . . and a reminder that anything is possible. After all, it miraculously came back to Calla here in Lily Dale after dropping into Mom's grave that rainy July day in Florida.

Passing Miriam, who gives her an admiring glance, Calla

heads for the stairs, her feet trying to get used to walking in a pair of high-heeled satin pumps that also turned up in the cedar chest. They're probably a size too small, but Calla chose to wear them anyway. They match the dress perfectly, and they were Mom's.

The mirror, every time she's glimpsed her reflection tonight, is like a window into the past.

Thanks to Leslie, who couldn't have known, Calla looks exactly like her mother does in the picture with Darrin.

Odelia was bowled over when she first saw her earlier.

"You could *be* her, Calla," she said tearfully, and hugged her hard. "I can't believe it."

Calla can't, either.

Because there are no coincidences.

So, what does it all mean?

It means I probably shouldn't be doing this, that's what it means.

Increasingly unsettled about what might lie ahead, Calla reminds herself that nothing bad is going to happen to her with Jacy around.

Something about him just makes me feel safe.

But when she reaches the top of the stairs to see Jacy standing below in the front hall, "safe" is pretty much the last word that comes to mind.

"Dangerous" is more like it.

Wearing a dark suit and tie, white dress shirt, and polished dress shoes, he looks about five years older—and so handsome she stops dead in her tracks.

Wow.

Calla reaches for the bannister and descends the first few

steps. Her feet wobble in the heels, and she remembers her mother on the steps back home, walking, falling . . .

No. Not tonight. Don't think of that tonight. Not now, anyway.

She reaches the foot of the stairs and Odelia is there, too, fluttering around, obviously thrilled to think that "romance might be blossoming," which is how she cringe-inducingly phrased it earlier, between Calla and Jacy.

"Peter got ahold of Jacy and bought him a new suit," she announces. "Doesn't he look great, Calla?"

"He does . . . you do." At last she finds her voice. Daring to look him in the eye, she sees a gleam that makes her heart beat even faster.

"You look good, too," he says simply, and holds out a florist's box. "This is for you."

"Thank you." She hopes he can't see how badly her hands are shaking as she takes it.

This isn't supposed to be happening.

Tonight is . . . well, it's kind of like a business appointment.

Oh, who are you kidding? You're into Jacy, no matter what else you've got going on, and you know he's into you.

Maybe when this is all over, and things are back to normal, the two of them can actually go out on a real date.

"Aren't you going to open the box?" Odelia prods.

Calla lifts the lid and the distinct floral scent hits her immediately.

Lily of the valley.

She looks up at Jacy, surprised and touched.

Looking over Calla's shoulder, Odelia says, "What an

exquisite corsage—white roses and lily of the valley? Those were your mother's favorite flower, Calla."

Yeah, no kidding.

"I know, Gammy." And so does Jacy. She told him all about it.

"Did Peter pick out the corsage, too?" Odelia asks, and Jacy shakes his head.

"Walt, then?"

"No. I did."

"Really? I'm impressed. I think that's a sweet coincidence."

"What is?" Jacy asks, as Calla slides the elastic band of the corsage over her wrist.

"That you happened to pick out a corsage with flowers—out of season, too!—that happened to be my daughter's favorite. Every time I smell lilies, I think of Stephanie." Odelia exhales shakily, then waves a limp hand in front of her face, as if to stave off tears.

"Gammy, are you okay?"

"I'm fine."

Hearing a car door slam outside, Calla looks out the window to see Russell Lancione arriving at the Taggarts' house. He's wearing a dark suit like Jacy's—though looking nowhere near as grown-up and handsome—and carrying a florist's box.

He hesitates at the curb beside his car, obviously nervous. Then he looks at his watch, visibly takes a deep breath, and heads up the walk.

Calla wonders how Evangeline is doing. Ordinarily, the two of them would have had a couple of phone conversations while they were getting ready for the dance. But Calla didn't feel right calling Evangeline under the circumstances, and the phone didn't ring here.

"We should really get going," Calla tells Jacy, not wanting the two of them to walk out the door at the same time as Evangeline and Russell.

"Let me just snap a couple of pictures first, and you guys can be on your way."

"You don't mind, do you?" Calla asks Jacy.

"Of course he doesn't mind," Odelia answers for him as she rummages in a closet. "Homecoming is a big deal."

Yeah. It is.

And they're not really going.

"Ah, here it is." Odelia pulls out a tripod.

"Gammy, you're kidding, right?"

"Kidding about what?"

In the living room, Odelia sets up the tripod with considerable effort, then attaches a camera . . . and attaches an enormous lens to the front of it.

Calla looks at Jacy, who grins. "It's fine. She's sweet."

"Okay, kids, all set! Candid shot. Say cheese!"

Calla tries to smile as a flash explodes in her face.

"Oops . . . lens cap!" Odelia giggles. "Sorry!"

She removes the lens cap and snaps some more.

Then she moves the tripod, poses them in front of the fireplace, moves the tripod again, tells Jacy to put his arm around Calla, and snaps.

"Great!"

She lugs the tripod across the room, poses them in front of the window, tells Jacy to pretend he's helping Calla to put on her corsage, and snaps again. And again. And again.

151

"Gammy . . . ," Calla says in a warning voice.

"You'll thank me later, when you have photos of this night to treasure for the rest of your life."

Calla thinks of her mother, going to the long-ago dance with Darrin. Was it Odelia who took the picture that's in Calla's bag at this very moment?

Before they can make an exit, Odelia carries her tripod to the front hall, poses them by the door, and tells them to gaze into each other's eyes.

That does it.

"Gammy, we really have to go!"

"Just this last picture . . . look at Jacy and smile!"

Calla does, but her mouth and jaw feel as strained as his appear to be.

"Oh, I don't like the light there," Odelia says, tripod in hand. "Let me try it from over here."

"I'm sorry," Calla says to Jacy with bared, gritted teeth.

"It's okay. She's just being a grandma."

Yeah. And he's just being a sweetheart about the whole thing.

"Now, let me just take it from a different angle," Odelia calls, removing her camera from the tripod and climbing up a few steps.

"Thank you for being such a good sport," Calla tells Jacy through her clenched smile.

"No problem."

"Do you two look beautiful together, or what?" Odelia glows. "Just one more, and then you can go have fun at your dance."

If only.

Right about now, Calla would give anything if she and Jacy were actually going to do just that, like carefree, normal kids their age.

Normal . . .

God, I miss normal.

It's such a cliche, not to have appreciated something until it's gone.

At last, she and Jacy are freed into the brisk, moonlit night, with Odelia calling, "Good-bye! Have fun!" and finally, naturally, "Be careful!"

A glance at the Taggarts' porch shows no sign of Evangeline and Russell, and Calla has to fight not to make a dash for the car at the curb.

Guilt, guilt, guilt.

Four tires and a steering wheel are about all Jacy's car has in common with Blue Slayton's BMW. This older sedan has duct tape on the side mirror bracket and smells faintly of mildew.

But Calla would rather be riding in this car with Jacy, even if they aren't going to the dance, than in Blue's car with him, on the way to homecoming.

More guilt. When she called Blue at the hospital today to see how he was, he told her again how sorry he was that he'd miss taking her to the dance. She had to say she was going with Jacy, though of course she was sure to make it sound as though he was doing her a friendly favor.

"That's good," Blue said, obviously not the least bit bothered. Maybe he doesn't consider Jacy serious competition. Or maybe he's just lost interest in Calla and doesn't care either way.

"At least you get to go," he told her. "I wouldn't want both of us to have to miss it. Have fun."

She was just glad he didn't say to be careful.

As Jacy turns up Route 60 toward Fredonia and the entrance to the thruway, she heaves a sigh and leans back in the seat.

He glances at her. "Are you okay?"

"I just feel horrible, doing this to my grandmother. And to your foster dads."

"I know. They were so great, making me buy the suit and everything . . . the only reason I agreed was because they said I'd need it anyway, for graduation in June."

"What if they find out we didn't really go tonight?"

"Peter and Walt?"

"And my grandmother. And everyone else," she adds, thinking of Evangeline and Blue and Ramona.

"Let's not worry about that now. You're only doing what you have to do. I mean, it's not like we're out joyriding."

Far from it.

The joyless drive to Geneseo takes almost two hours.

Calla spends most of it staring out the window, trying to fig-ure out how, in the grand scheme of things, she wound up here. Not just here with Jacy, tonight, but *here*—motherless, in upstate New York, with a newfound talent for seeing dead people.

If it weren't for Jacy beside her—and a whole lot of makeup caked around her eyes—she'd let herself have a good cry over the loss of her old, blessedly *normal* life.

"We're almost there."

She looks up and sees that the landscape, which had transi-tioned to more urban and suburban around Buffalo and

Rochester, is back to rural, and much flatter here than around Lily Dale.

Geneseo is yet another little town in the middle of nowhere, from the looks of things.

Gazing out at the silos and barns outlined against the night sky, Calla tries to zero in on her mind's voice, as Patsy taught them in class that morning.

"Listen to your psychic senses," she advised. "Be receptive to the energy. Look for information and answers to come to you from within."

Does Geneseo hold the key to what happened to Darrin Yates . . . and Mom?

Yes. It does.

She can feel it. Suddenly, her entire body is tense with apprehension.

"I feel like there's something here," she tells Jacy. "Like we're not wasting our time. What about you?"

"Yeah." He nods. "I feel the same way."

They pass SUNY Geneseo campus on the edge of town, and a residential neighborhood lined with century-old houses, many of them now obviously occupied by college students.

Kids are everywhere—alive and dead, from this era and eras past—walking with backpacks, cigarettes, groups of friends.

Main Street, in the heart of town, is dotted with towering oak trees and stretches for a few picturesque blocks, lined with bars, pizza and wing places, cafés and diners, and a couple of small stores.

In the center of it all, smack in the middle of the street, is a large, old-fashioned fountain.

"There's the bear!" Calla exclaims, pointing at the patinated

155

figure towering on a lamppost pedestal in the middle of the basin. "Jacy, you have to stop!"

He pulls into a vacant spot and she jumps out of the car before it's in park, barreling right over to the fountain, looking for . . .

What?

God only knows.

It's not as though she thought Darrin Yates would be standing right here on the street, waiting for her.

Still . . .

"It's just a fountain," she tells Jacy when he catches up to her, pocketing the car keys.

"Looks that way."

"I can't believe it. I really expected . . ."

"What?"

"I don't know . . . too much, I guess."

Why did she have to go and drag Jacy into this?

"Calla, we just got here," he points out.

Yeah, and he went to a lot of trouble to get her here. She has to at least try to see it through, hopeless as it seems.

"I know. It's just . . . the way that guy Bob talked about the fountain, I thought it meant something."

"It does. It got us to Geneseo, right?"

"Maybe we shouldn't have come."

In silence, Jacy reaches out and squeezes her hand.

Shoulder to shoulder, they gaze up at the bronze bear in the moonlight.

"What do you think we should do?" Calla asks Jacy, hoping he'll suggest that they drive back to Lily Dale in time for the last dance at homecoming.

"What do you want to do?"

She hesitates. This seemed like such a good idea when they talked about it last night.

Now . . . not so much.

What does she want to do?

Go home, that's what.

Her feet hurt in these shoes, and she's cold, and . . .

And longing for *normal*.

Longing to be held in Jacy's arms, swaying on a dance floor. That's what a girl her age should be doing with a cute guy on a Saturday night, right? Not looking for her mother's killer in the middle of nowhere.

Killer? You're positive Darrin killed her, then?

It's not something she's allowed herself to really think about lately. It's too painful to think of what happened to Mom on that awful day at the top of the stairs.

Now, she beckons the vision, tries with every ounce of concentration to focus on what her mind's voice is telling her.

And it's just not clear.

Logically, she should believe Darrin did it. Who else is there?

Every sign she's been given points in his direction.

Maybe you just don't want to believe it because it's too horrible to think she was killed by someone she once loved.

Why would Calla even doubt, though, that he's capable of murder?

Both Odelia and Ramona said Darrin was trouble. He was using a fake name when Calla met him in Florida, and there was something furtive about the way he and her mother were acting that day.

How difficult should it be for an intuitive person like Calla to put two and two together?

It shouldn't be difficult at all, and yet . . .

I'm just not sure.

If only she could find Darrin, come face-to-face with him, she'd know for sure.

"Okay," she tells Jacy decisively, "let's go look for him."

"Did you bring that snapshot of your mother and Darrin?"

"It's in my purse—I left it in the car."

"Let's go show the picture to some people. This is a small town. If he's been here, or lives here, maybe someone will recognize him."

"The only thing is, the picture's so old," she points out as they scuff through the dry leaves on the sidewalk. "I don't know if it's going to do any good."

"*You* recognized him from it," Jacy points out firmly, and gives her hand a reassuring squeeze. "Come on. It's worth a try."

FOURTEEN

Geneseo, New York
Saturday, September 29
10:16 p.m.

Calla is more ready than ever to call it a night.

Even if they left now, though, they wouldn't make the last dance.

What a waste of a potentially good—potentially great—evening.

Nobody she and Jacy have asked, mostly college students who are either hanging out or working at the businesses on Main Street, has ever seen Darrin Yates before.

"I guess old Red Beard Bob has a lot of work to do on his psychic abilities," she tells Jacy as they shuffle down the street again.

"Not necessarily. Maybe we shouldn't have interpreted his

vision so literally. Maybe there's another statue with a bear in it, in some other town . . . some other country, even. You just don't know."

"No, but I really felt like there was something here when we got here."

"So did I. The funny thing is, I still do."

So does Calla. That's the hard part.

She can't seem to ignore the gnawing idea that this place has some connection to Darrin.

Maybe he's not here now, but that doesn't mean he never was.

Regardless, she's exhausted and her feet are being tortured by these shoes, and it's really time to go, she concludes as they pass a couple of modern-day hipsters who are very much alive, and a 1960s hippie clad in a headband and bell-bottoms who obviously is not. He gives Calla a transparent peace sign before drifting into oblivion.

"Let's go, Jacy. Really."

"Let's just try this last place," Jacy suggests, pointing at a small café called Speakeasy, "and then we'll head back."

"Good idea."

The place is dimly lit, with high ceilings, exposed brick walls, and battered hardwood floors. There are stacks of freebie publications and a cluttered bulletin board covered in home-made fliers asking for or volunteering apartment rentals, room-mates, or ride shares to various locations over the upcoming break.

Between the door and the counter, almost all of the small, round café tables are full. Most of the patrons are very much alive: studious types sitting alone using laptops, boisterous groups of kids laughing and talking, couples who seem oblivious to everything but each other.

Yet there are a few apparitions hanging around, too, flappers with feathered headbands and dapper guys in pin-striped suits who could have stepped out of the Roaring Twenties. Hearing a faint Charleston playing in the background, Calla wonders if the place really was a speakeasy back then. Probably.

As she and Jacy wait for two alive-and-well coeds to place an order, Calla can't help but eavesdrop on their conversation. They're laughing and talking about what to wear to a party they're going to later, sounding as if they don't have another care in the world.

That's what my life will be like next year at this time. I'll be like them: totally on my own, with no one to tell me where I can go, or what time to be home, or to be careful.

For the first time in a long time, Calla feels a spark of excitement about next year.

Maybe tomorrow, she'll start working on that list of colleges for Mrs. Erskine.

The girls move on with their coffees; it's Jacy's and Calla's turn now.

"What can I get you folks?" The heavyset gray-haired woman behind the cash register is wearing a black Harley Davidson T-shirt and has a tattoo of a rose on her bare, fleshy lower arm.

Hovering behind her is the spirit of a beefy Hells Angel in a do-rag and a hideously bloody T-shirt. Calla tries not to look at him as Jacy shows the woman the picture and launches into the spiel they've been giving everyone they meet.

"We're trying to find this guy. This is an old picture, but

can you take a good look at it and tell me if you've ever seen him?"

"Sure, why not."

"He'd be in his forties," Calla tells the woman as she takes a step back and holds the photo to better light.

"He can't be in his forties. He looks like he's about your age—eighteen, nineteen."

Calla and Jacy look at each other. They've been through this repeatedly tonight.

"That's not me, in the picture," Calla tells the woman. "It's my mother."

"But . . ." She looks at the picture, then up at Calla, obviously confused. "You're wearing the same dress?"

She nods.

"Man oh man, do you look just like your mother or what?"

Calla wishes, again, that she weren't wearing the same outfit tonight that her mother has on in the photo—same outfit, same makeup, same hairdo.

It was eerie, the way people will glance at the picture, and then at her . . . as if she's somehow stepped right out of the photograph, and out of the past.

"So this picture was taken, what? Twenty, thirty years ago?"

"About."

"Well, I don't think I've ever seen him." Rose Tattoo shakes her head.

"Are you sure?" Jacy asks.

"He doesn't look familiar. Did he go to school at Geneseo or something?"

"I'm not sure," Calla admits, accepting the frame and tucking it back into her purse. "I don't know much about him."

"How come you're looking for him here?"

"Good question," she mutters, mostly to herself, then adds politely, "Thanks anyway."

"No problem."

"We might as well get going," Calla tells Jacy.

"You don't want to go around and ask the customers?"

"Why bother? I think if Darrin lives around here, we would have found someone who recognizes him by now. We've asked, like, a hundred people."

"At least. Okay. You're right. We can go. But first, let's order something." He gestures at the beverage menu written in colored chalk on a blackboard behind the counter, and she notices that the ghostly Hells Angel has disappeared.

"Oh, that's okay," Calla says, "I'm not—"

"Listen, Walt gave me ten bucks and told me to take you out for hot chocolate after the dance."

"That's really sweet."

"So . . . two hot chocolates?" asks the woman behind the counter, and they both nod. "Whipped cream, too?"

"Why not? Want a brownie or something, too?" Jacy asks Calla, and she's catapulted back in time to Florida and a rainy night and the scent of freshly baked brownies in the air.

Was it really only about nine months ago? How can that be?

The memory seems to belong to somebody else's life story, not hers. Not the person she is now, anyway.

But it did happen—to the person she used to be, living the life that was pulled out from under her without warning.

163

Kevin was home from Cornell that night, on winter break. She baked for him, and they snuggled on the couch, watching a silly eighties movie and eating molten brownies straight from the oven.

I really miss Kevin, she realizes with a pang. *A lot. Even now.*

Well, of course. He was her first love.

But maybe he isn't her last, as she concluded when he dumped her and it felt like her life was over.

She looks at Jacy, wondering if the two of them might ever become as close as she and Kevin were.

It's hard to imagine . . . but not impossible. If she's learned anything these last few tumultuous months, it's that nothing's impossible.

"Sure, I'll have a brownie," she tells Jacy, trying to sound casual, toying with the emerald bracelet, which Mom gave her last spring to help ease the pain of Kevin's dumping her.

Jacy orders two brownies, then catches her watching him and smiles a little. "What?"

"Nothing . . . just, thanks for doing this with me."

He grabs her hand below the bracelet and gives it a squeeze. "Don't be disappointed. Okay?"

Caught off guard by the pleasure of his fingers clasping hers, it takes Calla a moment to figure out what he's talking about.

Darrin Yates.

Hello? That's why you're here, remember?

She sighs. "I just really thought we were going to find him—or at least, find out something about him."

Behind the counter, Rose Tattoo squirts a generous dollop

of whipped cream on the hot chocolates, then covers them with domed plastic lids.

"It doesn't mean we won't find him," Jacy points out. "Just not here, and not tonight."

"What do we do next, though? Drive around the country aimlessly looking for neon purple houses?"

"Neon purple houses?" Rose Tattoo slides the cups across the counter to them. "Now that, I can help you with."

"What do you mean?" Calla asks.

"There's only one neon purple house here in town, and I happen to live on the same street."

Jacy and Calla exchange a glance.

"Maybe it's Darrin's house," he says.

"Nope." Rose Tattoo shakes her head. "I know the people who live there and it's not the guy you showed me in that picture. It's a mother and daughter."

"Maybe he lived there before they did," Calla suggests, trying not to get too excited, though it seems like they finally have a lead.

"Nope," Rose Tattoo says again. "Sharon Logan's owned the house for twenty, maybe almost thirty years now. I remember when she moved in—her kid was just a baby. She's all grown up now, in her twenties, and I think she must've moved out because I haven't seen her lately."

"So, there's not a man living there now?"

"No men. Never. It's not like that. The Logans keep to themselves."

Okay . . . but Calla refuses to give up on the lead. Maybe there's some connection to Darrin Yates. How many neon purple houses can there be in the world? And this one is right here in Geneseo.

"It's worth a look," Jacy agrees, and asks Rose Tattoo to write the directions on a napkin.

"I wouldn't go ringing their doorbell at night," she advises as she hands it over. "Mrs. Logan isn't the friendliest neighbor on my block, if you know what I mean."

Undeterred, Calla and Jacy thank her for her help.

A few minutes later, they're in the car, steaming hot chocolates sitting in the cup holders, all but forgotten.

Center Street isn't at all hard to find—it branches off Main, a stone's throw from the café (which Rose Tattoo confirmed to Calla really was once a speakeasy). She also said they could actually walk to the purple house from there, but Calla's toes are pinched in the satin pumps, and anyway, she's anxious to get there.

Her nerve endings sizzle with anticipation as they roll on up the dark street, past a lineup of old houses—most bigger than the ones in Lily Dale but definitely built in the same era. She can tell by the gingerbread porches, cupolas, fishscale shingles, and mansard roofs.

The neighborhood appears to be a blend of well-kept family homes, shabbier student rentals, and even a few fraternity and sorority houses marked with large Greek letters.

"You do know this might be another dead end." Jacy leans toward the windshield as he drives, straining to make out the house numbers, and paint colors, in the dark.

"I know it might. But it might not."

"I don't want you to be disappointed again."

"I won't be," Calla lies.

The truth is, she has a powerful gut feeling that they're about to find . . . well, if not Darrin Yates himself, then *something*. Some new information, another piece of the puzzle.

"It should be right around here somewhere." Jacy consults the napkin again, then slows the car to a crawl.

"There!" Calla points excitedly.

In the glow of the headlights and a nearby streetlamp, it's easy to see that the turreted two-story Victorian house is painted a bright shade of purple.

At the sight of it, an inexplicable rush of emotion sweeps through Calla.

She can't put her finger on why, but she's positive there's a strong connection between her mother and this house.

The instinct is so overwhelming that Calla jumps out of the car even before Jacy has come to a stop at the curb out front.

"Calla, wait!"

"What?" She turns back and sees that he, too, is out of the car, though his door is open and the engine is still running.

"I don't know if it's a good idea to . . ." He trails off and looks around them at the dark, deserted street. "I just don't know."

She nods, uneasily remembering all the warnings that have come her way lately. Still . . .

"You said you saw me struggling in the water. There's no water here."

He nods. 'I know. But to walk up to someone's door at night might be asking for trouble. You heard what the woman at the café said about the people who live here."

"I know, but we can't just leave."

"No," he agrees, "we can't."

Together, they walk up the leaf-strewn steps onto the shadowy porch, century-old boards creaking beneath their feet. Calla hesitates only a moment before ringing the old-fashioned bell. She can hear the loud buzz echoing on the other side of the door.

After what seems like a long wait, the overhead porch light flicks on and a face parts the curtains shrouding the door's glass window.

A woman's face, Calla realizes. Must be Sharon Logan. And Rose Tattoo was right, she doesn't look particularly welcoming.

In fact, there's something downright scary about the way her gaze narrows directly at Calla before she opens the door.

"What is it?"

At a loss for words, Calla is silent, taking in the formidable face before her. It isn't just that the woman is unattractive, with close-set, slate-colored eyes, sagging jowls, and a faint hint of fuzz across her upper lip. But her attitude is downright hostile.

"Mrs. Logan?" Jacy speaks up.

"No." The woman glares harder. "Not Mrs."

"Ms. Logan"—Jacy doesn't wait for an affirmation—"my name is Jacy Bly, and this is Calla Delaney, and we're in town looking for this man. Have you seen him?" He offers the framed photo, but the woman doesn't take it.

She merely flicks a glance at the picture, then back at them. "No."

Is she lying? Maybe.

But Calla isn't eager to toss out an accusation and risk the consequences.

"Are you sure?" Jacy asks, still holding the frame.

"Positive." Sharon Logan's gaze shifts from him to Calla. "Didn't your mother ever teach you that it's bad manners to go around ringing strangers' doorbells at this hour of the night?"

She closes the door in their faces without another word. A split second later, the overhead light is extinguished, leaving Calla and Jacy in the dark.

"Come on," he says in a low voice. "Let's get out of here."

"But I need to know about my mother," she says desperately. "And Darrin."

"You're going to Florida next weekend. Maybe you'll find something when you go through her things at the house, and check the laptop."

"Maybe."

Leaves rasping beneath their footsteps, they head down the steps and along the walk toward the car.

They're almost there when Calla feels a pair of eyes boring into her. She looks over her shoulder at the house again, expecting to see Sharon Logan in the window.

But instead, the silhouette of a man stands squarely on the front steps, facing her.

This time, it's no shadow ghost.

"Jacy," she whispers, heart pounding, "there's someone—"

"I know, shh, I see him."

Him.

Calla knows who it is even before he walks down the steps and into the moonlight, where she can recognize him.

"Darrin Yates," she breathes.

It's him.

It's really him.

She presses a trembling fist to her mouth.

After everything she's been through, trying to find him, here he is, walking toward them.

It's too good to be true . . .

Good?

Remembering that this man may have had something to do with her mother's death, Calla instinctively moves closer to Jacy's side and feels him slip a protective arm around her.

She shivers, noticing for the first time that the night air is cold, and leans into his solid warmth.

Darrin comes to a halt a few feet away. His eyes are wide. "Stephanie?"

Her mother's name on his lips catches Calla off guard.

She opens her mouth, but she can't seem to find her voice.

"You're so beautiful, baby . . . look at you." He's staring at Calla in wonder, shaking his head.

He thinks I'm her. He thinks I'm Mom, just like everyone who's seen that snapshot tonight.

Only Darrin Yates isn't comparing her to a picture. He's comparing her to the real thing—his lost love, Stephanie.

And the way he's looking at Calla, with utter reverence . . .

He's still in love with her.

That much is clear.

That, and the fact that he thinks he's seeing a ghost.

She glances at Jacy, who nods.

She clears her throat, manages to speak. "I'm not—"

"Stephanie, I'm so, so sorry." Darrin Yates falls to his knees in front of her, stunning Calla into silence.

Darrin looks up, his face ravaged with remorse. "I'm so

sorry for what I did to you. You had everything to live for—a husband, a daughter, a house, a job . . . you had a life."

Emotion clogs Calla's throat; tears blind her eyes.

So he did do it. He killed her.

"If I hadn't sent you that first e-mail, none of this would have happened. You'd still be alive. But—I don't know . . . it was Valentine's Day, and I was thinking of you, and . . . I just never meant to start anything. I never meant to hurt you. I never imagined where it would lead. Can you ever forgive me?"

He reaches toward her with trembling, pleading hands.

She inches closer to Jacy, a shudder running down her spine.

"Darrin—"

"No! No, don't call me that!"

"But—"

"It's Tom, Stephanie. Tom Leolyn. Remember? You'll get used to it. I did."

Calla gulps, manages to say obediently, "Tom, you have to tell me what you did. You have to tell me why I should forgive you."

She feels Jacy's arm tensing up on her shoulder.

He doesn't like this. He doesn't want her to go along with it, to let Tom think she's her mother.

But somehow, she's certain that the man kneeling before her isn't going to hurt her. Not now.

He already has.

All he wants is forgiveness.

"You know what I did," he tells her, his voice laced with despair. "I should have left it all alone. All those years . . . you

171

never would have had to know. But it was eating away at me. I couldn't let you go on thinking she was dead, when all along she was right here."

"What? What are you talking about? Who was right here?" Calla asks, heart pounding, trying not to strangle on the lump of dread in her throat.

But he's too far gone to even hear her. Words are pouring out of him, a heartfelt confession Calla knows she has no business hearing, and yet . . .

He blames himself for what happened to Mom.

He pushed her down those stairs. Why?

"I couldn't carry that secret with me for the rest of my life, Steph. I couldn't live with myself. I had to tell you, and I told myself I was willing to take the consequences. Now . . . look at me. I've paid the price. But so have you."

"What did you do, Tom?" Calla asks raggedly. "What did you do to me?"

"I never meant for it to happen. I've always loved you. There was never a day that went by that I didn't miss you, and wonder about you, and need you."

He's sobbing now, reaching for her.

Jacy steps between them. "No. Don't touch her."

It's as if Tom is noticing him for the first time, and his eyes narrow. "Who are you?"

"She's not who you think she is. Calla, come on. Let's go."

"But—"

"We have to go. I don't like this."

Jacy grabs her arm and pulls her to the car, all but shoving her into the passenger's seat before he jumps behind the wheel.

As they pull away, she looks back at Darrin, standing alone.

Then she turns on Jacy. "Why did you do that? He was telling us what he did to her!"

"He thought you *were* her."

"So?"

"I told you. It wasn't safe."

He's probably right.

Looking back on what just happened, Calla knows it probably wasn't smart to let Darrin believe she's her mother.

But she came here looking for answers. Darrin was giving them to her.

"What more do you need to know?" Jacy asks. "He said he was responsible."

"But he didn't say why."

"Does it matter?"

Yes. It does.

And she has the feeling she'll be haunted by Darrin Yates's ravaged face for a long, long time.

But . . .

Not Darrin Yates. Tom Leolyn. That was the name he gave. Apparently, it's the name he's been going by for all these years.

Leolyn, as in . . .

Leolyn Woods.

Odelia was dozing in her chair when Calla came in the door, but she stirred enough to ask about her night.

"It was great!" Calla told her, around an enormous yawn.

She didn't have to feign exhaustion—she was utterly

depleted by that time—but when Odelia started asking questions, she did have to work up a convincingly enthusiastic, and pathetically generic, description of the evening she and Jacy had supposedly just shared.

She talked about a punch bowl and crepe paper streamers and how a DJ would have been better than a live band. She said she and Jacy danced to a few slow dances, and she danced to the fast ones with her friends.

Every single school dance she's ever been to is the same old story. For all she knows, this one was drastically different, but she wouldn't bet on it.

Finally, carrying Gert up to her room with her as usual, she dropped into bed, exhausted, wanting only to sleep.

But sleep refused to come.

She's been lying here for hours now, staring at the shadows on the ceiling as the kitten purrs peacefully at the foot of the bed. She can't seem to stop her mind from working; she keeps going over and over what happened in Geneseo: the confrontation with the sinister Sharon Logan, and finding out that Darrin really did kill her mother, and wondering what she's going to find out in Florida next weekend.

At last, she feels sleep beginning to overtake her. Her eyelids close.

One thing is certain: first thing tomorrow, she's going to go next door to use the Taggarts' computer and check the name "Tom Leolyn."

She burrows into her quilt, absently wishing she had on warmer pajamas. It'll be good to get to Florida on Friday and feel warm again for a change.

For the first time, she allows herself to think past her

obsessive mission there and considers the fact that she's about to step back into her old life. What will it be like, weather aside, to be back in Tampa?

Again, she thinks of Kevin, missing him, remembering the good times . . .

Hearing Gert's startled meow and abrupt scrambling at the foot of the bed, Calla opens her eyes.

What the—?

Gert has fled the room.

And Darrin—Tom—is standing across the room, looking directly at Calla.

With a terrified scream, she bolts from the bed.

"Stephanie!" he calls after her. "Wait!"

"Gammy! Gammy!" Calla shrieks, and bursts into her grandmother's room to find Odelia sound asleep.

"Gammy!"

"Wh-what?"

"Wake up! Someone's in my room!"

"What?!"

"Someone's in my room!" Frantic, Calla looks around for a phone. "Call the police! Hurry!"

"There's no phone up here." Odelia grabs the table lamp from the nightstand, casts the paper shade aside, and yanks the plug from the wall, then barrels fearlessly toward the hall with it, Calla dogging her heels.

She pictures her grandmother hitting Darrin over the head with the lamp and can only hope he won't retaliate. Remembering the scene with the intruder—who meant to kill her—she has to force herself not to turn and run right down the stairs and out of the house.

Instead, she follows Odelia into her room . . . and stops short.

"There's no one here," her grandmother says, and bends to peek under the bed.

"Careful, Gammy!"

"No one." Odelia opens the closet. "No one here, either."

"But he was! He was here! I saw him!" He must have escaped from the room while she was across the hall. Either he ran off into the night, or he's still lurking somewhere in the house.

"Who was here?" Odelia asks.

"Darrin Yates."

Her grandmother's mouth tightens into a straight line. "I'm sure it was just a dream. A nightmare."

"No, Gammy, he was here. He must have . . ."

Followed me home from Geneseo, is what she was going to say. But she can't.

Her grandmother doesn't seem to notice. "It's only natural that you'd be having nightmares, after what you went through a few weeks ago with that maniac who tried to kill you."

"But it wasn't a nightmare. He was here."

Her grandmother hugs her. "I know how real it seems when you wake up from something like that—you think it really happened."

It did really happen, she thinks stubbornly. *He really was here. Why?*

Maybe he's lost his mind—he killed someone, he must be crazy, right?—and he really does think Calla is her mother. Maybe he's come after her to kill her all over again.

Or maybe he honestly believes she's her mother's ghost.

He grew up here in Lily Dale and his parents are mediums—he's no stranger to people seeing the dead; maybe he sees them himself.

"I guess I don't need this," Odelia says, gesturing wryly with the table lamp.

Calla says nothing.

"Most people just use a flashlight to see their way around a dark house at night. Leave it to me to go overboard, huh?" Odelia chuckles, then looks closely at Calla. "I'm trying to make you laugh."

"Oh. Sorry." She sighs. "Gammy, can you please check the house and make sure there's no one here? I'm really freaked out about this. I can't help it."

"Sure. Let's do it together. Come on."

They go through the house from top to bottom. Gert turns up downstairs, looking agitated—at least, in Calla's opinion.

Odelia scoops her into her arms and carries her around, making a big show of checking behind doors and curtains, under the furniture, even inside the kitchen cupboards, at which point Calla realizes her grandmother is strictly humoring her.

"There's nobody here," Odelia says. "Just you and me and Gert . . . and maybe Miriam. You don't think she's the one you saw?"

Calla shakes her head. "No. I saw Darrin Yates." Tom Leolyn. Her mother's killer.

"In a dream."

"I wasn't dreaming. Gert was on my bed, and he scared her, and I opened my eyes and there he was."

"Gert is down here, though," Odelia reminds her.

"Now she is. She was on my bed. She ran away when he showed up."

Odelia says nothing, just pets Gert in her arms.

I wish you could talk, Calla silently tells the kitten, who looks back at her with unblinking green eyes. *You know he was there. You saw him, too.*

Whatever.

The house really is empty, aside from Miriam, who flits somberly and silently from room to room with them.

"Ready to go back up to bed?" Odelia asks around a monstrous yawn, after checking all the locks.

"I guess so."

Maybe Odelia is right, and Darrin was never here at all.

Calla *was* starting to drift off . . . maybe she did fall asleep, without even realizing it. And of course Darrin Yates was already on her mind.

But what if Odelia is wrong?

What if he really was here?

What did he want with her?

And what if he comes back?

FIFTEEN

Sunday, September 30
7:30 a.m.

Ordinarily at this hour on a Sunday morning, a ringing telephone would wake Calla from a sound sleep.

Not today.

She hasn't slept all night. She just lay there, tense, keeping an eye out for Darrin Yates to prowl into her room again, maybe try to kill her like he killed her mother.

Finally, at about six o'clock, she got up and came down to the living room.

She's still there, brooding on the couch, fingering the emerald bracelet she can't take off her wrist, when the phone shatters the silence.

She reaches for it immediately, thinking it must be Jacy. He said he'd call her this morning before leaving for his cross-country meet, and she has to tell him what happened last night in her room. Maybe he'll agree with Odelia that it was just a nightmare.

The more Calla thinks about it, the more inclined she is to believe it.

Or maybe she just wants to talk herself into it.

"Hello?" she whispers into the phone, not wanting to wake Odelia, asleep upstairs. Not that that's likely. Her grandmother is such a sound sleeper, as she proved when Calla screamed for her in the night, that a tornado could lift the entire house around her and she'd probably still be there, snoring peacefully.

"Calla? Are you okay?"

"Evangeline?" Her heart sinks.

"Yeah. I hated to call this early, but . . . where *were* you last night?"

Uh-oh. Calla should have been ready for this. With all the tossing and turning she's done, there was ample opportunity to have come up with a suitable story about why they weren't at the dance.

Her grandmother seemed to buy her account of the evening. Probably because she was so groggy at the time.

Evangeline, however, sounds wide awake. And suspicious.

"Why weren't you and Jacy at the dance?"

"We . . . decided not to go."

"But I saw his car parked in front of your house before you left, and he was all dressed up."

Calla cringes at the idea of Evangeline spying on Jacy out her window, even though it's nothing new.

"We were planning on going, but . . . I just couldn't do it."

"Because of Blue?"

"Not really. Because . . ."

Okay, what can she possibly say that would make any sense at all?

"Because of me?" Evangeline asks.

Uh-oh. Definitely not that.

But Evangeline gives her no time to deny it.

"I knew it," she exclaims. "I *knew* you felt bad about this! I told my aunt all along that I didn't think you could do that to me. I mean, you've known from the start that I'm in love with Jacy."

"Come on, Evangeline . . . you're not 'in love' with him." Calla tries to keep the edge out of her voice, but she's still upset about last night, and she just doesn't have the patience for this. "It's just . . . a crush."

"Ex-*cuse* me?" Her friend sounds indignant.

Which, Calla realizes, is pretty unfair.

"Love," after all, is a strong word.

Maybe if Calla weren't so exhausted—physically, emotionally—she'd be able to go along with it. But the lack of sleep and all the stress are catching up with her, and she finds herself pointing out, "It's not like you and Jacy are—or even *were*—you know, going out."

For a moment, Evangeline is silent.

She *must* realize how ridiculous it is for her to expect Calla to stay away from Jacy because of her own crush—unrequited, at that.

"Well, it's not like *you* and Jacy are, either . . . is it?" Evangeline asks, not exactly sounding as if she's seen the light.

"I told you . . . we're friends."

"I know what you *told* me, but I'm not sure I believe you. In fact, maybe I don't. Are you?"

"Am I what?"

"Are you and Jacy really just friends, and that's it?"

Guilt twists Calla's stomach into a leaden knot. "Evangeline . . ."

"I'm right, then?" she asks shrilly. "There's something going on between you two?"

"It's not what you think."

"I don't even *know* what I think. What is it? Tell me."

Calla wearily examines her options, which are pretty straightforward.

You can lie again . . .

Or you can tell the truth.

Not the whole truth, though.

She can't risk telling anyone about Geneseo. If it ever got back to her grandmother, well, Calla hates to think of how Odelia would react to that.

All Calla can share is the truth about herself and Jacy: that they have feelings for each other.

But if she does that, her friendship with Evangeline might crash and burn.

Might?

Evangeline's made it pretty clear where she stands on this—fairly or not.

"It's not like you think," Calla tells her. "I mean, it's not like Jacy and I are going out or anything like that. We're just . . ."

"You *said* you were just friends."

Calla says nothing.

"You're more than that, aren't you?"

"Maybe. I don't know." Frustrated, Calla starts to rake a hand through her bangs, then encounters the hardened mass of goo that remains from last night's hairdo.

"Did you kiss him?"

She can't answer that. It will be too painful for Evangeline to hear it.

But she doesn't have to.

She can hear the tremor in her friend's voice as she says, "Whatever. I have to go."

"Evangeline—"

There's a click in her ear, followed by a dial tone.

Hearing the groan of old pipes upstairs, Calla knows that Odelia is running water for a morning bath.

Good.

Time to escape the house and check out Leolyn Woods, even if she has to go alone.

She doesn't have much choice, with Jacy at a track meet and Evangeline apparently no longer speaking to her. There's no one else she can ask.

But if what happened last night in her room was just a nightmare—and she's almost convinced now that it was—then there's no reason, really, for her to be wary of going into the woods alone.

And even if it wasn't a nightmare, even if Darrin really did follow her here to Lily Dale, she still has to go. She *has* to.

Maybe the circled X on the map has nothing to do with her, or her mother, or Darrin calling himself Tom Leolyn. Maybe it was pure coincidence that the book opened to that page when it fell. Maybe Aiyana wasn't even responsible for the book falling off the table in the first place. Except . . .

There are no coincidences, remember?

Calla hurries up to her room and grabs a jacket and her iPod, along with the now overdue library book containing the marked map.

"I'm going out for a walk, Gammy," she calls, knocking on the bathroom door.

"A walk? Right *now*?"

Hearing the water splashing into the tub, Calla is seized by a sudden, irrational flash of apprehension.

Huh? Where did that come from?

"It's, uh, a beautiful day," she calls back to her grandmother, disconcerted, "and I want to get out and enjoy it."

Odelia's cheerful reply is lost in the rushing water, and Calla wastes no time heading back downstairs.

The fear was fleeting, but so authentic that Calla wonders if she's channeling some frightening event that happened in that spot where she was standing, or perhaps in the bathroom.

Probably.

Just another perk of my "gift," she thinks wryly as she heads out the front door, where milky sunlight and a stiff breeze greet her. The sky isn't anywhere near blue, but at least it's no longer sodden with bruise-colored clouds.

Still, "a beautiful day" was stretching it.

Calla pulls on her jacket with a shiver, then descends the porch steps with a glance at the Taggarts' porch. No sign of

Evangeline, but Calla wonders if she might be watching from somewhere inside.

On the street, there's not a living soul in sight at this hour on a Sunday morning—though there are a few spirits drifting about. Things wouldn't be much different here at high noon on a weekday, though. Not at this time of year.

Will she ever get used to the postseason ghost-town feel to the place?

Ramona said she likes Lily Dale better this way; she finds the isolation peaceful.

It *can be* peaceful, Calla supposes as she heads down the street, head bent against the chilly wind off the lake.

But on off-season days when the sun doesn't shine, which is just about every day except today, there's something dreary, almost mournful, about the Dale.

Dappled shadows fall pleasantly from overhead branches as they move in the breeze, and the relentless rhythm of Kanye West in her earphones almost makes Calla forget that this isn't just an ordinary morning walk.

But it takes her only a few minutes to reach the entrance to Leolyn Woods, where the strange, ominous warning sign snaps Calla back to grim reality. She unplugs herself and tucks the iPod back into her pocket.

Wow. It's so quiet here.

Eerily quiet.

Branches stir overhead, sending down a gentle shower of red and gold leaves, but she's pretty sure the morning breeze doesn't qualify as "high winds."

Okay, you're good to go.

So . . . go.

185

Consulting the map, she wonders how far into the woods she has to go to reach the designated spot. Hard to tell. Probably not too far.

Still, Calla hesitates on the path, gazing around at the legendary old-growth forest, home to Inspiration Stump, with its powerful energy vortex.

Why did she have to come alone? What if Darrin is lurking, watching her? What if something happens to her in there? Something freaky, supernatural, like . . . Well, who knows what?

This is silly. Just get it over with.

She begins to tread slowly beneath the colorful high canopy of ancient trees, her sneakers scrunching through the dried foliage.

She checks the map again, adjusts her direction, keeps walking. The ground grows marshy in some spots, and she has to step over the occasional fallen log covered with moss.

If it weren't for the vague sense of foreboding, Calla would actually be enjoying the walk. Small woodland creatures, seen and unseen, dart playfully or furtively from her path. Her shuffling footsteps mingle pleasantly with the chirping of songbirds and the occasional whisper of wind through the leaves.

She inhales air heavy with the rich, earthy scent of autumn . . . and then it happens.

Her nostrils catch a hint of something else. Something familiar, unmistakable.

Lilies of the valley.

The scent can mean only one thing: Aiyana is here.

Calla waits for the telltale chill in the air, braced for a

glimpse of the spirit who, she's now convinced, led her to this spot.

But the only visible movement is a jet-black squirrel that hops onto a fallen limb, eating from its paws, seemingly oblivious to Calla's presence . . . or any other.

She checks the map in the book, looks around, gets her bearings.

Yes, this is it.

She's in the general area indicated by the X on the map. Nothing here but more trees, more logs, more fallen leaves layered thickly underfoot.

No Aiyana

The floral perfume hangs blatantly in the air, so potent Calla can smell nothing else . . . yet she still doesn't sense the ghostly presence that usually accompanies it.

But as she looks around, puzzled, her gaze comes to rest on something so startling, so utterly out of place, that she's certain she must be mistaken.

She takes a few steps closer, blinks several times, peers again.

She's not mistaken.

A small dirt patch of forest floor, maybe a couple of feet square, is curiously void of leaves, almost as if someone diligently swept the area clean.

Which is impossible, because there's not a soul in sight, and even if there had been, the breeze would have scattered and shifted more leaves.

Even more impossible: blooming in the bare spot is a clump of flowers.

Calla recognizes them not just by the distinct scent, but by the delicate clusters of bell-shaped blossoms perched atop straight, slender stems, poking out from pale green tuliplike foliage.

Lilies of the valley.

It wouldn't be unusual to see them blooming in the wild . . . in the spring.

But at this time of year, they should be dormant; the flowers would have long since shriveled, the foliage disappeared.

Calla stoops and reaches out, the emerald bracelet glinting on her wrist, to pluck one of the stems.

Is it a freak of nature?

Some kind of sign from Aiyana or . . . from Mom?

Calla presses the fragile white blossom to her nose and inhales the perfume, closing her eyes.

"Please, Mom . . . if you can hear me . . . please tell me what I'm supposed to do. Please . . ."

The breeze turns colder.

Calla feels the flesh rising on her arms and knows she's no longer alone. Her eyes snap open.

Aiyana stands before her, so solid, so real, that Calla fleetingly wonders, though she knows better, whether she's a spirit after all.

She sweeps a hand to indicate the extraordinary flowers, but she doesn't turn to look at them. Her black eyes are fastened on Calla's.

At last she speaks. "She isn't there."

A chill slithers down Calla's spine. "My mother?"

"No."

"You're *not* talking about my mother?"

"No."

"Then . . . who? Who isn't there? And where?"

Again, Aiyana points at the lilies.

Calla turns to look again at them, and all at once, it dawns on her. "Is this . . . is it a grave or something?"

At that, out of nowhere, a powerful gust of wind swoops around them, bringing a maelstrom of blowing leaves. Startled, Calla raises her elbows to cover her face.

The gust disappears as quickly as it came, and so, she realizes with dismay, has Aiyana.

She looks again at the lilies and notices that the wind has redistributed the surrounding bed of leaves. A solid, monochromatic object juts from the heap of gold-and-red confetti—a rock, Calla realizes.

She brushes away the leaves with a trembling hand. It's a smooth, oblong gray rock, roughly the size of a shoe box. It's not lying flat on the ground, but standing straight up as though human hands deliberately placed it there, jutting like . . .

Like a tombstone.

Her blood runs cold.

She sinks to her knees and runs her fingers over the rock.

She's not there.

Why would Aiyana say that?

Mom's grave is in a Florida cemetery; Aiyana must be aware of that because Calla saw her there, hovering on the edge of the crowd at the funeral that miserable day in July.

But I asked if she was talking about Mom, and she said no.

Who else would she mean?

"Who isn't there, Aiyana?" Calla calls out. "I don't understand!"

No response but the sigh of a gentle wind in ancient trees.

Calla shakes her head in despair, acutely aware that she's alone again.

She stands rooted to the spot for a long time.

Long enough for Mother Nature to do her work.

The sun climbs higher in the chalky sky and the breeze ebbs and flows. With it, leaves skitter across the earth and drift from laden boughs, coming to obscure, once more, the cold gray rock and the tender white flower blossoms that shouldn't, couldn't, be growing in Leolyn Woods.

As Calla turns toward home, she glimpses a face among the moving boughs, watching her.

Darrin.

She freezes, uncertain whether to scream, or run, or call out to him.

Before she can decide, the wind gusts and the branches shift again, obscuring his face and leaving her uncertain as to whether it was really there at all.

But she's not taking any chances.

She turns and runs, not stopping until she's safely back home again with the deadbolt locked behind her.

Calla spends the afternoon secluded in her room, unable to face her grandmother and any more questions about the dance last night.

It's bad enough that she's apparently lost Evangeline's friendship over it. The last thing she wants is for her grandmother to find out that she's a liar. For all Calla knows,

Evangeline has already told Ramona, and Ramona will tell Odelia, and maybe Dad, too.

And then he'll make her leave. Or Odelia will.

What does it matter, anyway?

Lily Dale isn't good for her, in her state of mind.

She doesn't need these people feeding her grief or fueling her nightmares and imagination.

Curled up on her bed, Calla tries to read her economics text, but she can't focus. Her eyes keep leaving the page to ensure that she's alone in the room. No Darrin Yates lurking . . . yet she can't seem to shake the eerie sensation that he's here, watching her.

Is it any wonder, though?

You're still upset about last night, paranoid . . . and totally wiped out.

Eventually, she goes from propping her head on her hand above a bent elbow to leaning back against the pillows, still trying to focus on the textbook.

Finally, the words on the page begin to swim, and exhaustion overtakes her.

Calla is back in the professionally decorated, tropical-hued master bedroom in their house in Tampa. She's her mother, humming as she gets dressed for work in a charcoal gray skirt suit and high-heeled black Gucci pumps, spraying on perfume that shouldn't smell like lilies of the valley, yet somehow does, today.

She pulls a brown manila envelope from beneath the mattress of the king-sized bed and looks at it, troubled.

"I'm sorry," she whispers. "I have to do this."

Leaving the room with the envelope in hand, she heads down the hall toward the stairs, past Calla's bedroom door.

It should be closed, but it's open. Puzzled, she starts to turn to look back. Too late.

Someone comes up behind her and pushes, hard.

She screams, falling, hurting, dying . . .

Drifting, floating, high above her own broken body now lying in a slowly spreading pool of blood. The crimson stream inches across the tile floor toward the fallen manila envelope.

Blood taints the edge of the yellow-brown paper in the instant before a hand reaches out to snatch it up. A left hand, thick fingers, the pinky adorned with a gold signet ring bearing a coat of arms featuring a heart pierced by three daggers.

"Calla?"

She awakens with a start to the sound of knocking and her grandmother's voice.

Dazed, she sits up, finding herself on her bed, fully dressed and shrouded in the dim gloom of Sunday dusk.

"Calla?" Odelia opens the door and a wedge of light spills in from the hall. "Oh! You're sleeping?"

"I . . . guess so."

Sleeping. And dreaming.

Mom . . . the envelope . . . the stairs . . . the blood . . .

Again.

But this time, there was more to it.

The hand . . . the ring . . .

"Are you feeling okay, sweetie?" Odelia flicks on a bedside lamp and Calla blinks.

Darrin's hand?

Darrin's ring?

"You look like you might be coming down with something." Odelia hovers over her looking worried, presses a hand against Calla's forehead.

Just like Mom used to do.

Without warning, the gentle maternal concern unleashes a tsunami of grief.

"Oh, my goodness . . . you're crying! What is it? What's wrong?" Odelia sits on the bed and takes Calla into her arms.

"I . . . just . . . miss her." Overcome, Calla collapses against her grandmother's ample, sturdy body with a sob.

"Oh, sweetie, I know . . . I know." Odelia strokes her hair, lets her cry, cries with her.

Finally spent, Calla accepts the crumpled tissue her grandmother produces from a pocket.

"It's clean," she says, and presses another to her own nose with a weary sigh.

Lost in their own thoughts, they wipe their eyes and blow their noses.

Then Odelia stands again and holds out a hand. "Come on."

"Come on where?"

"Downstairs. We can sit in front of the television and watch something mindless and trashy and eat dinner. I made soup."

"What kind of soup?" Calla asks warily. The last time

Odelia made soup, it was Spicy African Peanut Gumbo—which was pretty tasty, but not exactly soothing.

"Chicken noodle."

Calla raises an eyebrow. "Really?"

Odelia nods. "I had a feeling you were under the weather today. You've been so quiet, hiding yourself away. Come on. It'll make you feel better."

Calla doubts it, but she follows her grandmother downstairs, anyway.

A half hour later, she has to admit Odelia was right. A steaming bowl of soup—and the tail end of a Ben Stiller movie she's seen a million times—proves to be an effective remedy. She had been planning to make a beeline back to her room after eating, but instead she settles back against the couch cushions.

"I'll go see what I have for dessert." Odelia picks up their empty bowls and hands Calla the television remote. "See if you can find us something else to watch."

Left alone in the living room, she begins to channel surf past the evening news, a paper-towel commercial, a Hispanic soap opera, more evening news . . .

A stirring of uneasiness creeps over her again as snatches of her dream begin to filter back into her mind.

She finds herself glancing furtively around the room.

A sad-eyed spirit child she's seen around before is off in the corner, but that's not really a concern—not at the moment, anyway. She's not worried about dead people right now. Just live ones.

She looks at the windows to make sure Darrin Yates isn't out there in the night, peering in at her.

Impossible to tell in the glare of lamplight on the glass.

But I feel like he's around here again. Watching me.

She shudders. Maybe he really is.

Calla tosses aside the remote, gets up, and closes the curtains.

There. That's a little better.

At least now if he's out there he can't—

Turning back to the television, she gapes at the onscreen image of a white-haired woman with gold-rimmed glasses on a chain.

Calla recognizes her instantly.

Betty!

She's alive and well, obviously, and standing in front of a low redbrick house with dormered windows on the second floor.

"Oh my God." Calla fumbles for the remote and turns up the volume to better hear the newscaster's voice-over.

". . . and that was when Fredonia resident Elizabeth Owens discovered the theft from her home of several old stock certificates valued at close to seven figures."

The chicken soup is churning in Calla's stomach.

"They were left to me by my late husband," the elderly woman informs the on-the-scene reporter, "and they were hidden behind a painting I've had on the wall for years."

The scene changes to an interior shot: the reporter indicating the underside of a large wooden frame. "The certificates were cleverly concealed in a secret compartment behind the backing of this framed art. Ms. Owens believes the thief must have stumbled across them by accident, as she never told a living soul where they were hidden—or, for that matter, that she was in possession of the valuable stock."

"Only one living soul even knew I had the stock, and he did know that it was hidden somewhere in my house, but I never told him where. I guess he somehow figured it out."

Back to the voice-over. "That person is her current and estranged husband, Henry Owens, who met the longtime widow on a Caribbean cruise last spring and married her after a whirlwind courtship."

"I thought Henry was too good to be true," Betty's voice warbles, and her eyes are sorrowful. "I guess he was."

The reporter turns over the frame to reveal the other side.

"This painting," he says solemnly, "is worthless. Unfortunately for Betty Owens, the certificates concealed behind it were not."

Calla sinks onto the couch, sickened as she stares at the closeup on the artwork.

The painting depicts a large, gothic-looking house on a cliff overlooking the sea. It has a square center turret with an octagonal stained-glass window, and a widow's walk above.

The camera shifts to show a snapshot of the man Calla knows as Owen Henry, wearing a Hawaiian shirt with palm trees and standing in front of an aquamarine sea.

"Police now seek this man, Henry Owens, for questioning in connection to the theft," the reporter says. "Owens disappeared several days ago and is believed to have left the area. Viewers who may have information on his whereabouts are asked to call—"

"We're in luck." Odelia breezes into the room, carrying cookies. "I found a whole bag of Chips Ahoy in the cupboard."

"Gammy . . . I have to tell you something."

Odelia peers at her, sitting there on the couch. "What's wrong? Did something happen?"

Calla nods miserably. "I'm so sorry. I was only trying to help . . ."

Her grandmother puts the bag of cookies on the table and sits next to her, putting her hands on Calla's shoulders. "What is it? Tell me."

She does. The whole story.

And she braces herself for her grandmother's fury.

But shockingly, it doesn't come.

Odelia shakes her head a lot, and sighs heavily, but she doesn't yell or criticize or condemn or say *I told you so* or do any of the things Calla figures she has every right to do.

"You meant well, Calla. And you'll learn," she says heavily. "Just like I did. You'll learn when to get involved, and when to keep things to yourself."

"But now this poor old woman has lost all that money because of me. I thought he loved her and he was trying to reach her, and when I kept seeing her face, I thought she was a spirit . . . how could I be so stupid?"

"You're not stupid! You're just new at this." Odelia hugs her. "And you have a big heart. I know you want to help people. And you can. You can do a lot of good in this world using your gift."

"I can do a lot of bad, too. Maybe I shouldn't be trying to do anything at all with it. Maybe I should just forget I even have it."

As if that's even possible, she thinks, glancing at the sad-eyed little ghost girl in the corner of the room.

"You can learn to ignore it," Odelia tells her. "Some people do. But is that really what you want?"

"I don't know what I want. It's so depressing. I just feel awful right now, about that woman . . ."

About a lot of things.

None of which would ever have happened if she hadn't been thrust into this strange new world in Lily Dale.

Odelia ruffles Calla's hair. "You know what I think?"

"What?"

"That you should get a good night's sleep. Things will look brighter in the morning. They always do."

SIXTEEN

Monday, October 1
12:39 p.m.

Odelia is right about a lot of things, but she was wrong about this, big-time.

Things don't always look brighter in the morning.

On this particular morning, things couldn't have looked worse, and the afternoon isn't looking much better.

The day started with Evangeline going out of her way to avoid Calla. So she walked to school alone, trailing a good twenty yards behind Evangeline, also walking alone.

It seemed silly not to catch up to her and try to make amends, but it was really up to Evangeline to make the first move. Calla senses that her friend's pain is still too raw. And anyway, it's not as if Calla is willing to promise Evangeline she'll stay away from Jacy from now on. Not when they've finally gotten together.

When she got to school, Blue was there, on crutches. People were practically lining up to carry his books as he hobbled from class to class. He made a point of singling out Calla after first period to ask her how the homecoming dance was.

"It was okay," she said with a shrug, hoping he hadn't heard that she and Jacy didn't actually make it to the dance.

Luckily, he didn't press her for details, just asked if she wants to go to a movie next weekend.

"Thanks, but I can't . . . I'm going to Florida on Friday."

"Oh. Well, then, how about sooner. Tonight?"

"I have to babysit until late." Paula and Martin are going out to dinner. That means extra cash for her, and God knows she can use it.

"Okay . . . I have something going on tomorrow night, but how about Wednesday?"

"It's a school night." And her heart wasn't in it anymore. Now that she had been kissed by Jacy at last . . .

Why couldn't Blue, with his reportedly extraordinary perception, sense that she was no longer interested in him?

He definitely didn't, because he flashed those big Blue eyes and tilted his head at her and said, "We won't stay out late. Come on, Calla. I've been going stir crazy around the house. I could use some fun."

Frankly, so could she.

She found herself accepting the date, though mostly out of guilt.

She feels even more guilty now, though, seeing Jacy walk

into the cafeteria just as she sits down at her table without bothering to go through the lunch line.

"Where's your food?" Sarita asks, and Calla sighs inwardly, turning her attention to her friends.

"Oh . . . I'm not hungry today." Yeah, there's something about being stalked by your mother's murderer that really kills the appetite.

"I thought we might see you at homecoming Saturday," Willow says, uncapping her water bottle.

"Yeah, where were you, Calla?"

"You guys went?"

"Yeah, with a couple of other girls from the committee," Willow tells her. "It was fun. We danced a lot."

"Who needs guys?" Sarita flashes a metal grin and starts cutting into her apple. "Not that it wouldn't have been nice to go with a date. Weren't you supposed to go, Calla?"

"I was supposed to go with Blue, but then he got hurt, and—"

"I know," Sarita interrupts, "but I thought you were going with Jacy Bly."

"How'd you hear about that?"

"A couple of people mentioned it," Willow says, looking over Calla's shoulder. "And speak of the devil . . ."

"Hey, Calla," a male voice says, and she glances up to see Jacy standing there. He looks like his old self again in tattered jeans, sneakers, a gray hooded sweatshirt, and a baseball cap.

"Where were you guys Saturday night?" Sarita asks pointedly.

Ignoring her, Jacy tells Calla, "I need to talk to you."

Well aware of her friends' curiosity, Calla nods and pushes back her chair. "Sure. I'll, um, see you guys later."

"Later," Willow says with a knowing smile.

Jacy leads her toward the door. "Let's get out of here, okay?"

She looks around to make sure Evangeline isn't in the vicinity to see them together, even though she doesn't share their lunch period. It might be too late to protect her, but that doesn't mean Calla wants her to see the two of them together.

Good. The coast is clear. And she really does need to talk to Jacy.

"Okay," she tells him. "Where do you want to go?"

"Out," he says simply, grabbing her hand and heading toward the back exit on the ground floor, near the wood-shop classroom.

It's against school rules to leave the grounds during lunch period, but that never bothers Jacy. Today it doesn't bother Calla, either.

The feeling of his hand, warm and protective around her own, reminds her of the one thing that's finally right in her world: her relationship with Jacy.

Out in the cold wind beneath a sodden gray sky, she shoves her hand—the one he's not holding—into the pocket of her jeans for warmth, wishing she'd stopped at her locker for a jacket. As they head toward the seclusion of a wooded area at the back of the school property, she keeps a furtive eye on the shrubs and trees.

This time, she's on the lookout not for Evangeline, but for Darrin.

Do you really think he's going to jump out and attack you or something?

No. But she really thinks he might be lurking around here.

Sure, there's a good chance she dreamed that he was in her room Saturday night and merely imagined that he was in the woods yesterday.

But there's also a chance that after seeing her and mistaking her for Mom, he really did come back to Lily Dale looking for Stephanie, or Stephanie's ghost.

There's no sign of him today, though.

In the woods, Jacy sits on a fallen log and makes room for her. "So, how are you doing?"

"I'm . . . not so hot," she admits, sitting beside him, staring into the trees, looking for faces.

"You don't look so hot," he says without the slightest bit of irony.

"Gee, thanks."

Jacy's dark eyebrows furrow. "I just mean that you have circles under your eyes, and you look . . . you know, exhausted."

She is. But despite everything, she did try to cover up the circles this morning, taking some extra time to pull herself together for school—mostly for Jacy's benefit.

"I couldn't sleep at all Saturday night," she admits, "and I didn't sleep much last night, either."

"I didn't sleep much Saturday, either. That was pretty intense, with Darrin."

"Tom. Not Darrin. Tom *Leolyn*. Did you catch that?"

"Yeah, I caught it."

"What do you think it means?"

"That he's using a fake name?"

"That he's been using *that* fake name."

"I think it means he couldn't let go of Lily Dale. Or your mother, for that matter."

"I know. I wanted to get on the computer yesterday and check the name to see what I could find out about him, but . . ."

"But?"

But the only computer I have access to is over at Evangeline's, and she's not speaking to me because she's in love with you.

She's definitely not going to bring that up now. Or ever, most likely.

Anyway, there are other, more pressing things to discuss with him, that's for sure.

"The thing is, Jacy . . ." She trails off.

What if he doesn't believe her?

"The thing is . . . what?"

"I think he was in my room Saturday night, and he was watching me in the woods yesterday."

"What?" He gapes at her. "Who? Darrin?"

"Darrin. Tom. Whoever."

"He was in your *room*?"

"After you brought me home, I was lying there in my bed, and he was standing over it, watching me."

"Could it have been a dream?"

She sighs and toys with the emerald bracelet, still on her wrist. Maybe she'll never take it off again.

"That's what my grandmother said," she tells Jacy. "I woke her up, but by the time I got her back to my room, he'd taken off. *If* he was really there."

"Did he say anything to you?"

"In the dream? Or whatever it was?" She shakes her head.

"He just called me Stephanie again. He really thought I was her."

"He thought you were her ghost. He knows she's dead. You said he was at her funeral."

"Yeah. And that stuff he said Saturday night . . . about a secret, and that he should have left things alone after all those years . . . and how sorry he was . . . what did you get out of all that?"

"Something obviously happened between the two of them years ago. It sounds like he took off without telling her something he should have told her, and then—"

"And then he e-mailed her last Valentine's Day," Calla cuts in, "out of the blue, and told her about whatever it was. Right?"

"Sounded that way."

She nods, hugging herself against the chill—both outside and in. "I'm flying to Florida on Friday, Jacy. I'm going to get her laptop and find that e-mail."

"How are you going to do that? Do you know her password?"

"I'm sure I can figure it out."

He doesn't look convinced, and frankly, she isn't, either. But she has to try at least. She's been making a list for a few days now, writing down every possible password that occurs to her.

"What if she deleted the e-mail?" Jacy asks.

"What if she didn't?" she returns. "My mom was the most organized person you'd ever meet. She was really anal about keeping files, and copies of things. . . . I doubt she'd have deleted it if it were that earth shattering."

"She would have if she didn't want your dad to see it."

"He would never snoop in someone's private files. *Ever.* No way."

"Even if he was suspicious that she might be up to something with another man?"

Calla pushes aside the stubborn memory of her father telling her that her mother had grown detached from their marriage in the last few months of her life.

"I just don't know if you should be going to Florida and tapping into this on your own, Calla." Jacy brushes strands of windblown hair away from her face, looking worriedly at her.

Why did she agree to go out with Blue again on Wednesday night?

Because she felt bad about his being on crutches, and his thinking she had gone to the dance with Jacy.

Maybe she can cancel. Now that she and Jacy have connected at last, she doesn't want to be with anyone else.

Then again . . . maybe she'll use the opportunity to tell Blue she just wants to be friends, and nothing more.

Blue doesn't seem like he's in the market for a serious girlfriend, anyway. Considering the way the girls were hanging all over him and his crutches this morning, Calla doubts she'll break his heart if she tells him she's involved with Jacy now.

"Listen, Jacy," she says as his hand lingers on her cheek even now that he's brushed her hair away. "I don't have a choice about Florida."

"Sure you do. Don't go."

"I have to go."

"I keep thinking about you, flailing underwater . . ."

That does give her pause. "Can you tell if I am in Florida in your vision?"

"I don't know where you are. It could be anywhere. Here, even."

With a shudder, she thinks about the choppy black-gray waters of Cassadaga Lake, not so far from where they're sitting now.

"Well, I can't live my life not knowing what happened to my mother," she says resolutely, "and I can't live my life being terrified that something might happen to me around the next bend."

"I get that," Jacy says quietly, moving his hand away from her face at last. "I don't blame you. But I can't just let you go without warning you."

"Thanks."

"I wish I could go with you."

Her heart flutters at the mere thought of it, but only for a few seconds. Then he adds, "I can't, though. Even if Walt and Peter would let me—and could afford it, on top of the adoption expenses—I have a track meet on Saturday. I can't miss it. The coach is down on me for missing practice yesterday as it is."

"It's okay. I'll be fine on my own."

"I know, but . . ."

She smiles. "I know. It would have been good to have you with me. We should get going, I guess." She gets up, brushes off her jeans, and turns toward the school.

Darrin is clearly visible among the trees, watching them.

"Jacy!" She whirls toward him and clutches his arm. "He's here!"

"What? Who? Where?"

She points . . . then realizes he's gone.

"He was here! He must have seen me see him, and he took off!"

Without another word, Jacy starts running. He tears into the woods at high speed, expertly weaving around obstacles.

There's no way Darrin is going to be able to outrun him.

What's going to happen when Jacy reaches him?

Calla starts to chase after him, panicked. "Be careful, Jacy!"

She trips on a vine, nearly falls.

The sound of Jacy's running footsteps grows fainter. She'll never catch up.

Nothing to do but wait, her nerves on edge, for him to come back.

Please don't let anything happen to him. Please don't let Darrin hurt him.

At last, to her relief, Jacy appears in the distance . . . alone.

"Did you see which way he went?" he calls.

She throws up her hands helplessly, and he darts away.

Calla sinks onto the fallen log again and looks back at the spot where she saw him.

Or did she?

She wasn't dreaming this time.

Maybe you're just losing it.

Maybe everything—all the stress, and the emotion, and the lack of sleep—has taken a toll on her. Maybe something has just snapped inside her brain.

When Jacy shows up again—alone, of course—she apologizes.

"I really did see something." *Darrin.*

"I looked everywhere," Jacy tells her, "and there was no sign of him."

"I saw him."

No response.

What else can she say? "Maybe it was just a trick of the light."

"Yeah," he agrees. "Must have been."

He doesn't believe me. And I don't blame him. I don't believe me, either.

"Come on," he says, and hand in hand again, they make their way back to the school building.

Inside, Jacy asks, "Want me to walk you to your next class?"

Calla thinks of Evangeline and shakes her head, reluctantly pulling her fingers from his protective grasp.

"No, thanks. See you later, in math."

"Okay. Hey, what about after school? No track practice today. Maybe we could do something?"

"I can't," she says wistfully. "I'm babysitting. Maybe tomorrow?"

"I have practice. And Wednesday, too."

Right. And Wednesday she has her date with Blue.

I'm definitely going to tell him I'm seeing Jacy now, she decides. It's the right thing to do.

Even though the Lily Dale grapevine will wind the news right back to Evangeline.

Calla was dreading having her hands full with the Drumm kids after a long, exhausting day at school, but being around them seems to have worked some kind of magic on her mood. Despite everything that's going on, she actually finds herself smiling again.

"Again, again, again!" Ethan claps his chubby toddler hands and bounces his little butt on the couch, legs outstretched and blond curls flopping.

Calla reaches for his bare big toe. "This little piggy went to market . . . this little piggy stayed home . . ."

Ethan squirms with delight as she finishes the rhyme and tickles him.

"Again, again, again, again!"

She glances at his big brother, Dylan, kneeling on the floor in front of the coffee table, busily coloring.

"Why don't we do something together?" she suggests. "Dylan, do you want to play a game?"

"Okay. Candyland."

She should have known. She's played more rounds of Candyland in the past few weeks than she did in her entire childhood. Dylan loves it because, as he points out every time, his name is in the title. Ethan loves it because he loves life in general. He's the most exuberant kid Calla has ever known— and quite the opposite of his big brother.

Not that Dylan is a downer. He's just . . . intense. Especially for a five-year-old. And he's an incredibly gifted psychic whose imaginary friend, Kelly, Calla suspects, might actually be a spirit guide.

He actually warned Calla that a bad man with a raccoon eye was going to hurt her just before Phil Chase—sporting a black eye—attacked her.

She hasn't told Paula about her son's prediction being

legitimate—she doesn't dare tell anyone what happened to her—but she's been paying close attention to Dylan's mentions of Kelly ever since. Mostly, they just seem to play together, which is reassuring.

"Toes!" Little Ethan shouts, thrusting his feet at Calla. "Toes again!"

"No, Ethan, we're going to play Candyland with your brother now, okay?"

"Candyland! Candyland!" Ethan starts to dive off the couch with glee, and Calla collars him in the knick of time.

"Come on, Dylan, let's go upstairs and get the game." Calla struggles to hang on to a wriggling, giggling Ethan.

"Okay. This is for you." Dylan finishes his picture with a flourish and holds it up.

"Wow, for me? Thanks!" She sets Ethan on his feet and bends to look at the crayon drawing.

It shows a brown-haired stick figure girl, completely scribbled over in blue.

"What beautiful artwork, Dylan! Who is she? Is that Kelly?" she guesses.

"No, she's you."

"Oh, of course! Now I see. And I love how you made the sky so pretty."

And I must not be here in Lily Dale, because it's not gray, she thinks wryly.

"Hey, Ethan, not that way, get back here!" She scurries across the room and catches him before he can toddle toward the kitchen where his mother is trying to throw together dinner for Calla and the kids so that she can go get ready for her night out with her husband.

211

"That's not the sky!" Dylan informs her. "That's the water!"

"You mean the blue?"

"Uh-huh."

"Oh . . . so I'm in the water?" she asks, man-handling Ethan into her arms and trying not to crumple Dylan's picture in the process. "Am I swimming?"

"No. You're trying to get out, but you can't," Dylan says matter-of-factly.

Calla frowns. That was an odd thing for him to say.

Coming from any other child, it wouldn't necessarily bother her.

But coming from Dylan . . . and on the heels of Jacy's vision . . .

"Why can't I get out?"

"I don't know. Can we go upstairs and get Candyland now?"

"Candyland!" Ethan shouts, close to Calla's ear, and she winces and sets him back on his feet. He makes a beeline for the stairs with Dylan at his heels.

Calla follows, shooting another troubled glance at the picture before she folds it and tucks it into the back pocket of her jeans.

After dinner that night, as Calla sits at her mother's old desk in her mother's old room trying to study for a science test—and trying *not* to think about her mother—Odelia knocks on the door, then sticks her head in.

"Telephone, Calla."

"For me? Is it my dad?" she asks hopefully. Better him than Willow or Sarita, both of whom must still be wondering where she and Jacy were on Saturday night. She has yet to come up with a good story.

"Nope, it's not your dad." Wearing a mysterious smile, Odelia crosses the room and hands over the receiver.

"Who is it, Gammy?"

Her grandmother is already on her way back out of the room, saying, "Don't forget to bring the phone back downstairs," before closing the door behind her.

"Hello?"

"Hey, stranger."

"Kevin?" She almost drops the phone.

"How are you?"

"I'm good. I . . ."

. . . don't know why you're calling me. Didn't you break my heart into a million little pieces? Aren't you in love with some other girl?

Of course she doesn't say any of that.

"My sister gave me your grandmother's number. I sent you a card . . . did you get it?"

She fleetingly considers telling him that she didn't, just so she won't have to deal with his offer to come visit her.

But there's no point in lying, and anyway, he'll probably just repeat the offer on the phone.

"I got it," she tells him. "Thanks."

"I thought maybe I'd ride over and see you this past weekend, but I didn't hear from you."

Ride over? He makes it sound like he's just around the corner . . . which he literally *was,* back in the old days, in Florida.

"It was homecoming here. I went to the dance."

"Oh, right. I think Lisa mentioned something about that."

She *did*?

Hmm.

Maybe that explains why Kevin's suddenly sending her cards and wanting to visit. He's just jealous—as if he has any right or reason to be jealous when he has a serious new girl-friend himself.

Then again . . . Lisa didn't know about Calla's homecoming date with Blue until Wednesday, and Kevin's card was postmarked in Ithaca on Tuesday. Calla checked it. In fact, she analyzed everything about the card and envelope, as if she were a forensic scientist.

"Maybe this coming weekend, then," he says. "We have a semester—"

"I'm going to Florida this weekend."

Pause. "Really?"

"Yeah. Really. Friday."

Apparently Lisa doesn't tell him everything.

Just the stuff that will keep him on his toes.

Calla can't help but smile a little smugly as she says, "You know what? I'm kind of busy right now, so . . ."

"Yeah. I'll let you go. I just wanted to see how you are, and, you know, see if you need anything."

"No," she replies almost airily, "I don't need anything."

Not from you, anyway.

When I needed you, you weren't there.

"Okay. Take care, Calla."

"You, too."

She hangs up.

And finds herself on the verge of tears.

How is it possible to miss him so much—and care about him so much—when he callously broke up with her, and in a text message, no less?

At least you didn't let him know he was getting to you, she congratulates herself. *Good job of playing it cool.*

She let him know she has a new life now, and he's not a part of it.

She should feel good. Great, even.

And she probably will . . . just as soon as she lets herself have a good, long cry.

SEVENTEEN

Tuesday, October 2
5:32 p.m.

"No, listen, I know we're going to get this college thing straightened out," Calla's father reassures her over the phone. "You just have to get organized and figure out what you want in a school, and where you can go to get it."

He makes it sound like they're choosing a fast-food restaurant for lunch.

"It's not that easy, Dad." She spent a few hours this afternoon trying to read up on various universities. When she wasn't keeping an anxious eye out for Darrin Yates, or spotting spirits lurking around her. "I'm not sure what I want in a school."

"I've been looking into a few places I think you'd like."

"Where are they?" She folds the takeout pizza box from dinner and crams it into her grandmother's kitchen garbage.

"They're all over."

"Near here?"

There's a pause. "You didn't say you wanted to stay near there."

"The thing is Dad, I'm just not sure where I want to be."

"Then it sounds like you and I have something in common."

The dry comment catches her off guard. "What do you mean?"

"I'm thinking of getting out of California, Calla. This doesn't feel right for me."

"You mean, before the semester's over?"

He sighs heavily. "Yeah. I think so."

"Would you go back to Florida, then?" Her mind races. Would he want her to go with him?

A few months ago, that would have been a godsend. Not anymore.

"That would depend," her father says.

"On what?"

"On you. Would you want to go back to finish your senior year at your old school?"

Go back? And leave Odelia, and Jacy, and Lily Dale, and—

"No," she says firmly. "I don't want to go back. Not until the school year's over here, anyway."

"I didn't think so. I guess that means I'd better start looking for a place there."

"Where? Back home?"

"No," he says. "Lily Dale—or someplace nearby."

"What?!"

"It's not a hundred percent certain, but I'm thinking it

217

would be best for me. And for you. It's not good for us to be apart right now."

"But what would you do here?"

"I don't know. Get my head together. Read. Write. Something."

"Will the college there let you go?"

"Yeah. I've talked to the department about it."

"So when would you—" She cuts off, hearing a beep on the line. Call waiting cutting in.

Calla welcomes it. Yeah, she misses her father, but she isn't sure how she feels about him invading her turf. If he moves here, he's bound to figure out what goes on in Lily Dale, and he's not going to like it.

"Listen, I have to go, Dad. Odelia has another call coming in and I have to get it."

At the moment, her grandmother is behind closed doors reading a newly bereaved widow. Calla made a point of not being around when the woman showed up earlier. After what happened with that con man Owen Henry or Henry Owens or whatever his name is, she's steering clear of her grandmother's clients from now on.

"I love you, Cal'. Be good."

"I will." *And careful, too.*

She disconnects the call, then answers the new one. "Hello?"

"Calla, it's me!"

"Lisa! How are you?"

"F-ah-n," she drawls. "How was homecoming Saturday night?"

"It was good."

"Just good?"

"Well, Blue ended up getting hurt playing soccer, and I ended up going with Jacy instead, but it's a really long story. . . . I'll tell you when I see you this weekend." Or not.

At least her friends at school have dropped the subject . . . for now.

"Okay. So guess what?" Lisa moves on easily before Calla can spill the latest news about her father. "Nick Rodriguez broke up with Brittany Jensen and I heard he's gonna ask me out!"

"That's great, Lis'."

"Yeah." As Lisa fills her in on the saga, Calla pictures her best friend back home in Tampa, wearing big black sunglasses and a sky-blue two-piece bathing suit, her honey-blond hair falling long and loose over her shoulders as she lounges by the backyard pool beneath the warm late-afternoon rays. Country music—Trace Adkins, Lisa's current favorite—plays faintly in the background.

Remembering her vision of her father in his California kitchen munching an apple, Calla wonders if Lisa really does happen to have on big black shades and a sky-blue bathing suit out by the pool.

Before she can ask, Lisa changes the subject to college. There's just no escaping it, Calla decides with an inner sigh.

"I swear all I've done lately is fill out applications and write essays," Lisa says. "How about you?"

"Not yet. I'm still figuring out where to apply."

"Well, we always said we'd apply to all the same places, remember?"

"I remember. Where have you been applying?"

Lisa rattles off a list. Of course, her top ten schools are all in the Deep South.

"So get your butt in gear, and we can be roommates," she drawled. "Wouldn't that be great?"

Of course, Calla agreed that it would, out of habit. But the more she's been thinking about it, the more she wonders whether she might want to stay here in the Northeast next year.

There's something pleasant about the change of seasons, and she's even getting used to the cold, and most of the Ivy League schools are here . . .

And so is Lily Dale.

She just told her father she wants to stay through the end of the school year, but maybe even that won't be enough time. Whenever she thinks about uprooting herself again, leaving the new life that's just starting to feel comfortable . . .

Well, it isn't that she doesn't want to go to college.

It's . . .

Who knows what it is?

She has enough going on right now; she doesn't want to worry about college just yet.

Too bad she has to. Time is running out, according to Dad and the guidance counselor and even Lisa.

"Listen," her friend says, "you're still planning on coming down here Friday, right?"

"Definitely."

"Good." Lisa hesitates. "I wasn't going to tell you, but I probably should . . ."

"What?"

"Promise me you'll come no matter what?"

"No matter what," Calla says firmly, shoving aside Jacy's

latest warning about Florida. She has to get to her mother's laptop.

And get away from here.

The thought comes out of nowhere, but she realizes it's true. She loves Lily Dale, but she needs a break from all of this. Feeling like Darrin is stalking her, and seeing spirits everywhere she looks, and Evangeline still not speaking to her.

"I'm glad you're coming no matter what," Lisa says, "because Kevin's going to be here."

"What!"

"Yeah. He'll be home this weekend on a fall break. My mother just told me. I didn't even know about it till now."

Calla sighs inwardly. Kevin knew she was going to Florida that weekend, and he didn't mention any plans to be there, too.

Maybe that's because he didn't have any . . . yet.

But why would he want to see her, when he has Annie? That doesn't make sense.

Whatever. There's no way she's going to let his presence keep her from going to Florida next weekend. She'll simply pretend he doesn't exist.

Kind of like he must have pretended she didn't exist when he first met Annie.

After assuring Lisa she was still coming and hanging up, Calla lugs her heavy backpack upstairs to her room. She closes the door securely behind her, then hesitates for a minute before looking under the bed and in the closet.

No Darrin.

Today, Calla tried hard to convince herself she imagined Darrin ever being here in Lily Dale. She did her best to pretend everything is normal.

Going about her daily routine in school, despite being alienated by Evangeline and avoided by Jacy, definitely helped.

Takeout pizza for dinner was another dose of normal, and so, in a less welcome way, is the pile of homework now waiting in her backpack.

As Calla begins to clear a spot on the desk, she comes across the library book that led her to that spot in Leolyn Woods where the lilies were inexplicably blooming.

"*She's not there.*"

Aiyana's words keep coming back to her, and she still has no idea what they meant.

She riffles through the pages of the library book, as if the answer might magically appear.

Maybe she really should read it cover to cover. Just in case there might be some other clue to—

Wait a minute.

How can this be?

She's opened the book to the map . . . but where's the circled X?

Frowning, Calla holds the page directly beneath the glare of the desk lamp, figuring the mark must be too faint to see in regular light.

No.

It's still not here.

Various scenarios chase each other through her mind.

Someone could have erased it . . .

Except, who would come into her room and do such a thing?

Darrin?

Anyway, the mark was made in ink—old-fashioned-looking

ink, which couldn't be erasable, could it? And even if someone managed to erase it, there would still be a faint trace, wouldn't there?

Definitely. So this must be the wrong map page.

Except, it's identical to the one she saw before.

A thorough page-by-page search reveals that it's the only map in the book.

So there's only one explanation.

Spirit placed the mark there for her to see, and Spirit took it away.

Spirit wanted to get her to the woods, to see the flowers and the tombstonelike rock, and to know that "she's not there."

Wherever *there* is.

In the ground, beneath the rock and the lilies?

And she . . . who?

Not Mom.

Aiyana was pretty clear about that.

Spooked, Calla returns the book to the shelf, steps back, and narrows her eyes at it.

"What are you trying to tell me?"

Okay, you're talking to a book. You realize that, right?

In the grand scheme of things, that's the least of her problems, but still . . .

Come on. You can't freak out about this. Just do your homework. Get your mind off it for now.

Feeling helpless, Calla sinks into the desk chair, opens her calculus notebook, and wishes she could manage to shake the pervasive feeling that she's being watched.

EIGHTEEN

Wednesday, October 3
8:15 p.m.

"Want to come over for a little while?" Blue asks as they drive back to Lily Dale after a bad movie at the small cineplex in nearby Dunkirk.

Well, maybe it wasn't so bad.

It's not like Calla was paying all that much attention. Sitting there in the darkened movie theater, with Blue's arm around her shoulders, her thoughts were a million miles away.

She can't stop thinking about Darrin.

"Calla? Do you want to?"

"Hmm?"

"Want to come over to my house?" Blue repeats. "It's still early."

She glances at the dashboard clock. He's right. It's not even nine yet.

She's exhausted, though. Emotionally and physically. "I don't know . . . it's a school night. I think I'd better just go home."

"Come on. You said you'd take a look at that English essay I wrote—it's due Friday."

True, she did tell him, earlier, that she'd try to help him with it, when he confessed he'd gotten a D on his last essay. His grades, Blue said, aren't terrific, and he's worried about getting into a decent college.

"Isn't everyone?" Calla replied, and he looked surprised.

"I figured you were straight As all the way."

"I was, back home in Florida. Here, I'll be lucky if I don't fail math." She mentioned casually that Willow York is her study partner. No reaction from Blue.

"So do you want to come over?" he asks now.

She hesitates. She is exhausted and she's still so stressed . . .

And she hasn't told him yet that she just wants to be friends.

You really should, she reminds herself.

"Maybe you can meet my dad," Blue adds. "He should be home by now—he's been away since Monday morning, but he was supposed to fly in tonight."

So David Slayton left town the day after his son got out of the hospital, leaving him in the care of Mrs. Remington, their longtime housekeeper, as usual.

Wow. That's cold. If she were injured and on crutches, Dad would never leave her side.

"Okay, sure," she says reluctantly, feeling sorry for him. "I'll come in, just for a little while."

Blue laughs and shakes his head. "Works every time."

"What?"

"Nothing, just . . . everyone always wants to meet my dad."

"That's not why!"

"Just do me a favor and don't ask him for an autograph, okay?"

"But I wouldn't do that!"

"He loves it, actually."

"Huh?"

"My father," Blue clarifies. "He loves it when people ask him for autographs."

"Oh. Then maybe I should."

"Please don't feed the ego. It's a monster as it is."

Blue turns down Dale Drive, heading toward the big house on a knoll above the lake. The Slayton House has gingerbread trim and cupolas and a wraparound porch, but it's at least five times the size of the cottages located beyond the entrance gate, inside the Dale. Recently built, this is a neo-Victorian—not the real thing.

"These days, David Slayton is all flash," Odelia likes to say.

Calla knows that her grandmother, like many of the other mediums in town, doesn't entirely approve of Blue's father, who used to be "one of them" before he hit the big time. But Odelia's disapproval doesn't stem from professional resentment.

It bothers her that David Slayton spends so much of his time courting the cameras in New York City and Hollywood, leaving his only son alone with the housekeeper in their sprawling home.

Blue's mother took off years ago, Odelia told Calla.

Kind of like Odelia's husband—Calla's grandfather, Jack Lauder, who left when Mom was just a kid. Nobody ever likes to discuss him, though. Mom didn't, Odelia doesn't, and Dad is probably clueless about the details.

"Looks like he made it home," Blue mutters as he parks his BMW behind a black Mercedes at the top of the winding driveway, which circles around in front of the porch.

The oversized house is on par with those of Calla's private school classmates back home in Florida, but it's definitely out of the ordinary for this part of rural upstate New York. That's why she was surprised, when she first met Blue, to find that he went to public school.

Turns out he didn't always. He was kicked out of at least one private boarding school. Calla doesn't know the details, and she's probably better off.

Blue, always the well-bred gentleman, hobbles over on his crutches to open her car door for her, then leads the way up to the well-lit front porch. Balancing on one crutch, he opens the door and dismantles an alarm system—pretty much unheard of in the unassuming homes inside the Dale.

"Come on in."

Calla looks around with interest as he leads the way through an ornate first floor full of polished hardwoods, oriental rugs, heavy draperies, old-fashioned wallpaper, plenty of dark wood-work, and elegant antique furniture. It's as though someone was trying to re-create a grand Victorian home, and the result is a little too stagey and self-conscious for her taste.

Photographs of David Slayton are everywhere, as are awards and plaques—relics of his high-profile career.

"Wait here," Blue says when they reach the kitchen. "I'll be right back."

She settles on a stool at the marble-topped breakfast bar as he hobbles up a back staircase.

She really has to tell him she just wants to be friends. As she tries to figure out exactly how to phrase it in a gentle way, she notices that the house is extraordinarily still.

At Odelia's, the floorboards creak, the faucets drip, the pipes clang. Here, aside from the steady hum of the built-in refrigerator, which has a fancy wooden front made to look like an oversized cupboard door, it's quiet.

Quiet . . . but not, Calla realizes, quite as deserted as she thought.

Sensing a presence, she looks around, and out of the corner of her eye, spots not an apparition, but a shadow on the opposite wall. A human shadow, only without a human person to go with it.

This isn't the first time she's seen that phenomenon—a shadow ghost, Evangeline called it, when Calla described it to her. She didn't elaborate, but Calla later looked it up and read various theories: that the disembodied shadows are optical hallucinations or aliens, or—most troubling—demonic.

Apprehension creeps over her. Slowly, she turns her head toward the figure.

She can't tell if it's male or female; it's swathed in some kind of hooded cloak.

A shiver runs down Calla's spine and she's relieved to hear Blue making his way back down the stairs.

She turns toward him, then glances back to see that the shadow is gone—at least for now.

"I can get us something to eat. Are you hungry?"

She isn't; shadow ghosts have a way of killing a person's appetite, but she finds herself nodding anyway.

"But let me get it. You should get off your foot," she tells him.

"No big deal. I'm fine. You sit."

She watches him balance on one crutch as he opens the fridge, and can't help but wonder what he's going to come up with. This sterile place is a far cry from her grandmother's house, where the scent of cooking always hangs in the air and the appliances are well-worn from Odelia's constant use. Here, there's not a crumb in sight.

"Where's your dad?" she asks, keeping an eye out for the shadow.

"I don't know . . . he's probably sleeping," Blue says vaguely.

"It's early, though."

"Yeah, but he gets jet lag. What do you want to eat?"

"Oh . . . whatever. I can't, uh, stay long." Not if his father's not even around, and that freaky shadow ghost might still be lurking.

Blue produces a wedge of fancy cheese and some grapes from the fridge, and a box of imported crackers from a cupboard, along with two small bottles of Perrier.

"Cheers." He clinks his bottle against hers as he leans his crutches against the counter and sits on a stool beside her.

You have to relax, she tells herself.

She smiles at him, noticing that he really is incredibly good-looking. He's wearing a blue shirt, as usual. She's noticed that he does that a lot, as if he knows exactly how to bring out the intense shade of his irises. His wardrobe, like the home's decor, seems just a little too calculating.

She can't help but compare him to Jacy, who probably doesn't think twice before pulling on his usual worn jeans and soft T-shirts with faded lettering. He most likely gets his black hair cut at a barber shop, a far cry from Blue's salon style.

You have to tell Blue about Jacy. Just go ahead and say it. He'll live.

But she can't seem to get it out.

"So . . . ," Blue says, as she tries yet again to come up with the kindest phrasing in her brain, "you've been working on math with Willow, then?"

"Yup."

"Has she . . . uh, said anything to you? About how we used to go out?"

About to pop a grape into her mouth, Calla lowers her hand. "No. She's never brought it up, actually."

"That's so not surprising." Blue crunches into a cracker.

"Why?"

"She's pretty private, in case you haven't noticed."

"Nothing wrong with that." Calla has noticed, and figures she herself might be considered pretty private, so she's not judging Willow.

"Yeah, but . . . I mean, she was always so quiet."

Out of the corner of her eye, Calla sees movement.

Turning slightly, she glimpses the shadow darting across the wall.

"I could never get inside her head," Blue is saying.

"Whose head?"

"Um, Willow's?" he says, in a questioning tone that's more polite than a pointed *duh* would be.

Calla forces herself to look back at him, to focus on the conversation again. It's not that she isn't interested, it's just distracting to have some hooded being flitting around the room.

"Is that why you broke up with her, then?" she asks Blue.

"I didn't."

Her heart drops. "You're still going out?"

"No! I mean, I didn't break up with Willow. She broke up with me."

"Really? That's not what I heard."

"Yeah, people assume stuff. She didn't bother to set the record straight, so why would I?"

Calla shrugs, as if none of this matters all that much to her, when really, she's been wondering what happened between Blue and Willow . . . and where they stand now.

So Willow dumped him? Would they still be going out if she hadn't?

Evangeline has said she thinks Willow is still hung up on Blue, but maybe it's the other way around. What guy wouldn't be captivated by Willow, with her perfect porcelain skin, delicate features, and striking dark hair and eyes?

"Well, anyway, I just wondered if she'd said anything to you about . . . what happened with us. Since you two are friends now." Blue adds, "Hey, by the way, how's her mother doing lately?"

It's not a casual question, Calla realizes. That's the tone you use when the person you're asking about hasn't been well.

"Althea's hanging in there," she informs Blue, as though she knows all about it. Well, almost all about it. She can't help but ask, "What, exactly, is wrong with her? Is it cancer?"

"Maybe . . . something bad. I'm not sure exactly what. Willow doesn't like to talk about it. Althea's the one who told me. I was over there one day, and it was obvious something was wrong. I asked her about it, and she said she was sick. Really sick. She doesn't want people feeling sorry for her, so not that many people know about it."

"Not that many people know about what?"

Calla looks up, startled to see David Slayton framed in the doorway.

He's instantly recognizable. She's seen him on television plenty of times, discussing his work with celebrities and politicians, or solving high-profile crimes. She always thought he was impossibly good-looking, charismatic, flashy.

Kind of like his son.

Now here he is in person, even better looking than he is on TV. His wavy hair is more gray than brown, but not in an unappealing way, and he shares his son's intense blue eyes. He's wearing expensive-looking lounging clothes; the kind actors wear in movies, unlike real-life guys, who go around the house in holey sweatpants or boxer shorts before bed. Guys like Calla's dad, anyway.

Something tells her that her dad and Blue's dad don't have a whole lot in common.

"If people were supposed to know about the thing we're talking about, more people would, but since I just said they don't . . . don't ask." Blue's response to his father's question is punctuated by a look that makes it clear he isn't happy to see him.

"Keeping secrets from your old man again, are you?" He crosses the room and holds out his hand to Calla. "I'm David Slayton."

"Hi . . . I'm Calla Delaney."

"It's nice to meet you. You're not from here."

Caught off guard as much by the deliberate statement as she is by the intense scrutiny in his gaze, Calla stammers, "Oh . . . uh, I'm . . . no."

"The Southeast. Correct?"

"Florida."

He nods, looking so pleased with himself that she realizes he isn't just recapping what his son told him about her earlier.

In fact, she gets the distinct feeling Blue didn't tell him anything at all, because they don't seem to have seen each other in at least a couple of days.

"Do I have an accent?" she asks David, to break an uncomfortable silence. "Is that how you knew where I was from?"

"No accent at all. I just knew."

"He's magical," Blue says sarcastically. "Didn't you know?"

Ignoring his son, David Slayton mentions that he just flew in from California that evening, and is hoping to reset his body clock back into the right time zone.

"I swear by hot milk and honey," he comments, pouring some milk into a mug. "You should try it the next time you're jet-lagged."

Unsure whether he's talking to her or to Blue, Calla says nothing, watching him put the mug into the microwave and press a few buttons.

She notices that Blue is methodically plucking grapes from the stem, chewing and swallowing without the least bit of pleasure. You don't have to be a psychic medium to notice that there's plenty of tension between father and son. At least, there is on Blue's end.

David Slayton seems oblivious.

"You're living here now, in the Dale," he asks, or rather tells, Calla as he leans against the counter, arms folded, waiting for his milk to heat.

She nods. "Either you're really good, or Blue told you about me."

"I'm really good," he says simply, but not without a smug nod. "Blue hasn't told me anything . . . about you, or anything else."

"There's nothing to tell, and even if there were, you haven't been around all week."

"No. But I've called."

Blue shrugs. "Not every day."

"You're a big boy, Blue. Do you really want me bugging you every day?"

Calla watches Blue moodily rip the last couple of grapes from the bare stem and shove them into his mouth. Maybe he does want his father bugging him—or at least calling him— every day.

She remembers how strangely arrogant Blue acted the other day when she said she wanted to spend some time with her father instead of going out with him.

Maybe she had struck a nerve.

She thinks of her father. He always calls her every day when they're apart. And when they first laid eyes on each other at the airport that night after weeks apart, they flew into each other's arms as if it had been years since the last time they were together.

Maybe fathers and sons aren't quite as demonstrative as fathers and daughters, but Blue and his dad sure didn't have much of a reunion just now, after a week apart.

Suddenly, Calla spots the shadow again, out of the corner of her eye, and swivels her head to catch it. There it is, lurking in the far corner of the room.

"I guess he came in with you," David Slayton says cryptically.

"What are you talking about?" Blue asks.

Calla turns to see his father leveling a look at her. "You see him."

"Excuse me?" she says.

He tilts his head in the direction of the phantom being in the corner.

Blue turns in that direction with a searching frown but says nothing.

He doesn't see it, Calla realizes.

She asks David, "Who is he?"

He shrugs. "I have no idea. With shadow people . . . you never know."

She digests that and nods.

"So you're the real deal, then," David Slayton says to Calla.

"No, she isn't, Dad. Calla's not into that. She's just visiting

235

her grandmother." Blue is obviously thrilled to contradict his father, and something tells Calla it's better for her not to contradict Blue.

"Who's your grandmother?"

"Odelia Lauder. Do you know her?" Calla asks, though she knows the answer.

"Odelia Lauder." David smiles faintly and rubs his chin. "I've known her for years."

"How many years?" Calla wonders, suddenly, whether he knew her mother as well.

"Oh, fifteen . . . maybe twenty."

"Did you know my mother? Stephanie?"

His answer is straightforward. "No."

The microwave beeps and he turns to open it.

"She passed away over the summer," Calla tells him, not sure why she's offering the information. It's not like she needs his sympathy—or Blue's, for that matter.

His back to her as he stirs honey into his mug, David says only, "That's hard. I'm sorry."

She never knows what to say in response to that, other than, "Thanks."

Blue's father turns back to her, holding his mug.

"You're an unusual girl."

Disconcerted by his stare as much as the comment, she tries to make light of it, forcing a laugh. "Gee, thanks. I've been called worse."

He doesn't apologize.

"Dad, what the heck are you talking about?" Blue asks.

David doesn't even bother to acknowledge his son's

question. "You're gifted in a way that's very unusual for someone your age—or any age," he tells Calla.

"But . . . I feel like everyone around here is gifted. I mean, it's Lily Dale."

"Not this powerfully gifted. And not all of them." At last, he flicks a glance in Blue's direction, and it's almost disdainful.

Calla expects David to say something else, but he doesn't. He just looks at her again, so intently that she feels as though he can see right into her soul.

"Dad, can you . . . ?" Blue gestures impatiently toward the doorway.

"Get out of here and leave you two alone?" David Slayton's smile doesn't reach his eyes.

Carrying his mug, he crosses the threshold, then turns back. "Be careful, okay?"

"Careful with what?" Blue looks exasperated.

"Not you." David Slayton looks directly into Calla's eyes, and repeats, "Be careful."

Her heart pounds. "Me?" she asks stupidly.

"Yes. Spirit is warning you."

"But, why? What's going to happen?"

He hesitates. "It's not that something is 'going to' happen. Just know that you may find yourself in a dangerous situation."

"Does it have anything to do with . . . that shadow ghost?" she asks nervously, noticing that it seems to have disappeared again.

"Oh, I don't think so. Don't let those bother you." He waves it away like it's a pesky mosquito. "Shadow ghosts buzz around the room being distracting, annoying, maybe . . . nothing more."

"Are you sure?"

"Are we ever sure about anything, really?" he asks with an enigmatic half smile. "Just do keep your wits about you, my dear."

With that, he leaves the room.

"Cripes." Blue lays his own hand over Calla's trembling one, brushing against the emerald bracelet. "Don't let him bother you, okay?"

He's making a big effort to blow off what just happened, but Calla can tell he's rattled, too.

"It's not that I'm letting him bother me, Blue, but he warned me."

"Yeah, I know," he says flatly. "He likes to be dramatic. It doesn't mean anything."

"But it might. He's not the—"

She breaks off.

Blue's father isn't the only one who's warned her, but she doesn't want to bring up Jacy right now.

"Would you mind . . . can you just take me home?" she asks Blue instead.

"Leave it to my father to be a total buzz kill," he says with a good-natured sigh, but reaches for his crutches. "Sure. Come on. I've got an early doctor's appointment tomorrow, anyway, before school."

They make the quick drive to the Dale in silence. Now isn't the time for Calla to address the future of their relationship, or nonrelationship.

Calla is glad to see that her grandmother's home; the

flickering blue light from the television is spilling out into the night from the living-room window.

Blue leaves the motor running as he walks her up the steps. "Listen, I'll be pretty busy this week tomorrow and Friday, so we might not have much of a chance to talk until you're back from your trip, okay?"

"Yeah, sure, okay" Is he blowing her off?

Maybe. Because when he kisses her good night, it's just a quick peck on the cheek. Nothing like last time.

Problem solved. It seems like Blue, too, wants to be just friends. And she didn't even have to address the subject. She can't help but wonder whether he's read her mind. Everyone says he's a powerful psychic, just like his dad—not that Calla has seen any evidence of that until now.

Maybe he just took his cue from her. It's not like she acted the least bit romantic toward him. Or maybe he heard about her and Jacy. Or maybe he really is a player like everyone says, and he's simply moved on.

Whatever, she's totally fine with his losing interest in her. Or so she tells herself, trying hard not to feel the tiniest hint of wistfulness. For some reason, it isn't as easy as it should be.

"Thanks for tonight," she tells him as he heads down the steps.

"No problem. See you." Backing down the walk, he gives her a two-fingered salute. Then he climbs into his car and is gone.

Calla locks the door behind her, sliding the deadbolt—a new habit. Until last week, Odelia never even bothered to lock the door.

Her grandmother is in her usual chair in front of the

television. Surprisingly, she's actually awake for a change, and sets aside her knitting the moment Calla enters the room.

"*There* you are!" she exclaims as if Calla's late.

Which she isn't, since Odelia doesn't give her a curfew.

"How was the movie?"

"It was okay." She debates mentioning that she finally met the enigmatic David Slayton but decides against it. Not only because Odelia isn't crazy about the man, but also because she doesn't seem all that interested in the details of Calla's evening.

"What?" she asks Odelia.

"What do you mean, what?"

"Something's up, Gammy. I can tell by the look on your face."

Odelia wags an index finger at her. "Good. Very good. Something *is* up."

"What happened?" Calla wonders if she should be worried despite her instincts telling her not to be.

"You remember Betty Owens and the stock certificates?"

Calla nods. Uh-oh after all.

"I didn't want to say anything to you until I had something specific to report, but . . . I went to see her the other day."

"Did you tell her about me?"

"No. I told her I was a medium and that I wanted to help her find her lousy crook of an estranged husband. I told her he had come to Lily Dale looking for a psychic who could help him track down those hidden certificates in her house."

"What did she say?"

"Well, at first she assumed I was a crackpot—imagine that." Odelia offers a wry smile and eyeroll, and Calla can't help but grin. "But then she must have figured she had nothing to lose. I asked her to let me hold a shirt he'd left behind when he took off, and I did some meditating, and long story short, I figured out where he was."

"Where?"

"Mexico. I even got the right airport he'd flown into, and that he was staying in a pink stucco hotel near the beach. How do I know it was the right place, you're wondering?"

Calla nods, holding her breath.

"Because they found him there this afternoon and arrested him. With the stock certificates."

Calla throws her arms around her grandmother. "Oh, Gammy . . . you're amazing."

Odelia pats her wiry red hair and bats her eyes. "I am pretty amazing, aren't I? The police agree. Of course, when I first called that viewer hotline to tell them where to look for Henry Owens in Mexico, they thought I was a crackpot, too."

She laughs. "I can't believe you got all of that by holding his shirt."

"It's called psychometry. Basically, you make physical contact with something that belonged to someone, and you get psychic impressions. Patsy will cover it in your class, I'm sure."

"I'm sure."

"Anyway, I first picked up on a Mexico connection when I tried to read Henry Owens that day he came here, although I didn't realize it at the time. I wasn't getting any dead wife—or even the sense that he was widowed—but I did keep seeing a margarita glass."

"Margaritas . . . Mexico." Calla grins. "Psychic shorthand, right?"

241

"Right. Only I didn't get the connection. When my guides show me a martini glass it usually symbolizes a drinking problem, so when I saw the margarita glass I figured maybe Spirit was changing it up a little. I kept asking him if he had problems with alcohol, and he kept insisting he didn't. I figured he was just in denial. I should have just told him I was seeing that glass. See? I'm still learning even at my age."

"Yeah, but if you had told him you were seeing a margarita glass, he would have figured you knew he was planning to go to Mexico, and he probably would have changed his plans."

"I like to think I'd have found him, anyway. I just wish I had listened to my instinct that there was something off about him. And usually, when someone has a physical ailment, I feel it. He was trying to pass himself off as a feeble old man, with that cane, and I should have realized it wasn't ringing true."

"Yeah, but he was pretty convincing." Calla shakes her head, remembering how stunned she was when he shed the cane and ran out of the diner.

"It looks like he's made a career out of fooling people. From what the police told me, Betty isn't the first lonely widow he's conned. But all's well that ends well. That's what matters. Betty's going to be fine, and that con man is going to jail."

"You're like a superhero, Gammy."

"Maybe I should start wearing a cape."

"Um, no."

Her grandmother laughs, then kisses her on the cheek. "It's late. Go get some sleep. Your worries are over."

If only, Calla thinks wistfully as she goes upstairs to her room and checks under the bed and in the closet.

NINETEEN

Thursday, October 4
11:34 a.m.

On her way to social studies after third period, Calla rounds a corner and finds herself face-to-face with Evangeline.

For the first time since their Sunday-morning falling out, it's impossible for them not to acknowledge each other.

Or is it?

Evangeline quickly breaks eye contact and starts to move around her.

All right, this is ridiculous.

"Evangeline!" Calla grabs her arm. "Come on. Don't be this way."

She expects her friend's hazel eyes to flash with anger but sees only unhappiness.

"I'm sorry I hurt you," Calla blurts. "Really."

Evangeline shrugs. "Okay."

"*Okay?* What do you mean?"

"I mean okay."

Just okay. Not *I forgive you.*

Calla repeats, "I'm sorry. Really."

"I'm sure I'll get over Jacy," Evangeline tells her stoically. But she doesn't look sure. Not at all. In fact, she looks as though she's about to cry.

"Why don't we hang out later, after school?" Calla suggests, wanting to hug her, but sensing that Evangeline is determined to keep her at arm's length.

"Can't." She adds, a little less tersely, "I have Crystal Healing class on Thursdays."

"How about tomorrow?" Calla asks, then remembers. "Oh, wait. I'm going to Florida tomorrow. Next week, though, when I get back. Okay?"

Evangeline shrugs, murmurs something Calla can't hear above the noise in the hall, and they go their separate ways.

In the classroom, she takes her social studies notebook and text from her backpack. As she sets them on her desk, she hears Maggie, this girl who sits behind her, saying to her friend Gwen, across the aisle, "Oh my God, that is the funniest thing ever!"

A finger taps Calla on the shoulder. "Hey, Calla, did you hear?"

"Did I hear what?" she asks, surprised to be drawn into conversation with two of the more popular girls in the senior class.

"About Jill and Donald."

"Jill who?" Calla asks, pretty sure who Donald is. There's only one in school, as far as she knows.

"Jill Eggerton."

Oops, there must be more than one Donald after all, because there's no way a gorgeous brunette like Jill Eggerton would be connected in any possible way to Donald Reamer.

"Donald who?"

"Reamer!" Maggie exclaims as the bell rings, signifying the start of class. "What other Donald is there?"

"But—"

"All right, everyone in your seats, let's get busy," the teacher, Mrs. Atwell, calls as she shuts the door to the hall, then strides across the room.

"Jill challenged him to a chess game at lunch today. And he totally said yes!" Gwen tells Calla, lowering her voice.

"Like Jill even knows how to play chess," Maggie puts in, grinning.

"So, what's the point?" Calla asks uneasily.

"This morning she got him to give her that clunky old chessboard he's always lugging around. She told him she'll set it up since she gets to the cafeteria way before he does—you know how slow he is, lumbering around like a big old hippo."

That's it. Calla's had enough. She opens her mouth to protest, but Mrs. Atwell is rapping sharply on her desk.

"People! Quiet down! We have a lot to cover today!"

"Here's the punchline—Jill's going to superglue all the chess pieces to the board!" Gwen hisses as Calla obediently turns toward the front of the classroom. "Is that the best, or what?"

"Do you love it? Isn't it hysterical?" Maggie whispers gleefully.

Hysterical?

It's a sick joke, that's what it is. Literally. Calla feels nauseous.

Class begins and she does her best to take notes on the identifying characteristics of a mixed capitalist economy, but it's impossible to focus.

Poor Donald.

She can't let these cruel kids ruin the chessboard his father made for him.

When the bell rings at last, Calla bolts from her seat without a backward glance at Maggie and Gwen.

She races to the cafeteria, looking around for Jill Eggerton. She has to stop her.

The place is still almost deserted and Calla spots her immediately, across the room. She's crying, clutching her head. A couple of her friends and a lunch room monitor are gathered around her.

Calla spots Donald's chessboard on a table next to them, but the pieces are still in the box beside it.

Thank goodness.

As Calla goes through the line to buy an apple she doesn't feel like eating, she keeps a curious eye on the growing commotion surrounding Jill.

By the time she makes her way to her usual table with Willow and Sarita, she sees that Mrs. Musso, the school nurse, has arrived. She's got her arm around Jill, who's still clutching her head and sobbing hysterically.

"What the heck happened over there?" Calla asks her friends.

"I don't know . . . it looks like Jill hurt her head or something," observes Sarita, a gorgeous, sophisticated Halle Berry clone until she reveals a mouthful of braces. "She just keeps holding it and screaming like she's in pain."

Calla sees the chessboard still on the table and looks around to see if Donald's here yet. There's no sign of him.

No sign of Jacy, either, another quick glance reveals. She hasn't seen him all morning.

And she's definitely been looking. He must be cutting again.

Blue is here, though, a few tables away, eating his usual double lunch with his soccer friends. His crutches propped against the table and his leg outstretched, injured foot resting on a chair. He catches Calla's eye and gives a little wave, and she waves back.

She's not disappointed when he goes right back to his friends and his food.

Blue's a good guy.

He's just not Jacy.

Again, she looks for him.

Nope.

Where are you, Jacy? I miss you. I need you.

Glancing back over at the flurry of activity around Jill, Calla spots a familiar rotund figure hovering near the forgotten chessboard.

Donald Reamer's father.

He's watching Jill, Calla realizes, and wearing an almost smug expression.

"Hey, looks like Mrs. Musso's getting Jill out of here," Willow observes, and Calla sees the nurse leading an inconsolable Jill, whose hands are still grasping her skull, toward the cafeteria exit.

Now that she's gone, the crowd begins to disperse.

"So what time do you want to come over tonight to work on math, Calla?" Willow asks, unscrewing the top on a bottle of water.

"The earlier the better. I have to pack for my trip to Florida."

"When are you leaving?"

"Right from school tomorrow."

"Lucky you . . . you get to see the sun and go to the beach," Sarita comments, and of course Calla doesn't correct her.

She's letting her friends think this weekend is a pleasure trip, just as she's letting them think that she and Jacy were at the homecoming dance for a short time, but missed seeing them. That's what Willow guessed, and Calla didn't tell her she was wrong.

"Oh my God, you guys, did you hear what happened?" Pam Moraco materializes at their table.

"What?" the three of them ask in unison.

"Jill Eggerton was fooling around with this tube of super-glue, and she accidentally glued her hands to her head! It was like this freak thing. And now she can't move without tearing out huge hunks of hair. It's horrific!"

Calla turns to look over at Donald's father again, and a slow smile spreads across her face.

Donald is there, too, now, picking up the abandoned chess-board and looking around, for Jill, probably.

Calla pushes back her chair.

"Where are you going?" Willow asks.

"I'll be back."

Pam has already moved on to spread the news about Jill to the next table.

Calla sidesteps her and goes straight over to Donald, her grandmother's words echoing in her head.

"You have a big heart. I know you want to help people. And you can. You can do a lot of good in this world using your gift."

"Hey, Donald."

He looks up. "Hi."

"I'm Calla."

He just nods.

The older man beside him is watching her warily.

"Listen . . . this is going to sound crazy, but I just want to tell you something. I live in the Dale, and my grandmother's a medium and . . . well, so am I."

No reaction from Donald, but that's not surprising. A lot of the kids in this school can make that claim. No one thinks anything of it.

"I've been seeing someone around you, kind of . . . watching over you. I think it's your dad."

Something flashes in Donald's gaze behind those thick glasses, but he says nothing.

"It's an older man, and he looks kind of like you. He's got nice brown eyes, like you."

Those eyes, Donald's father's eyes, are grateful now, fastened right on her. "Thank you," he tells Calla. "Tell him that I love him. And I'm always with him."

"He loves you," she tells Donald, "and he's always with you."

She waits for a burst of emotion from Donald at last, but he's oddly stoic. "Anyone could say that about anyone who's passed."

All those years of pain at the hands of cruel classmates—no wonder he's unwilling to trust. He probably thinks she's setting him up. And why wouldn't he?

"Tell him his mother's going to love the cutting board."

Calla shakes her head slightly at the spirit, not understanding.

"Just tell him," Donald's father says. "He'll know."

"Your father says your mother's going to love the cutting board, Donald."

He stares at her in silence, but the guarded expression has given way, just slightly, to a hint of emotion.

"Tell him he should give it to her for her birthday, like he was planning to before he decided it wasn't any good."

Calla echoes the words from father to son, and at last, Donald seems to grasp what's happening.

"He's really here?" he asks, and she nods, and his cagey expression evaporates at last.

"I've been fooling around in his workshop a little . . . trying to learn how to use some of his stuff," Donald tells her. "I made this cutting board for my mom—it's shaped like an angel, and she, you know, collects angel stuff, so . . . but I didn't think it was very good."

"It is good. It's beautiful. He gets his talent from his old man," Donald's father says affectionately.

Calla repeats it with a grin, then realizes his father's energy is fading.

"He's going," she tells Donald. "But I'm sure he'll be back. I've seen him around you before."

"Really?"

"Yeah. I've been wanting to tell you, but . . . I guess I was afraid to butt in."

"I'm glad you did," Donald says. "It really helps to know he's with me."

"Yeah." She clears her throat. "I know what it's like."

"What do you mean?"

"Losing a parent. Missing them. Feeling like they're just . . . gone. But your father isn't, Donald. He watches over you all the time."

"I'm sure your father does, too."

"Oh, he's in California, so . . . but my mom, she's the one. She . . . died."

It's still not easy to say, even after all this time.

"I'm sorry."

"Yeah. It's hard."

"If my father's around me," Donald says, "then I'm sure your mother's around you, too."

Calla swallows hard, manages a smile—and no tears.

"Hey, do you play chess?"

"No."

Donald looks disappointed. "Oh."

"But I've been wanting to learn," she adds quickly, glancing over at the apple and the seat she abandoned near Willow and Sarita. She wasn't in the mood to eat, or chat, anyway. "Maybe you can teach me."

"Sure. Sometime."

"How about now? You just happen to have a set handy, I see."

"My dad made it for me."

"I know."

"You do?"

She smiles, nods.

"So, you want to play?" he asks.

"I'd love to."

After dinner with her grandmother, Calla walks the few short blocks over to Willow's to work on her math.

"That was really sweet of you today, playing chess with Donald," Willow tells her as she leads the way through the small house to the study.

"Yeah, well . . . I felt like he needed a friend."

"I know. I feel like that a lot."

Calla touches Willow's arm. "I hope you know you can talk to me, if you ever want to. I mean, we're friends, right?"

"Oh, I didn't mean that I feel like I need a friend. I meant I feel like Donald does. But thank you. And, I'll remember what you said. About being friends."

They share an awkward smile.

"Want to get busy? I know you've got a lot to do to get ready for your trip to Florida tomorrow."

"Definitely."

"Let's work on the floor, okay? The desk is too cluttered and I don't feel like clearing a spot."

Calla glances at the desk, which holds a computer and piles

upon piles of paper—junk mail, bills, newspapers. Althea York's housekeeping skills are similar to Odelia's, and Ramona's, for that matter.

Calla's mom was the kind of person who had a place for everything. Piles of stuff would have driven her nuts.

Is that why she left Lily Dale as soon as she was old enough to get out of town? Because she couldn't handle the clutter?

Ha. More likely, she couldn't handle the supernatural stuff, considering she never mentioned it at all. Not once.

I just wish I knew more about you, Mom. I thought I did, but you lived this whole life here with these people for eighteen years that I knew nothing about.

Calla kneels beside Willow on the rug and they start spreading out their textbooks, notebooks, calculators, and the latest batch of worksheets from Mr. Bombeck.

"Willow?" Althea calls from upstairs, sounding weak.

"Mom? Are you okay?"

"Yeah, I just . . . can you help me for a second?"

"Be right there," Willow calls. To Calla, she says, "Wait here—I'll be right back."

"She doesn't sound good."

"She doesn't feel good," Willow says simply, and leaves the room.

Left alone in the den, Calla rubs her tired eyes, wondering if she should tell Willow she really can't do this tonight. Math is the last thing on her mind, and she knows it will show in the work, so she might as well . . .

She frowns, realizing that there's a sudden chill in the air and that the bracelet around her wrist seems to be unusually warm against her flesh.

She looks around.

She can't see anybody.

But, feeling the whisper of movement beside her, she knows someone is here with her.

Again.

This is starting to get old.

Will she ever truly be alone in a room again?

Something brushes her shoulder.

Then rests there.

A gentle hand.

Calla goes absolutely still, not daring to turn her head, or even breathe, because she knows . . .

Mom.

It's her. She's certain.

I'm with you. I love you.

The words float into Calla's head as clearly as if her mother had spoken them aloud.

A sob escapes her throat and she turns, needing to glimpse her.

But the room is empty, and the hand is gone, and for all she knows she imagined the whole damned thing.

No.

I didn't see her, I didn't even hear her—not really, not out loud.

But she touched me. It was real. She was here.

Calla's gaze falls on the computer on the desk.

A few minutes ago when she looked at it, the screen was dark.

Now it's glowing.

She goes over, sits in the chair, and pulls up the search engine.

She types in

Thomas Leclyn.

The screen goes blank.

Then it comes back with a long list of blue links.

Of course. There are probably dozens of Thomas Leolyns in the world. Hundreds, even.

Calla clicks on the first.

The site belongs to a newspaper in Portland.

Portland . . . Maine or Oregon?

Before she can figure that out, she finds herself staring at a black-and-white close-up photo of the man she saw in Geneseo the other night . . . and in her room, and in the woods.

It's him.

On the first hit

With a trembling hand, Calla scrolls down.

And finds herself looking at an obituary.

Tom Leolyn—Darrin Yates—died last June in an unsolved murder.

Stunned, she reads, and rereads, the short article.

I'm not crazy. I really can see ghosts. I saw his—today and last night and at Mom's funeral back in July.

And that's when the shocking truth hits her, hard.

Tom couldn't have killed Mom. He died before she did.

So it was someone else.

Someone wearing a gold signet ring.

TWENTY

Friday, October 5
8:03 a.m.

"Hey, Calla . . ."

On her solo walk to school after yet another restless night, she turns and is relieved to see Jacy behind her, hurrying along Dale Drive.

Waiting for him to catch up, Calla notes that for a change, the sun is shining against a dazzling blue sky, a breathtaking backdrop for the hodgepodge of red-and-gold foliage. It's a perfect day—weatherwise, at least.

But Calla is sagging under the burden of her shocking discovery about Darrin Yates's fate, and Jacy is the only one she dares confide in.

"I got your messages when I got home last night—all four

of them," he says as he reaches her, "but it was too late to call you back."

"Where were you?" she asks, remembering that he wasn't in school yesterday. His face looks drawn, and the circles under his eyes are possibly deeper and darker than the ones under her own.

"I was down in Jamestown. We had a court hearing yesterday. About the adoption."

For the moment, Calla's own troubles evaporate. She lays a hand on Jacy's arm. "How did it go?"

"Great." He shrugs and kicks a stone, hard. "My parents aren't going to contest it, if that's what you consider great. I'm not sure if I do or not."

She doesn't know what to say, so she just squeezes his arm as they start walking again.

"So what did you want?" Jacy asks. "When you called."

Calla's grim reality slams back. In a rush, she tells him about Darrin being dead.

Jacy stops walking, stunned. "I can't believe I didn't realize he was in Spirit when we saw him that night."

"I know. I didn't either. What do we do about it?"

He shakes his head, looking thoughtful.

"I mean, his parents deserve to know, don't they?"

"Definitely. Except . . . they left last week to spend the winter in Arizona."

"Do you know how to reach them?"

"I'm sure the police do."

"The police!"

"Notifying the Yateses that their son is dead isn't our job, Calla."

No. She supposes it isn't, and she's relieved about that, considering the hostile confrontation she and Jacy had with the Yateses a few weeks ago. Still . . .

"We're the ones who have to tell the police, right?"

"I guess so."

"Can we do it anonymously? I really don't want the Yateses hating me any more than they already do. We could mail the police a copy of the obituary, right?"

"I guess so," Jacy says again.

"I'll do it," she tells him. But there's no rush. It's just going to have to wait until she gets back from Florida.

"So Darrin had nothing to do with your mom's death after all?"

"I guess not. I mean, he obviously had something to do with her life, and . . . what if he was murdered, too? By whoever killed my mother? I mean, how can they both have died so young, suddenly, so close together? That doesn't make sense."

"No," Jacy agrees, "it doesn't."

"Now all I can think about is the signet ring in my dream. I'm thinking that the heart pierced by three daggers must have been some sort of psychic shorthand but I can't figure out what it might mean, can you?"

Jacy shakes his head.

"Maybe when I'm on the plane later, I'll be able to think with a clearer head."

"So you're still going to Florida today?"

She nods. "I have to. Now more than ever."

"What about the police?"

"You mean, telling them about Darrin? There's no rush."

"There is if he was murdered, too. That means whoever killed him—and your mom—is still out there."

"I know. I have to get my mother's laptop and see what the two of them were e-mailing about."

"I think you should leave that to the police, too."

"No way." Calla shakes her head. "If the police get involved, my father gets involved. And if my father gets involved, I'm out of here."

"Well, maybe that's for the best. If you're in danger here, you need to leave."

"I am. At least, today. I have to leave school early to catch my flight, so I won't be in math. Can you get the homework for me?"

"Yeah. But Calla—I mean, come on. This isn't a good idea."

"What isn't?"

"Any of it. I just wish you weren't going." He stops walking and pulls her into his arms.

"I know. I have to, though. You get that, right?"

He nods. "But if anything happens to you . . ."

"It won't. What can happen? I'm going to get Mom's laptop, bring it back here, and see what's what."

"And depending on what you find out, we'll go to the police."

"Only if we have to."

"We're talking about murder. We have to."

"We'll see."

"You're stubborn." He shakes his head. "Did anyone ever tell you that?"

She smiles faintly. "Maybe."

A sudden gust off the lake flutters glorious golden leaves

down around them, and the look in Jacy's eyes flutters Calla's heart.

With all that's going on—let alone the fact that it's broad daylight in public—this isn't the ideal time or place for him to kiss her, but who cares? His lips brush Calla's and his hands flatten on her upper back, holding her close against him, and all logic seems to have been whisked from her head on the sweet-scented October breeze.

She smiles wistfully at him. "I'm going to miss you this weekend."

"Same here."

"I'll have my cell phone with me—there's no service around here, but it'll work down there. I can give you the number, so you can call me if you want. And I can call you, too. If you want."

"Yeah." He takes her hand, running his thumb over her knuckles. "That would be good."

Hands clasped, they begin walking again.

After a few steps, Calla senses a presence and glances over her shoulder. Is it Darrin, back to haunt her again?

No.

In the distance, she can see Evangeline trailing along behind them, on her way to school. Her head is bent.

Calla's heart sinks.

Did she see Jacy and Calla kissing?

Possibly.

Probably.

But what am I supposed to do? Calla wonders helplessly.

She herself is crazy about Jacy—and he seems to feel the same way.

Evangeline will just have to deal.

Calla loathes the callousness of that thought, even if it is the only rational way to look at the situation.

And she loathes the thought of losing Jacy far more.

Tampa, Florida
7:30 p.m.

"Calla!"

She hears Lisa's squeal long before she catches sight of her friend's familiar honey-blond head in the sea of strangers—dead and alive—crowding the Tampa airport terminal.

"Lis'!" Enveloped in Lisa's arms, Calla suddenly finds herself too choked up to speak.

"It's so good to have you here. Here, gimme your bag."

Calla nods mutely, allowing Lisa to take her carry-on.

"Come on, let's go find the baggage claim."

At last, Calla finds her voice. "Oh, we don't have to. I didn't check anything."

"This is it?" Lisa eyes the small duffel dubiously. "For an entire weekend?"

"That's it." Calla smiles at her expression, knowing Lisa would probably have a full suitcase and a hanging garment bag.

"I guess we're good to go, then. Come on." She dials her cell phone as she leads the way toward the exit, past towering palm trees in planters against plate-glass windows revealing the coral-streaked sky at Florida dusk.

"I found her," Lisa says into the phone. "Meet us next to the arrivals door."

Calla smiles, eager to be reunited with Mr. and Mrs. Wilson, too. They, and their home, were such a huge part of her life here.

With that thought comes the memory of all the times she shared with Kevin, and the realization that she's about to come face-to-face with him again, too.

She only hopes he didn't bring his girlfriend, Annie, home with him this time. Jacy or no Jacy, Calla isn't ready to see Kevin with his new love.

"You look great, Calla." Lisa hangs up her phone and tucks it into the back pocket of skimpy white denim shorts that bare her tanned legs and polished toes in sandals.

Walking along next to her, Calla feels totally washed out. "Come on, you're just being nice."

"No! I love your haircut."

"Thanks, but . . ."

"And did you lose weight? You look even skinnier than usual."

She shrugs, knowing she probably did. Her appetite has really taken a nosedive with all that's been going on lately.

"I'll have to fatten you up while you're here," Lisa says. "When was the last time you had, like, conch fritters? I bet they don't have them up in Lily Dale, do they?"

"Are you kidding?" Calla realizes her mouth is watering at the thought of one of her favorite Florida treats. Conch fritters, gator bites, fresh Gulf seafood, key lime pie . . . *Yum.*

As they pass a sign for the Ron Jon Surf Shop at the Galleria, she can't help but smile. Though she's well aware of the main reason she's back in Tampa, to unearth the truth about what happened to her mother, for the moment, all she can do is revel in familiarity.

Warm humidity envelops Calla the moment they step outside, and her ears tune in to the southern accents drawling all around her. She spots a lizard scampering along the rim of a large terra cotta planter filled with lush green fronds.

They pause at the curb, and Lisa searches among the headlights lining the roadway. Most of the cars are clean late models, the kind you rarely see around Lily Dale.

Wave after wave of nostalgia sweeps through Calla. This is—no, this *was*—home, all her life.

Suddenly, Lily Dale seems farther away than the faint yellow crescent moon rising against the tropical sky, and just as remote.

"There." Lisa points, and Calla spots the Wilsons' white Lexus pulling up. "Let's go."

The trunk pops remotely, and she tosses Calla's bag inside. "Get in the front, I'll sit in the back."

Seeing only a tall, broad-shouldered driver silhouetted beyond the tinted glass, Calla realizes she'll have to wait to see Mrs. Wilson until they get back to Lisa's house.

She climbs into the front seat, prepared to greet Lisa's father—but he's not the one sitting behind the wheel.

It's Kevin.

He's not as tanned as usual and his shaggy blond hair is a shade darker than the last time she saw him. Instead of one of his surfer T-shirts he's wearing a preppy looking navy polo, but in the open vee of his collar she can see the hemp and puka shell necklace she gave him back when they were dating.

"Hi," he says simply, and smiles at her.

Like everything else here, he looks really good to her, and achingly familiar.

Lisa leans in from the backseat. "Kevin flew home this morning. He offered to come back to the airport with me to pick you up because my parents are at this charity thing tonight, and you know how I hate to drive on the highway."

Lisa does not hate to drive on the highway. In fact, she likes to drive on the highway every chance she gets, and at breakneck speed.

But Calla doesn't call her on it. She just stares out the windshield as Kevin navigates the airport service roads, then the highway.

"Did you eat dinner on the plane?" he asks as they drive past a strip mall with a bunch of chain restaurants.

"Yeah," she lies. Actually, she slept on the plane, and it was a relief to get a break from all that's been on her mind in her waking hours.

Not only that, but the plane was teeming with spirits who apparently enjoy hitching rides or stowing away or whatever it is one would call a planeload of unticketed passengers. Calla has never seen so many ghosts concentrated in one place before, and it occurred to her that they might be fueled by all that excess nervous energy among the fearful fliers. She'll have to ask her grandmother about that someday.

Kevin doesn't say much else, just drives, but Lisa is full of questions and comments about Calla's life and her own, as always. Calla does her best to participate in the conversation, just glad Lisa's not asking about Mom's death, or what Calla hopes to accomplish by being here this weekend. Either she's being tactful because Kevin's in the car, or it's totally off her radar. Calla would bet on the latter.

They wind their way through the Wilsons' private gated

community just off of Westshore, in Calla's old neighbor-hood. The oversized modern homes surrounded by elegant royal palms and manicured lawns look foreign to her now, and she notices that there are very few people outside in their yards or on the street or chatting with the neigh-bors.

Not like in Lily Dale.

"Hey, how's your dad doing?" Lisa wants to know.

"Oh, he's actually thinking of leaving California."

"Are you serious? Does that mean you're coming back here?"

Lisa sounds so excited at the prospect that Calla feels a twinge of guilt telling her no, and another twinge of guilt when she blames it on her father. "Dad isn't ready to come back to Tampa yet. He'll probably rent a place near Lily Dale until the school year is over."

"I thought you said he's broke."

"He is, pretty much." Not that she thought to ask him about their money situation when he told her about the change of plans. "But everything is a lot cheaper there than it is in California—or here."

"Yeah, but he wouldn't have to rent at all if he just came home," Lisa points out.

"I don't think he wants to stay in that house just yet. Not after what happened to Mom there. I mean, neither of us could wait to leave after that, remember?"

"I thought you were dreading leaving."

"Was I?" Suddenly, it's so hard to recall her pre–Lily Dale life.

"Well, if you come back here you can always stay with

us—both of you, even—I kept telling you that before you left for New York."

Yes, and Calla kept telling Lisa the primary reason why she couldn't stay with the Wilsons: Kevin.

"Here we are, home, sweet home," he announces as the Wilsons' two-story home—stucco, Spanish-style, with a red tiled roof—comes into view.

At the sight of it, a ferocious lump threatens to strangle Calla. They all shared so many good times here. Her life was so normal then, so filled with promise . . .

But it's as if it all happened to somebody else—and really, it did. Calla is no longer the carefree girl whose biggest concern is whether to wear the white or black bikini to the beach.

Kevin insists on carrying her bag into the air-conditioned house, professionally decorated with warm tropical splashes of color against a pristine white backdrop.

"I'll put this in the guest room for you, Calla."

"Thanks." She waits till he's disappeared upstairs, then hisses at Lisa, "Jeez, why didn't you warn me he was coming to the airport?"

"I didn't know until you were already on your way. Anyway, what's the big deal?"

She's right. What's the big deal?

Sure, Calla once believed Kevin was the love of her life, but he doesn't mean anything to her anymore. He's just her friend's older brother. Period.

Yeah, right.

"Why don't you go up and get changed?" Lisa offers, eyeing Calla's jeans and sweater. "You look like you're all bundled up in that."

The clothing, which felt too lightweight against the October chill when she got out of her grandmother's car back at the Buffalo airport a mere few hours ago, does feel much too heavy down here.

"Go ahead. . . . I'll go get us some Cokes and find those pictures I was telling you about, from Billy Pijuan's party a few weeks ago."

"Great!" Calla tries to look as though she can't wait to check out photos of her old friends, when in reality, she hasn't missed them all that much.

Only Lisa still feels like a part of her life now. She suspects that the others, though she's known them since kindergarten, will probably fade into the past now that her era at the elite Shoreside Day School is firmly behind her.

Meanwhile, she's only known her Lily Dale friends for a month or two, and already they're among her closest confidantes.

Funny how things change. Funny, and kind of sad.

Alone upstairs, Calla sheds her layers for shorts and a T-shirt, finding that her arms, legs, and feet seem too pale and awkwardly bare. It wasn't so long ago that she was back in Lily Dale, first growing accustomed to the weight of jeans and fleece after a Florida summer interrupted.

I guess that proves you can get used to anything, Calla thinks as she opens the guest room door, the emerald bracelet reassuringly visible on her wrist.

"Oh, sorry." Kevin, just coming down the hall and about to crash right into her, stops short.

Why does he have to be right here again, right in front of her, making her remember all the chemistry they had between them once upon a time?

Never mind that, why is the chemistry threatening to pop up again despite all that's happened?

And why is she suddenly finding it impossible to hate Kevin for the unhappily-ever-after ending to their once-upon-a-time?

"Now you look more like you," he says, looking her up and down, and her heart skips a beat.

Cut it out. You can't do this.

No, she can't go around wistfully longing for the old days with Kevin. He's changed. She's changed. They're over. He has college and Annie; she has Lily Dale and Jacy.

"You mean I look more like the old me."

"Yeah."

"The one you broke up with."

He shifts his weight from one foot to the other. "About that . . ."

Trailing off, he looks at her as though waiting for her to interrupt, to tell him not to go there. No way. Let him fumble awkwardly. Let her be in control for once.

The least he can do—after breaking up with her in a text message, for Pete's sake—is make himself accountable to her.

"What about it?" she asks, all but tapping her foot and wearing an *I'm waiting* expression.

"Okay, I'll admit it. I was an idiot, and a coward. . . ."

"A jerk. Don't forget jerk."

He gives an awkward laugh. "Hey, don't mince any words, here."

She doesn't laugh. "Don't worry. I won't."

"I just hate that this has been hanging between us for all these months, unresolved."

"Who says it's unresolved?" She shakes her head. "You

resolved it for both of us, back in April. And now you have a girlfriend, so I'd say that's pretty resolved."

"Not anymore."

"What?"

"I broke up with her."

"In person? Or did you text her, too?" she forces herself to ask with a flip toss of her head, as though the news has nothing whatsoever to do with her. Which, she reminds herself, it doesn't.

"You're never going to forgive me for that, are you?"

"Probably not. I thought Annie was a great girl."

"You know her name?"

Oops. She shrugs, as though she could care less about her replacement—her temporary replacement, actually.

"She is a great girl," Kevin says.

"Then why did you break up with her?"

"A lot of reasons. Does it matter?"

"No," she says, "it definitely doesn't." Not considering that she herself is a great girl, and he broke up with her, too.

"Don't you think it's a huge coincidence," Kevin asks, his ocean-blue eyes fastened on her face, "that we both ended up in New York, just a few miles apart?"

"Ithaca and Lily Dale aren't a few miles apart," she points out, her pulse pounding. She wants to take a step back from him, but her bare feet remain stubbornly rooted to the cool tile floor. She needs to see this through.

"Well, in the grand scheme of things, Ithaca and Lily Dale aren't all that far apart, don't you think?"

Calla shrugs. This isn't the first time she's thought about that.

Yes, it's a coincidence that they both ended up in the same part of New York State—if you believe in coincidences.

Most people in Lily Dale do not.

But what can it possibly mean—Calla and Kevin finding themselves living in relatively close proximity again?

It doesn't mean that they're destined to be together after all. No, because . . .

Wait, why can't we be together again?

Annie is no longer in the picture, and . . .

Jacy.

You have Jacy now. Remember?

Jacy would never hurt you the way Kevin did.

Okay, six months ago, she'd have told herself that Kevin was incapable of hurting her, too.

But he did.

And she won't let herself forget it.

"I have to go find Lisa," she tells Kevin, stepping away from him at last, moving around him, past him.

"Fair enough," he calls after her, "but don't write me off just yet, Calla. Promise me you won't."

She doesn't bother to reply.

And as happy as she is to see Lisa again, all she really wants to do is get this Florida visit over and get back to Lily Dale, and Gammy, and Jacy.

Back where she belongs now.

TWENTY-ONE

Tampa, Florida
Saturday, October 6
10:41 a.m.

If seeing the Wilsons' house again last night after all this time was difficult for Calla, seeing her own house this morning is . . .

Well, heart-wrenching agony doesn't begin to describe the fierce emotion that grips her as she climbs off Lisa's bike and walks it slowly up the driveway.

Maybe she should have waited until Lisa could come with her after all.

But her friend had to work the senior class car wash this morning, and Calla had no desire to accompany her and see the old gang again. Lisa was surprised and disappointed—maybe even a little peeved. When Calla asked what time Lisa would be home, she said she had no idea and that Calla should just take the bike and ride over here herself.

"I just don't get why you want to go snooping around in your mother's stuff," Lisa said.

"Because I have to find out if there's more to it."

"Her death?" Lisa shook her head. "You can't obsess about that for the rest of your life."

"Sure I can," Calla shot back, resenting Lisa, whose mother was at that very moment downstairs ironing Lisa's T-shirt and shorts after whipping up homemade blueberry pancakes for breakfast.

Lisa didn't say a whole lot after that. Just got dressed, rolled her bike out of the garage for Calla, and wished her luck.

Oh, well. She'll get over it, and anyway, you can't worry about that now, Calla reminds herself as she jabs at the kick stand with her sneaker and leaves the bike behind.

No, she has more than enough to worry about.

She fishes in her pocket for the keys her father left with the Wilsons so they could keep an eye on things in the Delaneys' absence.

Then, hesitating on the walk, she squints up at her former home in the bright southern sunshine.

At three thousand square feet, the house seems gigantic to her, especially after spending two months among the modest gingerbread Victorians in Lily Dale. She can't help but compare the professionally landscaped grounds here to the chaotic, profusely blooming cottage gardens back in the Dale.

I like the flowers better, she decides as she passes clipped shrubbery on her way around to the side door.

She doesn't want to walk in through the front, where she would immediately confront the spot where her mother died.

Feeling distinctly uneasy, she glances at the house next door, across the fence, and spots a familiar sight: old Mrs. Evans sitting in her Florida room. Which might actually be comforting, if Mrs. Evans hadn't passed away two years ago.

I wonder if she's been there ever since she died, and I just couldn't see her until now.

Probably.

There are actually a lot of things around here that Calla couldn't see until now—and not all of them are ghosts.

The first thing that occurs to her, as she unlocks the door, enters the house, and relocks the door behind her, is that everything feels different.

Well, of course. The house has been standing empty for a couple of months now. The counters are bare, the rugs are rolled up, the houseplants all moved over to the Wilsons, and some of the furniture is shrouded in sheets.

Everything is dim; the shades are drawn against the sun. The rooms are blatantly empty and unnaturally quiet without the steady hum of the central air. The house is warm, humid, stuffy; an unfamiliar smell hangs in the air—a hint of old produce mingling with Windex and insecticide.

The house might as well belong to strangers. Calla can't imagine ever feeling at home here again. Not after all that's happened. And not without Mom.

Calla longs to turn and walk right out again.

But she's not here for old times' sake; she's here to look for clues, and to get her mother's laptop.

So she forces herself to keep going, moving through the first floor that was once filled with light, bustling with family life. She passes the gourmet stove where Mom whipped up all those healthy organic meals, the table where Calla used to sit to do her homework.

She passes the door to the changing room, with its stall shower and door that leads out to the inground pool, now tarped, the water beneath murky with chemicals.

Feet dragging, she finally makes her way to the front hall, and a chill comes over her.

"Mom?" she whispers, praying she'll materialize here, now.

But if her mother's spirit is hanging around, Calla can't see her, or feel her.

She glances at the spot where she found her mother's body at the foot of the stairs, and an image flashes into her brain.

Her mother, bloody, crumpled . . . and a figure bending over her. Before she can see who it is, the vision is gone.

"Oh, Mom." Calla grasps the edge of a table for support and lets out a sob, fighting the overpowering urge to flee.

You can't. You have to find out what happened to her.

She propels herself to the staircase and hesitates, poised to backtrack over the very last steps her mother took on that terrible day.

Maybe something more will pop into her head. Maybe she'll see the face of her mother's killer—and recognize it.

The stairs loom ominously above her. Heart pounding, she reminds herself that there's no real reason to be afraid right now.

Still, she pats her back pocket to make sure her cell phone didn't fall out while she was riding over.

Just in case she needs to . . .

What? Like, call for help or something?

That's a ridiculous thought, but Calla can't seem to rid herself of a nagging sense of dread.

Good. The phone is still in her pocket. Anyway, she promised Jacy she'd call him as soon as she finds something—or even if she doesn't. He called earlier this morning to check in, and to tell her he was headed to the library to research family crests.

Knowing he's out there somewhere, thinking of her, trying to help her, waiting for her, makes the task ahead a little less daunting.

Calla ascends the stairway and makes her way down the hall, past her own bedroom, where the killer hid on that awful day.

The door, like all the others, is closed. Maybe later she'll go in and see if anything strikes her.

Right now, she has tunnel vision.

At the end of the hall, she opens the door and steps into the master bedroom she last visited in her dream.

A hint of her mother's designer perfume lingers in the air.

But nothing else.

Not a hint of her mother's spirit; not a vision of the killer's identity.

Calla walks around the room, blinking away tears.

She remembers all the times she curled up on the Caribbean-blue bedspread, watching Mom get fixed up to go someplace. From the time she was a little girl, she was fascinated by the grown-up rituals: perfume and pantyhose, makeup and hairspray. She wanted to look just like her mother when she grew up.

But I didn't want to be like her.

No, she didn't want to become a businesswoman—a workaholic, Dad called Mom when they argued.

Mom always had to be doing something, going somewhere. She never relaxed, never took the time to just hang around the house, hang around with Dad and Calla.

It was almost like she was running away, Calla realizes now. And maybe she was.

Away from Dad? Or Darrin? Away from her past? Away from some nameless, faceless person who was stalking her?

Her jaw set, Calla opens the top middle drawer of Mom's bureau and fishes among silky undergarments for a key on a silken red cord. For a moment, she worries that it's disappeared.

No. Here it is.

Was Mom aware that Calla knew where the key was hidden? Probably not, or she might have come up with a better hiding place.

Closing her fist around it, Calla turns and leaves the bedroom, with all its memories.

With a purposeful stride, she heads toward Mom's home office on the opposite end of the hall.

There, she fits the key into the lock on the shallow top drawer.

Why didn't it ever occur to her that normal people probably don't keep their laptops locked away? That her mother might have something to hide? Something more than the financial documents she dealt with for work?

She had no reason to give it much thought. Not then. But now . . .

The drawer slides open and the laptop is right there, waiting for her.

Her breath shallow with anticipation, Calla lifts it out, plugs it in, and turns it on.

As it hums to life, she reaches into her pocket and removes the folded sheet of paper containing every possible password she could imagine.

The computer seems to take forever to boot up.

At last, she sits at the desk and goes right to the e-mail sign-on screen. Mom's screen name is saved there, but the log-in box is empty.

Calla gets to work methodically entering passwords from her list. There are well over a hundred, starting with combinations of names and dates and becoming more and more obscure. Like "Edgar," the name of Calla's pet goldfish when she was little. And "cottagerow," for Odelia's street back in Lily Dale.

Nothing works.

Frustrated, she closes her eyes, wondering what to do.

Then a thought pops into her head.

Maybe she could meditate on it, ask Spirit for the answer, the way she did that day in Patsy's class, reading billets.

Spirit, after all, led her to Geneseo and the purple neon house, and to Darrin/Tom.

"Leolyn!" she says aloud, abruptly.

It just popped into her head, but that's it. It has to be. She knows it before her fingers have even typed it out and hit Enter.

There's an endless pause as the screen flickers, goes blank.

Is it loading?

"Oh my God," Calla breathes, finding herself staring at Mom's e-mail homepage.

The in-box is full. A quick glance tells her it's mostly spam, advertisements, and stuff from people who didn't immediately realize she had passed away.

Clicking over to the archives, Calla knows right where to look. She scrolls through to last February 14 and scans the e-mails that arrived that day.

It isn't hard to pick out the right one: the subject line reads Hello, Stranger.

Her hand trembles as she moves the mouse over it and double clicks to open it.

Dear Stephanie,

It's been over twenty years now and I've never stopped missing you. I've been following you from afar—thanks to the Internet—and I see that you have created a nice life for yourself in Florida with a husband and a daughter and a great job. I'm really proud of you, and nobody deserves those things more than you.

I'm probably not doing you any favors by popping back into your life now, but I haven't been able to stop thinking about you, or everything that went wrong between us—or, mostly, lately, about everything that went right. There wasn't much, but when it was good, it was great. Anyway, I know it's an understatement to say that I'm sorry I left you the way I did, but at the time, I thought I had no choice. I definitely owe you an explanation. And I have one, if you're willing to listen.
Love always,
Darrin

Whoa.

Calla hurriedly clicks into her mother's Sent Mail archives. There is nothing from February 14, or the next day. But on the sixteenth, Mom did send a return e-mail.

> Darrin, I can't tell you how shocked I was to hear
> from you after all these years. I'm willing to listen. In
> person. Where are you? Steph

Darrin's response was immediate. He told her he was in New England, living under a new name, and that he would explain everything when they met. He would come to Florida, he said, the very next day if she wanted.

Mom wrote back that she happened to have a business trip planned to Boston the following week.

> How's that for fate? she wrote. Do you want to meet
> me there?

He did.

Of course he did.

Calla feels sick inside, reading the exchange between her mother and another man, arranging a clandestine meeting to discuss God only knows what. To do God only knows what.

There were no other e-mails for several days, over a week, and then the exchange began again. This time, Mom was the one who initiated the connection.

> Darrin (like I told you, I can never call you Tom, no
> matter what you want me to do, sorry!)—seeing you

yesterday was incredible, despite everything. You said you wanted me to think about what you told me, about what happened back then, and I've done nothing but that since you left me at the airport. A part of me can't believe it really even happened, but I know you wouldn't lie. Yes, you made some mistakes—terrible mistakes—but I understand why you did what you did. You were a kid, and afraid, and you thought you were doing what was best for me, and for you, and for

Calla looks up, startled, as a faint sound reaches her ears.

It's coming from somewhere downstairs—just the slightest rustling.

Is someone else in the house with her?

She sits absolutely still, sensing the stealthy movement below even before she hears the unmistakable tapping of footsteps on the tile.

It isn't a spirit. She's had enough experience to realize that they tend not to sneak about furtively, and they don't necessarily make human sounds, like footsteps.

It's not Lisa or Kevin, either. They wouldn't creep into the house; they'd holler from downstairs, just like old times. And anyway, they wouldn't have a key because Calla herself has the spare one Dad gave the Wilsons.

And she locked the door behind her.

Meaning, no one should be able to get in.

But someone did, once before. Whoever pushed Mom down the stairs snuck into the house, crept up behind her, and . . .

Instinctively, Calla closes the laptop, pulls the plug, and gingerly gets to her feet, careful not to squeak the chair. She moves as silently as possible to the storage closet across the room. It's jammed with office supplies, file boxes, and hangers draped with her mother's overflow wardrobe.

Slipping inside, the laptop clutched against her stomach, Calla pulls the door quietly closed and flattens herself against the back wall, behind the clothes.

Even if someone thought to look in the closet, she wouldn't be visible.

Someone . . . who can it possibly be?

Huddled in the closet, enveloped in terror and the scent of her mother's perfume, Calla wants to sob. Her heart aches in her clenched chest, racing so frantically that she's certain it must be audible.

Just don't panic. Stay absolutely still.

She can hear movement now through the thin panels of wood separating her and the intruder: footsteps in the hall, the creak of the den door being pushed open.

Don't move. Don't you dare.

She sucks in oxygen, eyes squeezed tightly closed, paralyzed with fear.

Someone is moving around in the den.

The closet door opens.

There's a pause.

Then it closes again.

Only when Calla hears the footsteps moving away, down the hall, does she dare to release her breath in a silent sigh of relief. But she stays right where she is, stays absolutely still.

Then a shrill sound pierces the air.

It's her cell phone, ringing in her pocket.

Panicked, she snatches it and flips it open to silence it.

"Hello?" she hears on the other end of the line.

Dear God. "Jacy, shh—"

"Calla, you'll never believe this."

She can hear the intruder coming for her now, no longer moving stealthily, but with deliberate footsteps headed right for the closet.

Oh, no . . . oh, please . . .

In her ear, Jacy says in a rush, "I found the coat of arms with the heart and daggers. I couldn't believe it, but I checked it a couple of times, and—"

The door jerks open, and the closet is flooded with light.

A bony hand reaches out and roughly jerks the hanging garments aside.

Calla gasps in recognition at the woman standing there, and she knows before she hears the name spilling from Jacy's mouth what he's going to say.

"Logan. The name is Logan, Calla!"

The woman who lives in the purple house in Geneseo— the woman who greeted them so hostilely the night they showed her the photo of Darrin—reaches for Calla with a menacing snarl.

She squirms out of reach, screaming into the phone, "Call the police! Jacy! She's here! Help me!"

She blurts her address so hysterically that she's certain there's no way he understood it. Then Sharon Logan is upon her, snatching the phone away with a hand bearing a gold signet ring.

She hurtles the phone and it hits the wall and falls to the rug in pieces, silenced.

Fury boils through Calla. "You killed my mother!"

The woman's thin lips curve a little, baring uneven teeth. "What makes you think that? Wait—don't tell me—you're a psychic. Like she was."

"My mother wasn't a psychic."

"Really." The smirk deepens. "Are you sure you knew everything about her?"

Calla falters. No. She didn't know everything about her.

Not by a long shot.

But she knows one thing.

"You killed her," she repeats, straightening her shoulders, defiant—perhaps foolishly so, but she can't help herself. "I know you killed her. And you killed Darrin, too."

A shadow crosses those beady black eyes, and Calla knows she's made a terrible mistake. She should have played dumb. Should have tried to escape immediately. Should have—

The hands reach out for her.

"No!" Still clutching the laptop, she writhes out of reach.

The hands claw at her.

She kicks upward, hard, hearing a gratifying grunt when her leg makes contact. Sharon Logan doubles over, clutching her stomach.

Calla darts for the door, taking an extra split second to slam it closed behind her.

Then she hurls herself for the stairs.

Please don't let me fall . . .

She can hear Sharon Logan coming out of the room, coming after her.

Mom, please don't let me fall . . .

She reaches the first floor and goes not for the front door, which would take too long to unlock with the chain and deadbolts, but toward the back of the house.

In the kitchen, she flounders momentarily, nearly overcome by panic.

Footsteps are racing toward her.

Calla runs into the changing room and locks the door behind her.

She leans against it, panting.

Is it safer to escape to the pool area, which is fenced in, or hide in here until the police arrive?

If they're even coming.

Could Jacy possibly have understood the address she blurted out?

Shouldn't she hear sirens by now?

No, it's probably only been a few minutes since she was on the phone with him. It feels like a lifetime.

Oh, Jacy . . . Oh, Mom . . . I'm so scared.

She listens for movement on the other side of the door but hears nothing.

She's not naive enough to think Sharon Logan abandoned the chase . . . but she could very well have moved on to the other end of the first floor, searching. It's a big house, and she might not have seen which direction Calla took at the bottom of the stairs.

She glances longingly at the door leading outside.

If she can make it across the pool area undetected, she can probably scale the fence. And scream for help.

Only, this is Florida.

It's not like Lily Dale, where people practically live outside when the weather is nice.

Here, they're all insulated in their climate-controlled homes. Calla hasn't seen a soul in the neighborhood other than the ghost of Mrs. Evans next door.

If she screams for help, there's a solid chance no one will hear.

And there's a chance she won't be able to make it over the tall fence. It's not like it's a chain link, easy to climb.

Then again, if she stays here, sooner or later Sharon Logan will find her.

She might break down the door, like something out of a horror film.

And then she'll kill me, like she killed Mom.

Calla has no choice.

She has to make a run for it.

But first, she opens the cupboard where they keep the bright-colored beach towels. She slips the laptop in among the stack, making sure it's not visible. There. At least it will be safe there until she comes back.

If I come back.

No. She can't think that way.

She peers through the blinds. The coast is clear. No sign of anyone lurking in the backyard.

It's now or never. Go.

Breath held, she quietly unbolts the back door . . .

Painstakingly turns the knob . . .

Opens the door . . .

Takes a step through . . .

Closes it behind her.

Immediately, she realizes that she forgot to turn the button in the knob, locking herself out.

There's no going back.

Swift-footed, she makes her way across the flagstones, toward the pool and the fence beyond. She glances over her shoulder at the house to make sure she's not being followed.

Too late, she realizes that the danger isn't behind her, it's leaped out in front of her.

The signet ring glints ominously in the sun as a hand closes around Calla's upper arm. "Where are you going?"

"Get away from me! Help! Someone, help!"

Fighting like a panther, Calla fends off her captor, breaks away. But only for a moment, then she's tumbled to the hard ground, rolling, scratching, wrestling.

Again, she manages to scramble out of reach, and for a moment, she believes she's free.

Then she realizes that the hard ground is no longer beneath her, and she's falling . . .

Landing on something pliant.

The covered pool.

The tarp holds her weight for a few moments.

Long enough for her to remember Jacy's vision of her struggling in the water.

Then the tarp sinks, and she's floundering in warm, rank water.

Is this how it's going to end?

Is she going to drown?

No! You'll be okay . . . you can swim . . .

Except the tarp is there, tangling around her like an octopus, and her attacker is there, too. In the water with her, on top of her, holding her under.

Calla struggles to break the surface, her lungs bursting hot with the need for air.

Viselike hands hold her under, suffocating her, and it's just like Jacy said, and she's going to die here, at this house, like her mother did.

And what about Dad? What's he going to do now?

With a mighty burst of adrenaline, she fights. Hard. Fights for her life. She breaks the surface, manages to gulp air before the hands push her under again.

No!

This can't happen.

She won't let this happen.

But she's weakening, and water is filling her mouth, and she's no match for Sharon Logan's shocking brute strength, and . . .

And suddenly, the hands are gone.

Gone, and she's floating.

Am I dead?

No.

She's alive.

Alive, freed, sputtering, lifting her head from the water, trying to force air past the water that's clogging her throat.

"Help her! Help the girl!" a male voice shouts, and Calla sees a police officer, sees several of them, sees a dripping-wet Sharon Logan in their clutches, just before she blacks out.

"What I don't get," Calla says to her father later—much later, that night, after he's arrived in Tampa, where she was waiting for him at the police station with the Wilsons—"is *why* she did it."

"Why she came after you?"

"No . . . Mom."

"Maybe we'll never know." Her father squeezes her shoulders. He hasn't let go of her since he got here.

"Ah think she's just a crazy person," Lisa drawls. "You know, one of those nuts who goes off the deep end."

Beside her, Kevin, who has been a quiet presence at Calla's side, shakes his head. "People don't just kill for no reason."

"Unfortunately, son, sometimes, they do," Mr. Wilson says somberly, and Calla is reminded of something Odelia told her.

"*Evil reigns in some souls. We can't explain it. We can only beware.*"

"We're just lucky Calla managed to get away," Mrs. Wilson says, giving her another hug.

"Yeah, thanks to your friend back in Lily Dale." Dad looks at Calla. "Jacy, was it?"

"Yeah. Jacy." Thank God for Jacy.

"You should thank him."

"I . . . I have." She spoke to him only briefly, though. Just to tell him she was okay.

"Are you sure?" Jacy had asked.

"I'm sure."

"What happened?"

"I'll explain it when I get home, but . . . what you said about the water . . . me, almost drowning . . . that's what happened, Jacy. In the pool."

"I told you to be careful."

"I was careful."

"No, you weren't."

"No. I wasn't. I was just so scared and I just had to get out of the house," she agreed. "And I just had to know what happened to my mom."

"And now you do. So come home."

She promised him that she would. And then she made him promise not to say anything to Odelia just yet about what had happened.

"I won't. I won't tell anyone."

As it turned out, Dad, whom the police called immediately after rescuing her, did get in touch with Odelia on his way to the airport. Gammy was reportedly horrified, of course, and wanted to jump right on a plane and come down here, but Dad convinced her to stay home.

"I told Odelia we'll both be back in Lily Dale in a couple of days," Dad tells Calla now.

"Both of you?" Mrs. Wilson asks, raising a professionally waxed, finely penciled eyebrow.

Dad nods. "Both of us. To stay. For now, anyway."

"You're not going back to California, then, Jeff?"

"Nope. I'm never letting Calla out of my sight ever again."

"You can't do *that* to her!" Lisa blurts out.

Calla has to laugh at her tone and expression; even Dad flashes a smile.

But he meant what he said. Calla can tell he's shaken up by what happened.

He's not the only one.

And he still doesn't know about Darrin. Or that Calla first saw Sharon Logan back up north, in Geneseo. For all he knows, the woman was just lying in wait for her at the house.

"How did she get here?" she asked Jacy on the phone earlier. "How did she even know I was here?"

"You said something about it when we were on her porch last weekend. She must have heard you. And she was obviously trying to keep you from finding something incriminating there."

Something in the laptop?

Could be.

There's still so much that isn't clear. Sharon Logan didn't immediately confess to Mom's murder, but the police are questioning her right now, somewhere in this building. They said they found a key to the Delaneys' house in her possession. She could very well have had it back in July, when Mom died.

When Dad heard about that he remembered, looking back, that he misplaced his own keys for a day or two last spring in his office on campus. And when they turned up, they were in the pocket of a jacket hanging on the back of the door.

"Your mother accused me of being my usual absentminded self," he said. "But I know I checked that jacket pocket a couple of times. And suddenly they were there. Who knows? So many people come and go in the science building. . . . Anyone could have borrowed them, made a copy of the house key, then put them back."

Calla shudders just thinking about it.

But if that explains *how* Sharon Logan got into the house to kill Mom, it still doesn't explain *why*.

"You look exhausted, sweetheart," Mrs. Wilson observes now, as Dad finishes signing the paperwork at the sargent's desk. "We have to get you back to our house and into bed. It's late."

"But my father—"

"Him, too. He can't possibly sleep in that house after all that's happened."

No. He can't possibly. Maybe neither Dad nor Calla ever will again.

She's in no hurry to go back there, that's for sure.

But she has to.

Riding with her father in the rental car on the way to the Wilsons', she asks, "Dad? Can we stop at the house? Just so that I can get a few things I need?"

He hesitates. "Okay. I guess I can use some stuff myself. I left California without a bag."

"What about all your stuff?"

He shrugs. "What about it?"

"Aren't you going to go back and get it?"

"Someday. It's not important."

Calla nods, wondering what this is going to mean to her new life in Lily Dale. She won't have time to get used to the idea, that's for sure. Not with Dad flying straight from here to New York with her.

The house feels more deserted than ever when they let themselves in the side door. Together, they walk through the empty rooms.

It's depressing, Calla thinks. It would be even if she hadn't just been through an ordeal here.

"Should we go upstairs and get our stuff?" Dad asks. "I don't really want to stick around here."

"I don't, either. Go ahead. I'll be right up. I have to get a few things from down here."

Looking reluctant to let her out of his sight, her father goes upstairs.

Calla immediately hurries to the changing room to retrieve her mother's laptop from beneath the beach towels in the cabinet.

She boots up the computer, and again it seems to take forever.

"Come on," she mutters. "Hurry!"

"Dad?" she sticks her head out and calls up the stairs. "How much longer are you going to be?"

"About five minutes."

Five minutes.

That should be enough.

At last, she logs back into her mother's e-mail address and scrolls to the note Mom wrote after seeing Darrin in Boston.

Calla picks up reading where she was when Mrs. Logan scared the living daylights out of her, creeping around downstairs.

but I understand why you did what you did. You were a
kid, and afraid, and you thought you were doing what
was best for me, and for you, and for our child

Calla gasps.

Their child?

Her mother's . . . and Darrin's?

A floorboard creaks overhead. "Are you almost ready, Calla?" Dad calls.

Is he even my real dad?

"Almost," she murmurs, clutching the edge of the counter, holding on for dear life as the room spins around her.

What if Darrin is her father? What if—

Wait a minute—he can't be!

No. Of course he can't.

Mom and Darrin hadn't seen each other in over twenty years. Calla is only seventeen.

Thank God . . .

Thank God Dad is my father.

For a moment there . . .

But . . .

Mom and Darrin did have a child together, and that means . . .

Somewhere, Calla has a half sibling.

AUTHOR'S NOTE

Having grown up a stone's throw from the gates of Lily Dale
in western New York, I've been familiar with the spiritualist
colony for as long as I can remember. My earliest visits were
for Sunday drives with my family along the tranquil shores of
Cassadaga Lake. Back then, I was more interested in not dripping my ice-cream cone all over the vinyl seats of our wood-
paneled station wagon than I was in what went on beyond the
mediums' shingles.

When I reached high school and college, my friends and I
started going to the Dale for readings—mostly to find out
what was going to happen in our futures. At that age, we—
especially I—had little interest in contacting the dead. After
all, I hadn't really lost anyone back then, other than great-
grandparents who had been closing in on their nineties when
I was born. Yet the spirits always seemed to have messages for
me anyway. Messages that often made perfect sense to my

Sicilian grandmother, whom I now suspect might just possess more than the standard five senses herself—not that she'll ever admit it! But it seemed that my grandmother's mother—my maternal great-grandmother, who had died when my mother was a child—always came through to me. To this day when I go to Lily Dale, she tends to pop up in my readings. Call me crazy, but I almost feel as though I've gotten to know her.

About a decade ago, going strong with my writing career, I decided Lily Dale would make a perfect setting for a novel. Though I had long since moved to the opposite end of New York State, I began visiting again at every opportunity, researching my books. Or so I thought.

Coincidentally—or maybe not—that was also around the time I entered the heartbreaking cycle of losing people I loved. First it was my paternal grandfather, the patriarch of our family. He was a strong character, and I was extremely close to him. The loss—though he was in his mid-eighties and had been ill—was devastating to me. Six months later, my paternal grandmother followed, having died (we all believed) of a broken heart. Then, my mother-in-law passed away— breast cancer, and she was far too young. Next, unexpectedly, I lost a close friend. Then my own mother; breast cancer again, far too young again.

With each loss, I found myself regarding my visits to Lily Dale and my readings with the mediums there in a whole new light. But I still wasn't sure what—or whether—to believe. I, after all, was there in the name of research.

A funny thing happened when I visited around the time I lost my grandfather. The medium—who of course was a complete stranger, with no advance knowledge of my loss—

claimed to be bringing through my grandfather. Her physical description was pretty unmistakable. She said he had a message for my father, and it had something to do with the song "Zippity Doo Da." She said he kept singing it, over and over, and wanted to know what it meant. I had no idea.

I later asked my father, who prided himself on being the ultimate skeptic. He was taken aback. Turns out the song "Zippity Doo Da" did have personal significance between him and his late father—and no one other than the two of them really would have known about it. He was shaken but insisted that if it were really my grandfather, he would have come through with his name.

"If he doesn't come through with his name, I don't believe it's really him," he said illogically, having disregarded the fact that the information I had been given was much more specific than a name.

"Anyone could come up with a name," I protested. The way I saw it, a charlatan could conceivably have somehow connected me to the late Pasquale "Pat" Corsi, but "Zippity Doo Da"? Even I hadn't known about that.

A year or so later, I went back to Lily Dale, to a different medium, for a group reading with my husband's sister and brother. Right before we went I had lunch with my father, still a die-hard skeptic. He said he wouldn't believe I'd heard from anyone on the Other Side unless they specifically came through by name. He was laughing about it, teasing me, really— but I knew darn well he meant it.

That reading began with some information for my sister-in-law. Then the medium said abruptly, "I have a Pat or Patrick here, and he's very persistent . . . ," and she turned to me. "I think he's here for you." She went on to tell me that he had a message for "his son." And the message was that he had to stop being such a "bullhead." I had to laugh at that. On my father's side of the family, people were always accusing each other of being bullheads. My father and grandfather were the two biggest offenders, and believe me, the shoe fit both of them!

In any case, I went home and told my father that my grandfather had done just what he'd asked—he'd come through by name. Not even by his formal name, but by his family nickname.

"Bah," said the skeptic. "His name wasn't Pat or Patrick. It was Pasquale."

"But everyone called him Pat—and Grandma called him Patrick!"

"Bah. You told me last time that anyone could come up with a name—a name isn't proof."

Oh, for Pete's sake. He was still determined to be a skeptic.

"What else did my father say?" my father asked me, after awhile.

"He told you to stop being such a bullhead."

My father's eyes widened and he thoughtfully rubbed his chin. Hmm. Maybe he did believe in this stuff, after all.

As for me, the tide had begun to turn the day I heard "Zippity Doo Da" from the Other Side. Since then, too many inexplicable things have happened to me in Lily Dale for me not to have an open mind.

I'll tell you another ghostly tale from the Dale next time!

COMING SOON:

LILY DALE
DISCOVERING

Having finally learned who was behind her mother's death, Calla Delaney still doesn't understand why it happened. Does the killer's motive have something to do with the shocking secret her mother kept hidden for more than two decades? Calla doesn't dare reveal that discovery to anyone—not even her father. Now that Jeff Delaney has moved to Lily Dale, he's a little too close for comfort—not just to Calla but to Ramona Taggart, the psychic next door. Calla figures it won't be long before Dad discovers not only that Ramona can see and speak to dead people but that he's just taken up residence in a town populated by mediums, which includes his own daughter.

Now Calla must call upon the spirit world to assist her desperate search for the stranger whose very existence has forever changed Calla's perception of her late mother—and herself. Because somewhere out there, someone shares the powerful psychic abilities that allow Calla to see not only into the past but to the Other Side—someone who apparently doesn't want to be found.

Will Calla's journey lead to the closure that will allow her family to start healing at last? Or will it force her to accept yet another loss and forever wonder what might have been?